The girls of *Haute* would become women of privilege...

There were charge accounts at Bendel's, Saks, Bloomingdale's, and Bergdorf's, with instructions that the bills be sent to accountants someplace "for handling."

They had come to *Haute* to find themselves and were, for the first time in their carefully insulated lives, exposed to rasping, carping, unforgiving, insulting criticism from Miss Harrington. All for slave wages. Girls at *Haute* seldom made more than two hundred dollars a week in the glamour jobs. The secretaries, the telephone operators, the cleaning women—all made more than the editorial assistants and the fashion associates who were proud to have their names printed on the *Haute* masthead.

The pay was not important to them. The aristocratic comers and goers on the masthead were never there for the money.

Haute was an experience.

HAUTE

HAUTE

HAUTE

JASON THOMAS

KNIGHTSBRIDGE PUBLISHING COMPANY
NEW YORK

This paperback edition of *Haute* first published in 1991 by Knightsbridge
Publishing Company

Originally published by PaperJacks in 1987

Published in the United States by
Knightsbridge Publishing Company
208 East 51st Street
New York, New York 10022

ISBN 1-56129-078-5

10 9 8 7 6 5 4 3 2 1
First Edition

To Marcella Todd — she knows who she is.

HAUTE

Chapter One

Sylvia Harrington always enjoyed the first few minutes of the morning most. It was during the calm start of her day that she truly could appreciate her life and the power that she had attained. No wake-up call or alarm clock was ever needed. Ever since she had been a child — though some people doubted that Sylvia Harrington ever had been a child — her eyes would open precisely at the designated moment. It did not matter where she was — in her Manhattan apartment, at the Georges V in Paris, or, God forbid, in California. It would not have mattered if she were on the moon. Waking up was simply part of the life she planned so carefully. She would wake when she wanted, not a minute earlier, not a minute later.

The night before, she had decided that 6 A.M. would be the moment she would start this Monday morning. At exactly 6 A.M. her small eyes opened.

And closed again. For, while the actual moment to begin another day was carefully planned, it did not mean that she immediately left the luxury of her rose satin — always rose satin — sheets. This was the part of the waking-up process she enjoyed the most. As her eyes opened, an observer would notice — if there had been an observer, though in fact there never was — she would always be curled into a tiny fetal ball in the center of the huge bed, with its layers of coverlets. It was the tight, guarded position of an animal instinctively protecting itself. Slowly, she unwound and stretched.

Her long thin legs pushed gradually outward from the small aura of warmth her body had created in the nest of satin, the flesh cringing as it touched the colder satin.

It had been the same every morning for the previous three decades. First, the warm ball of flesh and bone and the satin it touched. Then the stimulating coldness of the rest of the satin, so much more stimulating than warmth. Today, in the midst of the New York winter, the temperature of the fabric seemed exceptionally austere, almost bringing a smile to Sylvia's thin lips. Almost. The iciness of the fabric felt so good, so right. It was better than sex, richer, more caressing. She closed her eyes and let the sensations flow over and under her body.

Her eyes opened again.

As usual, there was that dependable glow. Sylvia almost smiled again at another favorite sensation. The steady blinking glow of the square push buttons on the business-style phone next to her bed. The constant blinking, so silently, was always reassuring; people wanted to talk to her. It was late morning in Paris and the middle of the night in Los Angeles, and people, important people, already hoped to talk to the important Sylvia Harrington.

The humor in this never ceased to amaze Sylvia. On the other ends of those silent blinking lights were the rich and the famous. Maybe a few were merely glamorous. But they all wanted, needed, to talk to with her.

The silent blinking lights were connected to the most private lines at *Haute* magazine. She seldom answered — there were those who thought she never did — any of those always-important and almost-always-to-remain-anonymous blinks at her apartment. The numbers were semisecret. Other than a few of the world's top fashion designers and people who had infil-trated the penthouse executive offices of *Haute*, only a smattering of jet-set types and some of the still-rich nobility were awarded the numbers.

Sylvia enjoyed imagining just who was ringing her up at such an early hour. It was all so *very* delicious.

"Good morning," she said aloud.

Nobody heard her words. Nobody ever heard her first words of the day. She spoke in her usual clipped voice with the accent of an American who had received much education in Europe, perhaps at some remote and selective girls' boarding school somewhere in the Swiss Alps. Sylvia Harrington almost smiled once more. There had never been an exclusive girls' school in her background. But there was that slight accent.

"Go ahead, blink, blink some more. I am not going to answer," she told the phone.

In her very public life, there was only one place of total privacy. Her apartment. Few people ever were in-vited there, and the most private part of the so-very-private apartment was the rose-and-burgundy bedroom, a nest within a nest. No one had ever been invited into her satin shelter. The bedroom was for Sylvia Harring-ton — alone.

Sylvia even cleaned the room herself. The latest in a long succession of maids had been surprised at first, then relieved, when Miss Harrington listed endless in-structions for the arrangement of the kitchen, the dusting of the mostly Regency antiques in the living room, the exact spots to which each piece of furniture had to be returned after the daily vacuuming; to be warned never at any time to open the double doors to the rose-and-burgundy bedroom came as a relief.

Actually, the order was unnecessary, because the doors were always kept locked. Among the few who knew her intimately, the very few she chose to permit into her personal life, the legend of the forever-locked bedroom had sparked a few attempted raids. Beverly Boxard had tried only the night before.

Mrs. Boxard was the editor of *Architecture Now,* the most successful interior design magazine in the world. Her story was not unlike Sylvia's. She had taken a nearly dead trade publication that dealt mostly with hardware and building specifications and transformed it into a sleek and gossip-crammed consumer success. The two women were comparable, if not equal, successes. *Haute* was a much larger and much more popular magazine. Still, the success of *Architecture Now* had entitled Mrs. Boxard to admission to one of Sylvia's very few "at homes."

After a number of glasses of champagne — ten — and a huge chaser of fine French brandy, the formidable Mrs. Boxard had begun her siege of the secret room. Sylvia gleefully remembered the incident.

At one moment, Beverly Boxard had been admiring the Chagall, a gift, that hung above the almost-Adam fireplace. The colors of the large room — the only really large room in an otherwise small apartment — were based on the blues, greens, and the burgundy of the Chagall.

"Sylvia," Beverly had said in her most charming cocktail-party voice, a tone she seldom used since her magazine had become so successful and so very socially desirable, "this room would photograph beautifully. When do we do it?" This was editor-to-editor conversation. None of the usual social banterings and hedgings before asking or being asked, just the mating of two journalistic tigresses.

"I think not, Beverly," Sylvia had replied.

"But, why?" her guest had asked innocently.

"I don't need it."

There was bite to this remark. For almost ten years, Beverly Boxard had fought to convince the rich and the important to permit the privacy of their mansions and villas to be invaded on the full-color pages of her magazine. It had been difficult, damned difficult. Most of the quality rich did not want the publicity. For years, the pages of *Architecture Now* had been filled with film-star glitz and the expensive excesses of the new rich. But slowly Beverly had lured a few of the truly rich and the really important into *Architecture Now,* and she had felt smug about it. Still, a very few, the most secure in their wealth and power and the most demanding of their personal privacy, remained unreceptive to her overtures.

Photographing Sylvia's apartment, especially the forbidden bedroom, would be a coup in the battle to break down the final barriers of exclusivity that blocked *Architecture Now* from rising to the ultimate level of acceptance.

"Sylvia, everyone would die to see your little place and know how very cleverly you have done everything," said Beverly. For a moment, Sylvia thought she was the recipient of a bitchy putdown. But, no, not even Beverly Boxard would dare to tread on Sylvia Harrington. "I bet you did it all yourself," Beverly continued. "I must see the whole place. Is the bedroom up those stairs?''

Beverly started swaying toward the two steps that led to a tiny hallway and pair of scaled-down double doors. Sylvia made no effort to stop the assault. The other guests stopped their conversations to watch as Beverly paused at the top of the two steps to get a second wind.

"Forget it," said Barry Dobene, one of Beverly's pet designers, to break the sudden silence.

"Beverly, dearest," Sylvia purred, "there is absolutely nothing special about this place. I could never have it photographed. Why, I have never even used it for a background in *my* magazine."

Beverly swayed, just a little drunk. "What a shame. If the bedroom is as beautiful as the living room, my readers would love it. I really must take a look."

Everyone leaned toward the doors. The legend of Sylvia Harrington's secret bedroom seemed about to be revealed. Beverly turned and grasped the antique gold handles that Sylvia had found twenty-five years before in an antiques shop on Fifty-seventh Street. She twisted the fragile handles. Nothing happened.

Startled, Beverly let go of the handles and turned toward the curious onlookers in the living room. "Locked . . . she keeps her bedroom locked. How strange." She seemed incapable of selecting the right words. "How very strange," she repeated.

"You probably couldn't have published that room in a family magazine after all," Barry Dobene said, desperately trying to cover up his embarrassment for Beverly, his discoverer, benefactor, and publicist. "I understand that it is all done in black leather," he added, laughing, but his laughter faded as he realized that nobody else was reciprocating. No one wanted to run the risk that Sylvia Harrington might not be amused. Offending was a practice that had been honed to an art form in the chic tower apartments of Manhattan, but it was seldom practiced on the very powerful. No one ever dared to offend Sylvia Harrington — at least, not to her face.

"Don't get your hopes up, darling," Sylvia snapped at Dobene. "It isn't one of *your* rooms, you know."

Sylvia made a mental note to tell her editors to let a year or so go by before again permitting one of Dobene's expensive interiors to appear as a backdrop for a *Haute* fashion layout. He had nervously joked himself into journalistic exile.

Sylvia liked the memory of the evening.

The bedroom was still hers, hers alone, she thought before rising. She leaned back against the huge bank of satin-covered pillows. In a rustle of satin and silk, she leaned to the edge of the bed and pressed down the only button that wasn't lit up. Her long Arden-sculptured fingernails tapped out the familiar number.

"Sandy."

The voice at the other end did not answer, and it was not her habit to wait for him to respond. After twenty years of chauffeuring Sylvia Harrington, Sandy Peterson knew simply to wait for his morning orders.

"Have the car brought around at seven-thirty today," she said.

"Yes, ma'am."

Sylvia Harrington would be in her office at twenty minutes to eight. She enjoyed arriving at unexpected times each day. When she was earlier than the staff, she regarded herself as an inspiration. When she arrived later than nine, everyone worried. They worried about being caught not looking industrious. They worried about being caught exchanging a morning pleasantry that could be interpreted as a lengthy while-the-boss-is-away talk. Mainly, just they worried. The staff hated the late-arrival days more than the mornings when they would see the big limousine curbside, indicating Miss Harrington was already ensconced in her top-floor office. Today was to be an early day.

The morning-at-home ritual always took exactly an hour. This was the time that Sylvia devoted entirely to herself. Outside, beyond the heavy velvet drapes, cars were starting to crowd the Fifty-ninth Street Bridge, but none of the city sounds entered the bedroom. The double burgundy drapes and the padded and upholstered rose satin walls stifled even the garbage-can-hour din of Manhattan. Daylight never entered the rose bedroom. Sometimes at night the drapes were opened to permit the electric glitter of the city to enter. But only rarely. The lighting in the room was carefully subdued. No harsh wrinkle-revealing shadows here.

Not that it would really matter. There were no mirrors in the bedroom to reflect those wrinkles.

When the sacred bedroom had been created twenty-five years earlier, the last thing Sylvia Harrington wanted to see first in the morning was her face. So the bedroom had no mirrors. Even when she discovered the mirrors of the *Queen Mary* had been tinted a rose color to add a more flattering hue to seasick first-class passengers and decided that if this trick could help green plutocrats, it might help her, no mirrors were added to the bedroom. She had installed the mirrors in a second bedroom that had been transformed into a closet and dressing room.

Sylvia stood up, her feet sinking into the carpeting that Edward Fields had designed exclusively for that twelve-by-fourteen space, and the morning officially began. Sylvia lived in luxury, that expensive luxury crafted by people with names that had become synonymous with costly extravagance. Of course, Fields had given her the rug. The men who laid the rug and the upholsterer who padded the walls were the last people, other than Sylvia, even to enter the sanctum. She had brought all the furniture up the two steps from the living room and arranged everything herself. She even scrubbed the carpeting herself. Maybe the place was getting a little tattered, she suddenly thought. But in the dim controlled light of the rose bedroom, who could tell?

The dressing room was a different matter.

The light was brighter. It had to be, for the makeup. Even the mirrors were not enough to give Sylvia's gray-tinged skin a hint of natural color before her daily dousing of paint. It just did not seem fair. There she was, the person who decided what clothes would be beautiful that year, what kind of body would be chic, what hairstyles would be right. She gave the world her standards for beauty, and she was . . .

. . . ugly.

God! Damn! *Ugly!*

It had never been fair. She was tall. Some said the passion for tall models started with Sylvia Harrington, who had attempted to exact revenge on every coquette of her Midwestern childhood. She was painfully thin. Yet, the folds of flesh seemed to hang at her neck and from her arms. Throughout her life, she had always been twenty pounds underweight, but still there were those folds.

And the face matched the body.

The nose was hawklike. The hair was thin, teased, and forced into a severe chestnut-dyed helmet. The eyes were small, but they were the least of Sylvia's problems, since they were always hidden behind gigantic sunglasses, which were skillfully designed to draw the eye away from her face.

Plastic surgery had been suggested ever so tactfully over the decades, but there were always excuses. Most of those who knew Sylvia well enough to be part of such a conversation thought she was afraid. Her favorite reason for avoiding the surgery seemed to prove their supposition. "I'm a terrible bleeder," she said regularly to the proponents of surgery. But that was not the real reason. Her ugliness had caused more pain to Sylvia Harrington than would ever have been caused by any amont of surgical cutting and rearranging. The purple swellings and skillfully chipped bone could never exceed the pain caused by the intense inner anguish suffered because of that nose, that long thin face, those tiny eyes, the thin lips that were almost no lips at all, the body that was already thin and twisted at an age when other girls' bodies were at their most physically alluring, and the thin, yet coarse and brittle, hair. Nothing could hurt more than those years of teasing and insults — unless it was the clumsy attempts at kindness and pity.

There were the boys who asked for dates out of a kind of sympathy. Or, worse, there were the men who pursued her because they thought she would have as little interest in them as they did in her. That hurt the most. That tore, more than a surgeon's knife could — ever. No mere surgery could cause more pain than being ugly in a world where everyone was beautiful. Sylvia Harrington could have endured any operation — a dozen operations — if she thought there was a surgeon in the world who could repackage her.

Only she did not think there was.

She was afraid that after the surgeon had finished,

after all the bandages had been removed, she would *still* be ugly. Maybe less ugly, but not beautiful. Never beautiful. She could not settle for less than beautiful, so there never would be plastic surgery.

Sylvia looked at the haggard face in the mirror. Slowly, she started applying the custom-blended cosmetics. Estée Lauder had sent over four girls from her General Motors Building offices to supervise the skin and coloring analysis to create just the right bases and shades to attack the sallowness of Sylvia's skin. Even the eyes that would always be hidden behind the huge sunglasses were lined and mascaraed. Lips were rediscovered, defined, and widened. Parts of the face were heightened, parts subdued. Slowly, the public image of Sylvia Harrington appeared in the rose mirror. Finally, every nuance was right, not too much or too little. The technique was perfection yet the result was always disappointing. Without makeup she was an old woman. With makeup she was a painted old woman.

The former second bedroom of the apartment, which was now the dressing room, stored each season's clothing. Every fashion season, the best and most expensive designers flooded Sylvia with their pieces. "This could look good only on you," each lied. "I want you to tell me honestly what you think of this," each flattered. But mostly everyone just bribed. At the end of each season, she sold the dresses, many of which had never been worn, to an expensive "previously owned" dress shop.

This added thousands of dollars to her income. Always, she knew, the closets would be refilled. More shoes from Italy. More suits from Dior and Beene. More evening clothes from Blass and de la Renta. More Saint Laurent. More Halston. More Fendi furs.

The closet was fitted with the kind of revolving racks

found in dress shops. On one tier were the office outfits each coordinated with suitable blouses and a bag of shoes; a bag of costume jewelry hung on the same hanger with the shoes. Once an ensemble had been conceived, it was never redone. The shoes would be worn only with the same skirt, suit, or dress. The evening clothes were similarly arranged, though she seldom wore any jewelry at night. This was because Tiffany and Cartier seldom gave away expensive jewelry, not even to such as Sylvia Harrington. Since Sylvia thought borrowing jewelry was tacky, and she refused actually to buy anything, she had decreed not wearing jewelry a sign of chicness.

The racks waited. The morning paint session was almost completed. If Estée Lauder ever painted the makeup version of the Sistine Chapel — once, before Michelangelo, deemed the ugliest roof architecture in the world — it would be the flesh of Sylvia Harrington.

"Not bad." She was still checking to hear if her voice was working properly, not offering professional criticism. She adjusted a pair of side mirrors to see if the artistry had missed any of the grayish flesh. No. In only a matter of minutes the first of many polite someones would lie and say, "You look very nice today, Miss Harrington." Or the real phonies would gush, "You look beautiful" — or "ravishing," or, in the case of hairdressers, "dazzling." A few people would attempt to maintain a trace of personal integrity while still stroking the boss by commenting, "What a fabulous suit. I love your taste."

She had long ago become used to the daily compliments, but she still classified people according to their comments. Those who flattered her clothes were "ethicals." Those who praised her looks were "phonies." She approved equally of both groups.

Dressing went faster than the makeup application. The luxury of her expensive one-of-a-kind ensembles provided the same kind of security as the satin sheets. She could disappear into layers and layers of costly fabrics. There were those who said the layered look was created only as a hiding place for Sylvia Harrington's body, a burial ground in Saint Laurent.

In four long strides, she crossed the living room. Up a pair of steps to a small but pretentious black-and-white marble entrance hall — Beverly Boxard made fun of the "itsy grand hall de la dame" — and finally into the kitchen. In less than two minutes the coffee machine dripped the Jamaica Blue Mountain into a mug that was not a part of her antique gold-and-red lacquered china, a gift of the French government for conducting a trade mission in the sixties. She downed a cup and noticed the blinking light on the wall phone.

Pressing a vacant line, she dialed another number that had long been a reflex.

Ring.

"One," she counted.

Ring.

"Two."

Ring.

"Three."

Ring.

"Miss Harrington's residence."

"You must be very busy today." Sylvia demanded her answering service to be as vigilant as her office staff.

"Oh, Miss Harrington, I'm sorry. It has been so busy this morning, and one of the kids is sick. I am very sorry —"

"My messages," Sylvia interrupted.

"Melissa Fenton said that she was called out of town suddenly by a family emergency and will not be able to do the Tuesday shooting. She did not leave a number."

Sylvia felt a churning in her stomach. *The little bitch is probably still stoned from her weekend,* she thought. *Either that, or she can't walk because she nearly fucked herself to death. The time has come to do something about Melissa Fenton.*

"Did you get that, Miss Harrington?"

"Go on," Sylvia snapped.

"Mr. Spense said to remind you of his showing this morning and the party at the Sixes. He said to be sure to tell you that you promised to come."

Where does Spense get off? I have already seen the collection. No, I will not be at the show. The Sixes! That place is barely a step above a gay bar, but for Spense, I guess I can go to his little party. The right people always go to Spense's parties.

"Miss Caldwell wanted to remind you that you have scheduled an editorial meeting on the June issue for 10 A.M."

Jayne, always so careful. Always so tactful. She knows that I never answer the phone in the morning, but she leaves a message anyhow. The office's little Miss Perfect.

"I know about the meeting," Sylvia said, becoming bored with this part of her daily routine. "Are there any foreign messages? Skip the rest and leave them with my secretary."

"No, nothing, Miss Harrington."

"Nothing from Paris?" Sylvia asked.

"No."

"Check again." Sylvia waited impatiently as the operator studied the pile of messages attached in front of 555-8007, the private line of *Haute* magazine.

"I have checked very carefully, Miss Harrington. There is nothing from Paris. Not for you."

"What do you mean, not for me?" Sylvia was instantly alert.

"Miss Caldwell received a call from the Paris office of Mr. Lagerfeld."

"Read it."

"But it was Miss Caldwell's message."

"Miss Caldwell is my employee. She is paid by *Haute* magazine, as are you. Now read me that message, you stupid little . . ." She stopped. It was too early in the morning for her to be profane, even with faceless telephone answering services.

"Mr. Lagerfeld's associate . . . he was speaking very bad English, so I hope everything is correct. He said that all the seats were in order for the special February fashion showing, and he asked if she could please call him to discuss the arrangements. That was all, Miss Harrington."

Sylvia banged the receiver into its resting place. "That incompetent bitch," she muttered.

Across the city at a crowded telephone answering service, a girl by the name of Nellie Washington flashed her middle finger at 555-8007.

The black coffee was too hot and too strong. Sylvia drank another cupful, then walked into her small foyer, unlocked the three security locks, and left her cloistered private little world.

The eighth-floor hallway was stark and cream-colored. The floor was covered with tasteless imitation-brick tiles. Sylvia always ignored the cheapness of the hallway, with its fake Monet painting and its dusty dried flowers sitting lifeless in a pot that was bolted to an aged mahogany commode that was, in turn, bolted to the fake-brick floor. She pressed for the elevator and stared at the worn brass button in an attempt to intimidate the aged elevator to strain faster in its creaking trip to the eighth floor.

It was 7:29 A.M.

The elevator cringed to a halt, not quite meeting the eighth floor. Sylvia stepped down into the cage. She had learned long ago to yell only at things that could be expected to cringe in response to her wrath. Elevators received only exasperated sighs. It took more time for the apartment elevator to drop eight floors than was required for the elevator at *Haute* to rush more than fifty floors to the executive offices. Finally, the dim light behind the floor panel started to glow weakly behind the part of the panel that had been cut out to spell the word "Lobby." Sylvia burst through the opening doors like a racehorse, startling the workmen in the lobby.

"Careful, lady!" one of them called.

Sylvia ignored them. Anyone who did not know who she was . . . A piece of jagged metal caught on the silk lining of her sable coat; the sound of shredding fabric, expensive fabric, punctuated the workman's warning.

"Told you, lady. These dames never listen. Just don't send us the bill, lady. Hey! You hear me, lady?"

Sylvia swept past, ignoring the workmen. They were nothing but stupid and irritating machinery. It was going to be a rough day for the office staff of *Haute* magazine.

Sylvia had detested this part of the morning ever since plans had been announced to change the ugly brick building that stood twelve stories above the intersection of First Avenue and Fifty-ninth Street into a co-op. When she first moved there in the late fifties, the only name for the building had been the address, 400 East

Fifty-ninth Street. That had been good enough for the kings and queens of fashion who had been grateful to be invited to her apartment. It was enough for a New York cabby. But now a new brass sign proclaiming SUTTON BRIDGE had been bolted to the newly sandblasted brick outside the doors. "Bridge," indeed! Most of the building was not so much overlooking the none-too-graceful Fifty-ninth Street Bridge as squatting under it.

Still, it was a good address, just on the extreme north edge of exclusive Sutton Place. Thirty years before, she had wanted that address badly, back before she was the famous Miss Harrington, back when she needed to have status instead of creating it. It was almost Sutton Place back in the days when Sylvia Harrington sometimes settled for "almost good enough."

"Co-op, shit!" Sylvia mumbled to herself as the Iranian doorman halfheartedly made a lunge at the heavy double doors. Outside the serenade of morning horns proved that it was once again Monday in New York.

She had no intention of paying the four hundred thousand dollars that was being asked for her apartment, her home for more than twenty-five years, especially when it was rent-controlled and cost only four hundred fifty dollars a month. The sales agent, a small blond type who was obviously wearing her most fashionable clothing when she called on Sylvia, seemed surprised at the reaction to the asking price. "Perhaps I could talk to the owners," the agent said, worried. She had been telling people that one of the more famous residents was the Sylvia Harrington of *Haute* magazine. The unexpected attitude could hurt sales.

"Tell the owners to go straight to hell!" Sylvia had roared without removing the security chain from her narrowly opened door.

"I'm sure —"

The door slammed in the agent's face. She had been so sure that the rich and famous Miss Harrington would have been eager to pay four hundred thousand dollars to be the owner of her treasured apartment. She was so very sure that the Harrington name would be one of her major selling tools in the marketing of Sutton Bridge. "After all, she still lives here. I shall simply tell people that she lives here instead of . . . of saying she bought the apartment." Relieved, the agent replaced her smile and pressed the next apartment buzzer. There would come a time, when all the rest of the apartments had been sold, to deal with Miss Harrington.

"Stupid little bitch," Sylvia recalled as she left the apartment building.

She paused a moment. First, she would be crazy to give up rent control. A rental apartment like hers would cost at least two thousand dollars a month in this neighborhood. And, second, she did not have the four hundred thousand. Famous? Definitely. Rich? No. Her salary, a secret known only to herself, the publisher, and a bookkeeper, actually a computer, was only seventy-five thousand a year. Editors of sports magazines with a fraction of *Haute*'s circulation made twice that amount. It was rumored that Beverly Boxard pulled down a quarter of a million, plus stock options. The trouble was that Sylvia had all power at *Haute* except the power to grant herself a raise. To get that raise, she would have had to ask Richard Barkley, the publisher, for his approval, and she never asked Dickie his approval for anything.

Seventy-five thousand dollars! For a single person with no tax shelters, the government took fifty percent. On the other hand, Sylvia never really needed money. Everything in her life seemed to be free. The secret gifts of clothing. The furniture. Even the art. Most came from people who wanted to influence, or keep influencing, Sylvia Harrington. The company provided the first-class travel budgets and the always-waiting limousine at the curb. After all, it would not be proper for the editor of *Haute* to go steerage. The luxury was there. But four hundred thousand was not. It never would be. The smug little girl from the management office would never know that she was one of the few people on earth who could actually send a shiver of fear into Sylvia Harrington.

Maybe a deal could be made, Sylvia thought suddenly. *Maybe I should tell them I want a consideration, a very large consideration, for the use of my name. I bet they are really squeezing the most out of the Harrington reputation. Let me think about that some more.*

Sandy, the *Haute* magazine driver, was standing beside the gleaming Cadillac limousine, which did not have a hint of dirt on its enameled finish in spite of the slush of the gray January day. A freakish warm spell had melted a layer of snow, to the consternation of chauffeurs throughout the city. Sandy was glad that the garage was only two blocks away. Sylvia cleared her throat as a warning as she walked toward the curb. Sandy opened the rear door with a single practiced flourish and then closed it with a hard, reassuring thud of heavy metal against heavy metal. Sylvia sat in the exact center of the seat.

"Good morning, Miss Harrington." Sandy did not bother with flattery. After twenty years of this ritual, there was an unspoken truth between the man in the front seat and the woman in the back. "Unusual day."

"When did it warm up?"

"A front came in about midnight."

"This will melt the snow." A January thaw was always a depressing time for New Yorkers. While most of the northeast was eager for a warming trend, the January thaw produced a disgusting mess in pet-crazed Manhattan. Weeks of collected animal droppings surfaced to ruin the latest clothes and the latest shoes and to stain and disgust those of high style. "I should have worn boots." Sylvia was again attacked by forces she could not control.

She leaned back in the red velvet plushness of the upholstery. The interior of the car was scented by a spray bottle of Saint Laurent's Opium, no spray freshener from the grocery store for the *Haute* limousine. The crystal vases attached to the doorframe each contained a single deep pink rose and a small fern backing. The Waterford decanters and tumblers in the bar tinkled crisply as the great car moved soundlessly through the streets. A puddle of slush was gathering around Sylvia's feet and soaking into the thick wool carpeting. Only ten feet from the building to the curb and the delicate Italian leather shoes were ruined. They would never be worn again. Yes, she should have chosen boots.

The long car circled the block and headed toward Park Avenue.

Chapter Two

The building always amazed Marcella Todd. In a city like New York, where the powerful and famous wore their offices like designer jeans, the twelve-story red-brick building in the heart of the Seventh Avenue garment district was unpretentious. Yet the aging building, with its boarded windows, represented status. Inside its stained walls were the showrooms of the best and the most successful fashion designers in America.

Marcella had often thought about the oddness of the building. The tiny lobby, with its battered-by-a-thousand-clothing-push-racks walls, led to some of the most expensive fashion showrooms in the world. The creaking elevators, with their unpolished brass grates, stopped at floors that had been remodeled dozens of times, each time more expensively than the time before, until the fittings, the carpets, the teak or walnut paneling, the furniture on any one of the twelve floors seemed to exceed the value of the entire brick building. In an industry that constantly offered some new fad that would impart instant status, the building was a corporate status symbol. Only the designers who had made it and made it big were there. Most had slowly devoured an entire floor by taking over the space of somone whose dream of success had been lost in ledgers filled with fiscal mistakes or, worse, dreams that had not inspired the whim of the public. They had failed. There was no room for failure in that grimy brick building on Seventh Avenue.

The elevators, as always, were slow.

"Good morning, Miss Todd," said a beautiful girl, not more than seventeen years old. She was lugging a huge duffel bag, and a Hermès silk scarf covered her curlers. "God, how I hate these morning shows. You would think that somebody like Spense could have his shows later. He's famous enough."

Smart designers at the beginning of their careers often tried to have the first showing of the day so that the photographers would have plenty of time to develop their shots and get them on the wire services in time for the following day's morning newspapers and a few of the faster-moving evening newspapers. But Spense — who used only one name, his middle name — was not a new designer. He was just a careful businessman who understood that proper timing meant publicity in the fashion business, and publicity meant profits.

Finally, the elevator creaked to a halt in the lobby. The model and Marcella Todd slipped into a corner.

"You girls working the Spense show?" asked a heavyset man, enthusiastically crushing into both Marcella and the model. He turned so that they faced one another, the women against the wall of the elevator, the man a smiling pinstriped lump of Midwestern joviality in the middle of the car.

"Yeah!" The model muttered in a voice that immediately sent a chill through the man.

He turned his head and applied his complete attention to Marcella. "How about you, little lady?"

"No, I'm not," she replied.

"You're kidding. With your looks you should try modeling. I know about these things. Did you ever hear of the Birdcage?" He did not wait for an answer. "It's the classiest little dress shop in Quincy. That's Illinois, not Massachusetts. People are always getting that mixed up. Why, we carry real designer stuff. Get customers all the way from Moline coming to the shop. I handle all the advertising, and, believe me, you would be perfect for the Birdcage." He was talking fast because, even in the slowest of elevators, a twelve-floor trip to Spense's penthouse showroom took less than two minutes. "It could be a great opportunity for you, young lady."

"I used to be a model. I don't do it anymore," Marcella said firmly.

Mercifully, the elevator doors opened and the cramped occupants pushed into the gray-suede-upholstered anteroom of Spense Design. The first showing of any major collection was always crowded with press, the buyers for stores that purchased a lot from Spense, some of his rich customers, and a smattering of movie and Broadway stars who got free clothes from him in exchange for guest appearances at his openings. There were always too many people fighting for too few folding chairs at such moments.

The model with her giant duffel bag headed for a rear door behind a haughty and scowling combination of gatekeeper-receptionist. The door opened for an instant and the model disappeared into a room filled with naked bodies and twelve-hundred-dollar — wholesale — dresses.

"Don't worry," said the man from the Birdcage, still looming at Marcella's elbow. "I'll get us a seat. Spense is a friend of mine."

"It's all right."

He had pushed his way through the crowd to a mirror reflection of the guardian of the models' room. She was standing alert at the door to the main showroom. "Hi, there, missy." He beamed at the crone. "I'm Cecil Fine, from the Birdcage."

"Are you on the list?" The harpy made an impatient scan of a carefully typed three-page memo.

"We had two trunk showings at the Birdcage last year." Fine was doing his best salesman bit. "We do a lot of Spense business."

"Everyone does." The harpy was unimpressed.

"By the way," Cecil Fine added, "I'll need an extra place for my little friend here."

"I'm sorry, but there is no extra space," said the harpy, not even looking up. "You said your name was Stein?"

"No, Fine . . . and there must be a place for —"

"It's all right," Marcella interrupted. "I believe I'm on the list."

The harpy froze at the familiar soft voice. She looked up and paled. "Oh, Miss Todd. I didn't recognize you in this mess. Please, you and Mr. Fine can go right in. There are some refreshments in the private reception room. You know where it is."

"Thank you."

The padded suede-covered doors to the Spense inner sanctum opened. Marcella strode into the room with her usual long-legged model's walk, followed by Cecil Fine.

"I guess they know you," Fine said with admiration.

"I guess."

"Where do you want to sit?" the man asked.

"I usually sit over there by the door to the inner showroom," Marcella replied, walking to a chair upon which was emblazoned MARCELLA TODD - GOLDEN

LIMITED. To each side of it was a chair labeled GOLDEN LIMITED - ASSISTANT and GOLDEN LIMITED - PHOTOGRAPHER.

"What's Golden Limited?" Fine asked. "Some big chain or something?"

"It's a chain of newspapers. I write for them."

A look of recognition was followed by a look of awe spreading across the face of Cecil Fine. "I know that name. One of the newspapers in the Quad Cities carries your column. And in St. Louis, too."

"Those are good newspapers." Marcella smiled at her now-nervous escort. "The *Times Revue* is a Golden Limited-owned newspaper. The one in St. Louis buys my column from the Golden Syndicate."

"Wait until I tell my wife." Suddenly, Mr. Fine looked embarrassed. He had not meant to mention his wife, but it was too late. "She is always quoting your column. We have the one about the practicality of investing in furs framed in our fur salon."

"How nice of you." Marcella felt a kind of affection for the pudgy man from the Birdcage of Quincy-the-one-in-Illinois.

Cecil Fine was about to settle into the Golden Limited - Assistant seat when a slightly shrill voice echoed through the room.

"Where is she? Where is my Marcella? Darling, where are you hiding?" The black-clad slender form of Spense jerked into the room. His motions were halting and almost clumsy, self-conscious.

"There you are. God. I'm glad you could come. I'm so nervous." The cocaine-sunken eyes peered through dark glasses at Marcella. "It's moments like these when a person needs his friends."

"I'm sure everything will be fine." Marcella was

polite but unimpressed. This was not really a very important collection, and Spense did not really fear failure. But before the next hour passed, he would say approximately the same speech to dozens of his "needed friends."

"Just wait until you see the evening gowns . . ." Spense stopped in mid-sentence and stared at Cecil Fine. "And *who* is this?"

"Cecil Fine of the Birdcage in Quincy," Fine said, beaming. "We had two trunk showings from Spense Design last year."

"How thrilling." There was an edge in Spense's voice. Then he remembered that for some strange reason, this large lump of semipressed flesh was with the beautiful Marcella Todd. An instant smile enveloped his face. "The Birdcage. Of course. Lovely place, Quincy. Did you take the train down?"

"No, I flew."

"From Quincy," Spense remarked, making conversation. "Seems a waste. Isn't the time on the train about the same?"

"The train would take a day and a half."

"From Massachusetts?" Spense was becoming bored. "What abominable service!"

"But . . ." Fine started to explain.

"Oh, there is Liza." Spense jerked away. "Liza, darling, God, I'm glad you could come. I'm so nervous."

Marcella smiled at Cecil Fine. "Spense has a lot on his mind. He does get confused sometimes."

"Yes, he must," Fine said, looking hurt. "I guess that the Birdcage must seem like nothing to him. We sold almost two hundred thousand dollars retail of his crap last year from those trunk shows. That's a lot of money. Maybe not a lot to him. Dammit! He should have remembered."

Marcella suddenly felt sorry for Fine. "I am sure he does. That *is* a lot of business. It sounds as if the Birdcage is a fine store."

"It is. It really is. Counting the storage room, we have almost three thousand square feet and two floors. It's all class stuff. It's the best place between Davenport and St. Louis."

"It must make you very proud." Marcella smiled.

"It sure as hell does."

"You know, my assistant is not coming today," Marcella said to the man. "I would appreciate it if you could sit with me and give me your opinions of the collections. A lot of my readers do their shopping at stores just like the Birdcage, and I would really like to know what you think."

"I would be glad to help." Cecil Fine brightened, sitting down. "You know, we like the classic stuff. The faddy junk just does not go over in Quincy." He was perking up.

"I know," Marcella continued. "I was born in a little town in Ohio and lived there until college. I bet it is a lot like Quincy."

Suddenly, Marcella felt a strong hand come to rest on her thigh, *high* on her thigh. This had happened before. There was something about Marcella's long legs that seemed to attract a man's hand. She breathed deeply and turned to face her unwanted admirer.

"Burt!"

"Surprise!" Burt Rance, the publisher of the widely circulated daily fashion publication, *The Business*, smiled his perfect smile at her. She was familiar with both the

Burt Rance smile and the Burt Rance hand. It had been on her leg before. She shivered at the instant of memory.

"I didn't know you came to these things," Marcella said.

"I don't. I just took a chance that you would be here. I wanted to find out if you still hate me."

"I hardly hate you."

"Then there's hope," Rance said eagerly.

"Burt, we discussed this. I like you. I just do not want to be another head in the Burt Rance emotional trophy room."

Burt kept his tanned fingers tight against Marcella's upper leg. She did not remove the hand. It felt good, and nothing more could happen in this crowded room. Nothing more was going to happen ever again, she vowed.

"Have you been south?" Marcella asked.

"Yeah, the Bahamas," Burt answered. There was enough vanity in the handsome man to make him go south several times each winter to keep a real tan on his well-conditioned body and the right streaks of blond in his curly brown hair. "You look great."

"Thanks," Marcella said simply.

"Really great." Burt continued gazing deep into her eyes.

Cecil Fine was staring at Rance. "Might I introduce myself? I am Cecil Fine of the Birdcage." He stretched out his hand across Marcella to the other man.

"I'm Burt Rance. Glad to meet you, Cecil. What the hell is the Birdcage?"

"Burt Rance? The guy who owns *The Business*?" Cecil was in heaven. "That's my Bible at the Birdcage. Really glad to meet you."

"The Birdcage is a store in Quincy, Illinois,"

Marcella added. She felt ill at ease. Burt was still staring at her. To him, no one else in the room seemed to have any existence but Marcella.

"I need to talk to you," he said, his voice low and urgent.

"There isn't anything to talk about," Marcella replied. "We have said everything, and we will never agree. Please, Burt."

"You haven't changed your mind?"

"No!" Marcella was uncomfortable knowing Cecil Fine was overhearing every word.

"You will. I promise. Look, I don't want to sit through this thing. I just came to see you, not the latest overpriced Spense creations. I'll call you."

"Burt!"

He stood and headed with long strides toward the door, cutting through the tidal wave of chic and would-be chic people who were fighting for the seats.

Marcella felt a tear begin to form and fought it successfully. Damn, she could pick them. The men in her life. Her husband . . . well, ex-husband, then Kevin O'Hara, and most recently Burt Rance. They always seemed to be mistakes. Something was always wrong. They were out of sequence. Her husband wanted her to be exciting at a time when she only wanted to be a mother and a housewife. Kevin did not know what he wanted from her. Now Burt. For a while it looked as if that might just work. But only for a while. Burt wanted the traditional wife and lover at a time when Marcella was just beginning to feel secure in herself as a career person and an independent individual. They were all so out of sequence. Damn!

Marcella fought to organize her mind to cover the Spense show. It was time to work.

Suddenly, the suede-covered doors opened and the throng that had been impatiently corraled in the posh hallway broke into the main showroom and flooded over the chairs that lined that runway.

Through the throng of fashion seekers came a tall young man with a pair of Nikon cameras hanging around his neck. In a business and a town where image was everything, Zackery Jones had the perfect photographer look. His hair was thick and darkest brown, eyes blue. His body was good enough so that he was able to look perfect in a fashionable place wearing only tight jeans, a Polo pullover, and cumbersome-looking running shoes. His horn-rimmed glasses gave him a slightly studious look that was instantly charming when his frequent, shy smile appeared. Zackery Jones was often mistaken for a carefully tanned and gym-honed male model, but Jones's place was behind the camera, not in front of it. He had tried modeling when he first came to New York from Andover, Ohio, and could not get a job even as a photo assistant; he was too self-conscious and shy. His face froze in front of the camera. But behind a camera Zackery Jones was gifted.

"Hey, Ohioan!" Jones slid into the Golden Limited – Photographer chair.

"Hi, Zack." Marcella Todd had both affection and admiration for the photographer. His enthusiasm had impressed her when he had come looking for part-time work at Golden Limited to supplement his income as staff photographer — one of many and low men in seniority — at *Haute* magazine.

"Jeez!" Zack said with his best shy smile. "I hope this thing starts soon. I have to be back at *Haute* by nine-thirty for the warm-up."

"Warm-up?"

"Yeah, my boss always gives the troops a little coaching before the weekly staff meeting with Miss Harrington.

"She's quite a legend," Marcella observed.

"You better believe. Sometimes I'm glad to be low man on that totem pole. I might just be the darkroom boy, but I don't have to take the hassle that the stars do."

"You'll be a star someday," Marcella said, really believing what she said. When she had looked through Zack's portfolio, filled with photos of some of the highest-priced models in New York — who had posed for Zack for free — she had recognized the potential. That was why she employed him on a freelance basis instead of using one of the Golden Limited staff photographers.

"Yeah . . . I can hope."

A new harpy walked along the front row, passing out sheets recording the run of the show, listing each outfit and its wholesale price. Marcella circled a few outfits on her sheet, then passed it to Zack.

"This is a pretty good spot," Zack said as he surveyed his shooting area. "Some good natural light coming from the windows, and that archway for a background. Yeah, it should be all right."

"Is there anyone here from *Haute*? Marcella asked.

"Heck, no," Zack answered. "The queen arranged a private showing of Spense's best stuff last week for her and the girls. He's even pulled some of the stuff from this show so it will be seen first in *Haute*."

Zack turned and started setting his exposures and adjusting lenses. The room was overfilled and the air conditioning was needed, even though outside it was the middle of winter.

Marcella's reportorial instincts were aroused. *If this is such a nothing collection this time, why the big secret showing for* Haute? she wondered. Spense had to be planning something, and knowing Spense, she guessed that it must be good.

Cecil Fine had been intently studying the arriving crowd. "My God!" he said suddenly. "There's Miranda Dante."

It was indeed the famous Miranda Dante. Movie star. Wife to seven of the richest or most interesting men in the world. Owner of the Star of Madeira diamond. The semiconstant cover of every gossip magazine on the planet.

"She must be thinking of divorcing the Vice President," Marcella mumbled to herself.

"How do you know?" Fine asked eagerly.

"I have this theory on Miranda Dante's marriage habits. Whenever she goes on a diet and loses fifty pounds or so, she is always about to dump her latest husband. See! She's thin again."

"She looks great!" Fine gushed with admiration.

"That is exactly what I mean. When she married Senator Parker, she gained a ton. Remember the Presidential campaign photos? She was buried in yards of carefully draped Spense taffeta."

"Uh-huh."

"She eats when she is happy and diets when she is miserable. It's a pattern with her." Marcella was sure the gossip columns would soon be buzzing again.

Zack had bounded across the room to where Miranda Dante was posing in a doorway. Her famous lavender eyes sparkled in the explosion of flashbulbs. "Now, boys," she cooed, "what do you want to take pictures of a fat old matron for?" She kept smiling her Academy

Award-winning smile. "Now I am going to find my chair — if they have saved a place for me."

They had saved a throne. The spot directly in the center of the room across from the best place to photograph the models had been reserved for Miranda Dante. She would appear in thousands of publications sitting straight and demurely behind the latest Spense collections. Spense was no fool.

"Hello, Marcella," Miranda said, waving a lavender silk scarf across the runway toward Marcella.

"Hello, Mrs. Parker," Marcella answered.

An instant look of pain crossed the carefully calculated face of the star. Only a few months earlier, she had clung to her new husband's arm and told the press she was "just Mrs. Parker." Now that title caused an instant twinge of pain. Marcella's reporter's instinct told her immediately that husband number eight must be already in the planning stages. Too bad. Marcella had liked Miranda Dante in spite of her reputation for being self-centered and demanding. She had written in an inteview:

Perhaps Miranda Dante's ability to feel, that ability that has made her such a sensitive actress, is what causes her lack of success in marriages. She might be *too* sensitive. Too quick to feel rejection. And too demanding, not just of others, but of herself. But in an age when many women with her beauty and wealth would be content to have affair after affair, Miranda Dante keeps trying to find that perfect marriage. She does try.

Miranda had sent Marcella a handwritten note commenting on the story.

"Great skin," Zack said, impressed. "She must be pushing fifty, and the skin is still clean and taut. She isn't even wearing a ton of makeup."

Suddenly, some trendy taped music blared through several huge speakers, indicating the fashion show was about to begin.

Spense walked onto the makeshift runway that rambled through the space of the vast showroom. This was highly unusual. Usually, the designer waited until the end of the show to appear, and even then he'd arrive only after being coaxed by waves of carefully planned applause.

"My friends," Spense started. Zack and his fellow photographers sped toward Spense, focusing frantically. "I have made a change in the program because there is something I want to show you."

Marcella pulled out her felt-tipped pen and notebook.

"The last few years have been confusing economically. While Spense Design has done well, I feel we could have done a lot better. As you might have heard, there has been a rumor that my clothes are considered . . . well . . . perhaps a trifle expensive." A murmur of laughter wafted through the room. Spense's clothes were *too* expensive.

"So, for the last eighteen months I have been working on what I have called Project X. Doesn't that sound very mysterious?"

More murmurs.

"Now I want you to see the results of Project X . . . my new Project XSPENSE Collection."

A group of towering black beauties jumped onto the runway and stormed the length of the room wearing the simple draped silk dresses that had made Spense famous. His simplicity and draping were his trademark.

He had a talent for creating clothing that could either cling to a great body or flow in disguising layers around a more ample figure. Any woman would look her best in a Spense drape dress.

"There is something very unusual about this Spense dress," Spense said, looking at the expression of the crowd. "I know what you are thinking. Spense knows. You think it is the same dress I have been doing for years." More murmurs. "It is. But this dress will retail for under three hundred dollars."

Some scattered applause came forth from the audience. Spense's famous classic dress usually cost more than nine hundred dollars.

Cecil Fine was paying very close attention.

"There are differences, of course. Less hand-sewing. The lining is a lesser silk. The label is not in gold thread. But now more women can be Spense women."

Applause.

"I must go back and see to the girls, but the first part of the show will be a special segment of some of the Project XSPENSE Collection. I hope you love it," the designer finished, blowing kisses to the applauding crowd.

The music started again. More girls came onto the runway. This time they were wearing the famous Spense raincoats in shades of navy, white, mint, yellow, pink, powder-blue, and gray.

"The navy, powder-blue, gray, and pink ones will sell for me," Fine muttered as he jotted sale numbers in his notebook. "The women would like the white, but it would never survive a Midwestern winter. I think he made a mistake by not offering them in black, beige, and grape. They aren't new colors, but they always sell."

Marcella looked at Fine and made a note of his comments. Zack was bent on one knee, waiting for the perfect moment to photograph the raincoats. "Tasha," he said, "hold it there a sec." Tasha, a model who had already appeared in one of Zack's test photos, paused dramatically in the archway while the rest of the show slowed behind her.

"Anything for you, Zack." She smiled, then glared her best sexy-model glare at the Nikon. "Got it?" Then, with a sweep of the trenchcoat, she lunged onward.

A collection of simple draped one-shoulder evening dresses in prints was followed by the same styles in solid reds and blacks.

"The blacks will sell like crazy." Fine beamed. "Nobody could tell that they are not the real expensive stuff. But the prints really look too Hawaiian. Women will never buy those, because everybody will always remember the dress after they had worn it once."

Some simple two-piece business suits were paraded down the runway by a gaggle of models carrying identical briefcases and wearing identical horn-rimmed glasses. The suits were in the same colors as the raincoats.

"I can't believe it." Fine was visibly upset. "No blacks. No tweeds. Who in hell wants to wear a mint-green suit all winter? The price is only three-twenty-five retail. I could sell dozens of them, but not in yellow and mint-green."

Marcella took more notes. The Project XSPENSE Collection was limited and brief. It was over in ten minutes. Then the regular costly and abundant Spense Design collection began. An hour later it was all over, and the crowd stampeded toward the elevators.

"Come on," Zack said, going toward the door. "Let's take the back stairs."

"Just a second," Marcella whispered as she leaned toward Zack. "See that man over there next to where I was sitting?" She pointed toward Cecil Fine, who was frantically writing in his notebook. "Shoot some candids of him."

"Sure." Zack pulled the 180-mm lens from his camera bag for some close-ups of Fine's serious expressions. A few clicks and he was finished. "When do you want them?"

"Give me the roll. I'll have them developed at my office." Zack looked wounded at Marcella's suggestion. He took pride in developing and printing all his own shots.

"You sure are in a hurry," he said as he emptied the last rolls from the cameras and sorted through his film bag for the rolls he'd already shot.

"I want to move a story on this right away," Marcella said. She could see Zack's disappointment. "I'll make sure you get a credit line on this stuff."

"Wow!" Zack beamed. "Great!"

Fine looked up. Marcella Todd waved good-bye, and she and Zack slipped through the rear door to the back stairs. Only a few of the models and people who were very familiar with the old brick building knew of the existence of the back stairs. The echo of spiked heels resounded throughout the twelve floors.

"Good luck at your staff meeting," Marcella said.

"Heck," Zack answered as the pair arrived at Seventh Avenue, "nobody will even know I'm there." He turned and walked east toward Park Avenue. She walked north toward the Golden Limited offices on

Sixth Avenue. She could have taken a cab, but Marcella Todd had learned long ago that the fastest mode of transportation in midtown Manhattan was the feet. And right then she wanted to move fast.

Minutes later she was sitting at her cluttered and battered desk in the well-used Golden Limited offices in one of the skyscrapers in the new section of Rockefeller Center. The furniture had always been newspaper functional, and a decade of coffee stains and desk-eaten lunches had added a certain journalistic patina of worn edges and a tarnished finish.

"Jake," Marcella said to the wire editor, "can you squeeze some time for me on the afternoon transmission? I think I have something special."

"For you, anything." Jake was one of the original members of the cigar-chomping, brusque-talking, big-hearted school of jouralism. He loved to stare admiringly at Marcella's legs.

Marcella turned toward a computerized videoscreen and keyboard that stared back at her in shades of mute green blankness. Her long fingers flashed across the keyboard. She typed onto the screen:

Log on code . . . Fashion / Marcella.

She pressed another button and the screen filled with a listing of stories she was in the process of releasing to the wire service. At the bottom of the list she added:

SLUG Quincy.

The screen cleared. Then she typed:

By MARCELLA TODD
The Golden Syndicate

Today New York's designer for the rich and the famous decided it was time he did something for the rest of the world. The great Spense might be able to offer that famous Spense look at, if not bargain prices, costs that are only a third of his normal costliness.

But will the Project XSPENSE Collection play in Quincy?

"Maybe," says Cecil Fine, who, with his wife, Cynthia, owns and operates the Birdcage, the largest fashion store between Davenport, Iowa, and St. Louis, in the small city of Quincy, Illinois.

While Spense has always been the designer to the chic and instantly with-whatever-is-new set in New York, Chicago, Houston, Dallas, and Beverly Hills, what will happen to the king of Seventh Avenue as he attempts to storm Main Street?

Forty-five minutes later, Marcella Todd typed "END" to the story and pressed the store button that instantly committed her newest column to the computer's memory.

She picked up the phone and dialed the photo desk. "I want the proof sheet pronto," she told the editor. "I need them for an eleven o'clock deadline."

"Thanks a lot, Marcella." The photo editor enjoyed complaining almost as much as he enjoyed beating tight deadlines.

By the deadline, the story on Cecil Fine and his Birdcage and the new Spense collection, complete with four photos, would be transmitted to newspapers across the nation. It would be treated more like a fast-breaking news story than a fashion piece. Some papers would run the story on the business pages instead of in what was still called The Woman's Section. The Quincy, Illinois, paper would put the story on page one.

A week later, Marcella Todd would receive a grateful note from Mr. and Mrs. Cecil Fine. Fine would be asked to speak at the next Midwestern Fashion Conference in Chicago. And instead of selling twenty thousand dollars in Spense clothing that year, he would nearly break the hundred grand mark in Spense goods.

Marcella Todd sipped a Pepsi Light and started through her mail, smiling. It was a good story.

Chapter Three

It had been Sylvia's idea to move the *Haute* magazine offices to a Park Avenue address. Dickie — only Sylvia ever called him Dickie — Barkley, the publisher and grandson of the founder of Pendlington Publications, would have preferred to keep the offices on Madison Avenue in the depths of Publishers' Row. But, as usual when Sylvia and Dickie disagreed, Sylvia got what she wanted.

"For Christ's sake, Dickie!" she had roared. "*Haute* has gone from being a silly woman's magazine to serving as the voice of fashion, interior design, entertainment, gossip, and beautiful people for the entire world. It just does not look right for us to be in these crappy offices."

"Maybe we can add another floor of space." Dickie honestly had been trying.

"Bullshit!" Sylvia had exploded, sending Dickie, as usual, scurrying to the security behind his grandfather's massive desk, a desk that had outlasted the old man by more than three decades. "This is a class magazine, and I want a class address. *Haute* deserves Park Avenue.

You can stay on Madison Avenue if you wish. I am taking the magazine to Park.''

And again, as usual, Sylvia had been right. She signed the lease — or, rather, she forced Dickie to sign — for the top four floors of one of those black monster buildings at Forty-eighth Street. Part of the deal was that the letters H-A-U-T-E be installed at the top of the building. At night, it was eye-catching, one of the focal points of one of the most glamorous strips of cement in the world.

And why not? Sylvia thought as the car inched into the NO PARKING OR STOPPING ANYTIME zone in front of the *Haute* building. More than eight million people bought *Haute* (three dollars a copy at the newsstand) every month in the United States alone. The French and Italian editions added another three million in worldwide circulation. Income generated in the last fiscal year exceeded fifty-four million dollars. All this came at a time when postal-rate increases and dwindling advertising had forced dozens of magazines, including some of *Haute*'s competition, out of business.

Haute definitely deserved Park Avenue.

Sylvia waited for Sandy to open the heavy door of the stretch limousine. The few seconds that Sandy took to exit on the driver's side, walk around the car, and open the passenger's door were a favorite part of her day. It was a neat end to her morning privacy period and a start of the hectic daily world of *Haute*. Sylvia approved of well-defined endings and beginnings to everything.

"Will you need the car for lunch?" Sandy asked.

"I don't know."

Sandy would wait, reading the *Times* first, then the *Daily News*. He had not read the *Post* since its fashion editor had referred curtly to Sylvia as "the grandmother of the American fashion press." It would never do for Miss Harrington to find a shred of the *Post* in her limousine.

Sylvia swept through the marble-and-glass lobby to the express elevators that led up to *Haute*'s offices. A brass sign outside the elevators read *HAUTE* RECEPTION: FORTY-NINTH FLOOR. She took a key from her purse and turned a special lock where the button should have been for the fifty-second floor. Only she and Dickie had such keys; the staff and the rest of the world had to stop first in the forty-ninth-floor reception area, with its posh silk Oriental rugs, Louis-the-something-or-other furniture, and curving staircase that did not really have much purpose but was very dramatic.

The doors opened at the fifty-second floor.

The walls were of bleached teakwood and were lined with paintings, all expensive. A few even were good. All had at one time or another adorned the pages of *Haute*. Erté. Miró. Even a few Picassos. Only the Ertés were actually "fashion." The rest, including some superb Georgia O'Keeffes, were bought by Richard Barkley for his own amusement, and Sylvia had humored him by insisting that they be used in some of the magazine layouts. Thus, Barkley was happy, and the investigators from the Internal Revenue Service were satisfied that these rather large expenditures really were for business purposes.

The carpeting was black and very thick in order to swallow any sound that might dare to intrude on the atmosphere of the fifty-second floor. The only color came from the paintings, hung in identical heavy gold-leaf frames and lighted brilliantly by dramatic pinpoint spots. The rest of the lighting in the reception area was dim. At one end stood a large semicircular teak desk that matched the walls. Some pinpoint spots illuminated the executive-floor receptionist. Besides the paintings, she was the only color, the only sign of life evident at first glance. Even the plants seemed to have been freeze-dried and mummified at their moment of perfection.

"Good morning, Miss Harrington," the receptionist said, jumping to attention. One of the few enjoyments Sylvia permitted herself at the office was the succession of nameless receptionists and their reactions to her and her legend. The female employees of *Haute* usually were extremely homogeneous. With only a few nearly invisible exceptions, they were rich or well bred, often both. They had recently graduated from suitable schools and wanted a career in "exciting New York." After their brief career fling, they usually married someone suitably rich and/or well bred. They all had family subsidized apartments filled with ferns somewhere on or near Central Park West.

The girls of *Haute* would become women of privilege.

There were charge accounts at Bendel's, Saks, Bloomingdale's, and Bergdorf's, with instructions that the bills be sent to accountants someplace "for handling."

They had come to *Haute* to find themselves and were, for the first time in their carefully insulated lives, exposed to rasping, carping, unforgiving, insulting criticism from Miss Harrington. All for slave wages. Girls at *Haute* seldom made more than two hundred dollars a week in the glamour jobs. The secretaries, the telephone operators, the cleaning women — all made more than the editorial assistants and the fashion associates who were proud to have their names printed on the *Haute* masthead.

The pay was not important to them. The aristocratic

comers and goers on the masthead were never there for the money. *Haute* was an experience. It was a place to be for a few months before returning to the Junior League world back in Gross Pointe, Lake Forest, Brentwood — thank God, Sylvia thought, not many Californians were interested — Shaker Heights, and always Scarsdale. The term "editorial assistant" reeked of prestige and glamour. The receptionist outside the executive offices was an editorial assistant. She would never write a word, except in letters back to Scottsdale — or was it River Oaks? — extolling the benefits of her time in Manhattan, and she would go for coffee and politely answer the phone and graciously wallow in the mire of Sylvia's cutting remarks.

"Who did your hair?" Sylvia demanded as she passed the receptionist, never breaking her stride. The girl smiled graciously; she was used to receiving compliments. She had, indeed, spent hours in the beauty shop having her black hair sheared and permed and streaked. Now, Miss Harrington had noticed, and her clever little plan was working perfectly.

"Antonio. He has a *wonderful* little shop on Madison near Grand Central." The speech was carefully rehearsed to fill the few seconds that it took for Miss Harrington to pass her desk. "He used to be with Kenneth, but he felt his talent was being stifled, so he opened his own place. It's just *adorable*. I really think he's a *genius*. Perhaps we could mention him in the book." Magazine people called every issue of a magazine "the book," and editorial assistants loved using the term. "Don't you think he might do some work for —"

"You look like a whore," Sylvia snapped. "Fix it at lunch."

Thus, poor Antonio, with his dreams of being made

famous on the pages of *Haute*, was to remain un-
discovered in the shoestring shop on the wrong part of
Madison Avenue. He was doomed to anonymity and a
life of fifty-dollar permanents instead of two-hundred-
fifty-dollar creative cuts. The receptionist would cancel
a lunch date at the Dove with a rich and well-bred boy to
rush a few blocks to Saks to buy a turban.

Sylvia realized no one had ever before called the little
girl from Scottsdale a whore. The pampered princesses
who were part of her court had always been carefully
sheltered from insults and hurt. While many young girls
often suffered all manner of degradation as part of
growing to adulthood in the unsheltered world of public
schools, most *Haute* staffers were raised and educated
in expensive and carefully cultured institutions of pro-
priety in Switzerland or the hills of Virginia and Pennsylvania.

True, the word "whore" was not exactly new to
them. Even well-bred girls today exchanged insults and
profanities. But being called a "whore" by someone
they desperately wanted to impress was crushing. Sylvia
realized that. She had experienced similar scenes hundreds of times over the decades. She considered it a contribution to the education that the girls of *Haute* should
receive during their months in the big city. She enjoyed
being the teacher . . . God, she enjoyed it.

Jayne Caldwell watched the brief scene from the open
door to Sylvia's office.

"I rather liked her hair," she said in her clear Boston-
accented voice, which was in no way an affectation. As
Sylvia stuffed the sable into her private closet in the
anteroom outside her office, Jayne continued her ever-
so-slight upbraiding. Jayne Caldwell was one of the few
people who could challenge Sylvia Harrington in any

way. No one on the outside of *Haute*'s innermost circle could understand why this was tolerated. Shy, "Plain Jayne" — her nickname among the slick and glittering members of the staff — could, in her careful, soft way, reprimand her boss and get away with it.

Sylvia was bored with Jayne. She had probably always been bored with her. But she needed Jayne and her ability to plod through the endless daily operations that were required to produce the magazine. And Sylvia took care to tolerate whatever was absolutely essential to her or to *Haute* magazine.

To make a point of something as insignificant as a receptionist's hairstyle, Jayne, too, must have had a bad morning, Sylvia thought to herself. "You must be joking," Sylvia said. "You liked *that*?" The voice carried out to the reception area. "Perhaps this whatever-his-name might have the appropriate talent for some other publication. Maybe something like the *National Enquirer* or the *Police Gazette*. Does he do corpses?"

Jayne did not bother to respond. Instead, she opened the double doors to Sylvia's huge office, which overlooked the entire east side of Manhattan. She walked across the Oriental rugs to a twenty-foot drawing table covered with black Formica. Cardboard-mounted pages of the May issue of *Haute* were arranged to neat rows on the table awaiting the initials "SH" to be inscribed and circled in each upper right-hand corner.

"We need final authorization for the Blass layout for May," Jayne began.

There was a kind of time warp in the magazine business. The calendar might indicate that it was the middle of a cold and snowy January for most of the real world. But in the magazine business, it was already spring and a time of billowing dresses and light coats. It would be very easy to become disoriented in a world where it was necessary always to live in the future. Even though the weather was miserable, some of the girls of *Haute* magazine already were wearing light cottons and silks they had managed to glean from the designers in advance of the season.

"Let's see," Sylvia said, exchanging her sunglasses for matching tinted reading glasses. The plastic-covered pages were handed to her in pairs so that she could see them just as her eight million-plus readers would view them when they read their May *Haute*.

"What ads are against this?" Sylvia asked as she checked a blank page marked "Saks."

"It's for a Blass raincoat," Jayne answered instantly. "They requested special position opposite the lead page of the Blass layout."

"Will it conflict with anything in the layout?" Sylvia detested the idea of repetiton of merchandise in an issue, either in the editorial sections or in the advertising pages.

"The coat is not in the layout, and the lead page is mostly text and a photo of Bill. It's only a small insert photo in the center of the text block. I see no conflict."

"I suppose." Sylvia scanned the remaining pages. "Hmm, nice. Get a better transparency of this one. Move this photo. Good God! What's that? Add some bugle beads there and reshoot. That looks too heavy. This is almost summer, you know."

"Would you like to read the copy?" Jayne asked. She already knew that Sylvia did not want to see the story. She never read the copy. She was a terrible writer. Sylvia Harrington had absolutely no appreciation for the printed word. In fact, when she first took over *Haute*, she practically banished words from the magazine and opted for huge dramatic photographs. Actually, the famous editor was almost illiterate. Jayne always handled all the nonphotographic editorial content of the magazine. But she knew always to ask.

"Any problems with the copy?" Sylvia questioned.

"None. We have an excellent interview with Hubert de Givenchy. You know how shy and boring Hubert usually is? Well, this interview is different. He talks about more than just fashion."

"Hmm," Sylvia muttered. *There is nothing more than fashion,* she thought.

"Perhaps we could give the story some promotion," Jayne suggested carefuly.

"No. The photographs are not strong enough. Use the Blass in the television ads." Sylvia did not really believe that any of the readers of *Haute* read. They preferred photographs — big, glossy, dramatic photos of haughty-looking women in expensive settings.

Sylvia knew she could have promoted the Givenchy story. If she had suggested the idea herself, the advertising people would be planning a commercial in a matter of hours. But she did not want to agree with Jayne. Sylvia Harrington did not like Jayne Caldwell. Jayne had become too necessary to *Haute.* It was Jayne who had added the new interest in writing to what had become basically a picture magazine. The readership surveys had shown that the younger audience so much desired by the advertising department liked something to read, something with insight, as well as pretty pictures to look at. Jayne, the managing editor, had had a job that dealt mostly with checking spelling and proofreading. Then she had started adding her feature stories.

A profile of a designer here, a gossip-packed look in a star's closet there. She always seemed to have dozens of ideas.

The response had been impressive and immediate. More than one hundred thousand new readers sent subscription money during the first month of Jayne's "written-word experiment." Sylvia never could understand why. Jayne Caldwell did and it made her indispensable. It also made Sylvia Harrington nervous.

Jayne had always been a wallflower. Her hair was plain and mousy; her face was well scrubbed and uninspiring. Her clothes were practical Pendleton knits. Her shoes were sensible. She was always very Boston. But at least she kept her mouth shut while Sylvia was accepting all the praise for the new changes in *Haute.*

All this bothered Sylvia. It was one thing to take credit for the work and talent of others; that was normal in the publishing business. But Sylvia hated the changes. She thought they were mistakes, every one of them. Yet they were successful changes, and the circulation started expanding with a transfusion of young and affluent readers. Sylvia worried. She worried that something new was happening that she could not understand, something that made someone else necessary for the future of *Haute.*

"Is Dickie in?" Sylvia was ready to change the subject.

"Mr. Barkley is due at ten."

Good, Sylvia thought. After more than twenty-five years of uselessness, Dickie had finally given up pretending to have any effect on *Haute* magazine and fallen into a schedule of arriving late, going to lunch, and leaving early. He no longer attempted to become involved in the day-to-day editorial aspects of the magazine, which was exactly the way Sylvia wanted it. Let Dickie busy himself lunching with some advertiser or something.

"Anything in the mail?" Sylvia asked.

If there had been anything important, a major showing, a request from an important advertiser, or a note from Jackie or that dreadful Truman, it would have demanded immediate attention. There wasn't.

"How about Dickie's mail?"

"It's here." Jayne detested opening Barkley's mail but did it because ever since the time in the mid-seventies when a Chicago food company had tried to buy the magazine, Sylvia had wanted to see the corporate mail before Barkley saw it. She fortunately, had found out about the buy-out offer in time to browbeat Dickie into not selling. No more chances with the mail had been taken since then.

"Just some garbage," Jayne said.

"Put it there."

Jayne placed a pile of about thirty envelopes on Sylvia's rosewood desk, turned, and left the somber office, headed for the relief of the constant editorial hubbub among the writers and artists on the floor below. While she had impressive offices on the penthouse floor, Jayne really preferred the chattering and confusion — and the creativity — of the editorial, art, and photographic departments.

"The meeting at ten?" Jayne reminded Sylvia as she stood in the doorway.

"All right." Sylvia motioned her away with a wave of her hand.

Jayne gently closed the double doors as she left and Sylvia glanced at the mail. Her practiced eyes could instantly sort through the envelopes without reading the return addresses. There was the junk mail. The invitations. Pleading notes from publicity people whose large salaries hinged on the number of appearances they wheedled for their clients in magazines such as *Haute*. She tossed the duplicate invitations for parties and showings into the wastebasket. She disliked it when Dickie attended the same showing as she did. This tended to confuse people about who should be the center of attention. He did, after all, own the magazine. She did, everyone knew, run *Haute*.

Then her eye noticed the postcard.

It carried a photo of Rio, showing the statue of Christ standing atop Corcavado. On the back, where the message should have been, was just "Tom A." Nothing more.

"So that's where he is," Sylvia said softly to herself.

Satisifed with her mail inspection, Sylvia gathered the surviving letters and the card and walked through an archway to a second pair of doors, which opened to a huge pale green drawing room that stretched between her corner office and Richard Barkley's corner office. The sixty-foot room was designed to resemble the salon where she had first seen a showing of Dior back in the early days at *Haute*. The showing had been in some château outside Paris. She no longer remembered the name of the castle, but she had never forgotten a single detail of the magnificent room.

The delicate clouds painted on the ceiling. The gilt furniture. The aging mirrors that were a century past giving accurate reflections. When the time came to create the penthouse offices, she recreated the salon as a drawing room high above the canyons of Manhattan. Perhaps the ornateness of the drawing room was at odds with the austere design of the entrance corridor. So what! she thought. This was the room where the people who filled the pages of *Haute*, the proud and the beautiful and the rich, would come to pay homage to the magazine and the woman who created it. It was the throne room of the kingdom of *Haute*. The penthouse floor was, indeed, a palace of publishing.

It was the setting for the public Sylvia Harrington.

The executive floor also boasted a complete kitchen and bakery, where two shifts of chefs and kitchen staff toiled over the preparation of sumptuous lunches and occasional dinner parties. The wine was always brought from a storage area in the basement of the building, lest even the slight structural swayings of the skyscraper damage the integrity of the delicate Margaux and Latours. There was only French wine in the cellars of *Haute*. No California vintages.

The dining room could seat fifty, though it was usually set for not more than a dozen. There was a library filled with leather-bound volumes, a few of which were collector's items. Waterford decanters waited there filled with sherry and port. There was a pair of bedrooms; they were seldom used, but they were most impressive to the people who managed a look or an evening in the *Haute* penthouse. The dining room was probably the most popular of all. It was a status symbol for a designer, a model, a photographer, an employee, or an advertiser to receive an engraved and hand-delivered invitation to eat in its Haviland & Co. splendor surrounded by walnut walls torn from some ancient English country house.

Sylvia walked through the drawing room doors that led to Richard Barkley's suite. The carpeting changed from mint-green to pale blue. There were more expensive Oriental silk rugs. The paneling was solid mahogany. The room was dominated by the desk. In spite of the careful refinishing and restoring, the heavy carved-oak desk — originally bought by William Randolph Hearst and stored away in a warehouse near his California palace for thirty years before being added to the Barkley family image — remained a clumsy and dominating piece of furniture. In spite of the five pale blue upholstered wingback chairs gathered in a semicircle in front of the desk, the desk overpowered the large room. Sylvia silently walked across the ancient blue-and-ivory Oriental rug and piled the mail neatly on the blotter, the postcard placed conspicuously on top.

"More busy work for you, Dickie, dear," she hissed.

The view from the windows of Richard Barkley's office included the entire lower portion of the island of Manhattan from the Hudson River, around the Battery, to the East River. It was the sort of view available only to the richest tycoons with exorbitantly priced leases.

Maybe the office was larger than Sylvia's. But it was not the heart of *Haute*. He might have the title and all those shares of stock, but she had the power. It was a fair trade. No, she did not want his office.

She returned through the thick silence of the nearly empty penthouse floor to the endless blinking of her mute phone. It was time to deal with a few of the more important or interesting calls.

First to be taken care of was Melissa Fenton, the beautiful Melissa Fenton. Sylvia had created Melissa Fenton. Certainly, Melissa had been beautiful the morning three years before when Eleanor Franklin of Franklin Models had personally asked Sylvia to "take a look at this girl." There was something so special about Melissa's look. She was, of course, tall. Her hair was black and so thick it had a perpetual wild look. Her pale gray eyes seemed to change colors with her mood. Her body was graceful, with tight, firm breasts. But what was unique about Melissa Fenton was her fabulous alabaster skin, perfection on every square inch of her body. Sylvia had marveled at the skin as she watched Melissa change from one high-fashion outfit to another. It was so opposite her own pasty coloring.

Melissa Fenton's first legitimate modeling assignment was to pose for the cover of *Haute*. Sylvia's orders. And she had been used in every issue since. Her modeling rate had climbed to five thousand dollars a day under the careful guidance and support of Sylvia Harrington. Sylvia had done everything for Melissa. She had given her fame and money. All she wanted in return was total loyalty and devotion, something Melissa was incapable of giving to anyone.

Lately, Melissa had been disappearing for days. Nobody knew where. A dozen calls to her answering service were always fruitless. Yes, Sylvia Harrington was going to have to teach Melissa Fenton a lesson, a lesson in gratitude.

Instead of placing the call to Eleanor Franklin through her secretary, Sylvia dialed the special Franklin Models number herself. A few blocks away, the private line on Eleanor Franklin's desk rang its two-tone chime.

"This is Eleanor Franklin." The voice was husky and slightly sensual.

"This is Sylvia."

"Darling." The voice was filled with calculated charm.

"What can I do for my favorite magazine editor?"

"We have a problem today, Eleanor," Sylvia started. "It's Melissa Fenton — again." Sylvia had never complained about her pet Melissa before, but she knew others had and thought the "again" was a nice touch. "She left us in the lurch today. No reason. She just left a message on the service."

"That's shocking." Eleanor's mind was racing at the possibilities.

"It's quite a problem for us."

"I'll send someone over immediately. Who would you like?" Eleanor sounded efficient.

"That's unnecessary. We got someone really fabulous from Ford Models, a new girl." Sylvia was lying. She knew this loss of business and clout with *Haute* would damage Eleanor. "What I'm worried about is Melissa. Does she have a drug problem?"

"Don't they all?" Eleanor answered. "I really don't think she is any worse than most of the other models."

"I think she's been photographing a bit drawn lately," Sylvia continued. "Perhaps *Haute* should refrain from using her for a while. She's *associated* with our magazine, you realize, and if she were to get some bad publicity — some drug publicity, let's say — it could reflect on *Haute*."

Eleanor tensed. If *Haute* were to drop Melissa Fenton, there would be lots of gossip. If she got a reputation as an undependable druggie, she might rapidly go out of fashion with all Eleanor's other clients. What Sylvia Harrington was quietly threatening was the destruction of Melissa Fenton's career. Eleanor did not give a damn about Melissa; there were always more beautiful women. What she did not want to lose was her commission, the current high esteem with which she was regarded by Sylvia Harrington, and the constant access Franklin Models had to the pages of *Haute*.

"What do you suggest?" Eleanor asked tactfully.

"It really is not my problem. But if I were you," Sylvia continued, "I would give the girl a much-needed rest. She evidently cannot take the strain of some of the really big jobs. There's another point: a cut in income might bring her back to reality."

She wants me to dump Melissa, Eleanor thought. In a business where a model could be instantly hot, then instantly cold, Sylvia Harrington was cooling Melissa Fenton.

"You're quite right," Eleanor said. "I'll shift some of her clients. Quietly. Melissa does need the rest."

"I think that would be good for both of you," Sylvia added. Both women knew what Sylvia meant. It was either shift the business away from Melissa to one of the other Franklin models, or lose the commissions to another agency that would be all too willing to court the favor of Sylvia Harrington. "I knew you'd understand," the editor cooed into the phone. Then she replaced the ornate receiver and turned toward her fine view of New York. She had won again.

Eleanor Franklin held the phone in her hand, forgetting for a while to replace it in the cradle. What had Melissa Fenton really done to cause her benefactor to assassinate her? "I thought Melissa really had that situation under control," she mumbled to herself. "How could she have blown it?"

Back at her *Haute* office, Sylvia was buzzing her personal secretary. "Get Spense," she growled into the intercom.

A few minutes later, the secretary buzzed back. "He's on line five, Miss Harrington."

Sylvia waited a few minutes before picking up the receiver. There were few people who could keep the haughty and arrogant Spense waiting on a dead phone early on a Monday morning, but one of them was Sylvia Harrington.

Finally she picked up the receiver. "Spense!"

"Sylvia." Spense was dripping with warmth. "I should be furious. Just furious with you. You didn't come to my show this morning. I was devastated."

"You'll survive."

"It was beastly."

Spense, Sylvia thought, was overdoing the fake emotion.

"There was no one from *Haute*," the designer continued. "Not a person. Do you hate me?"

"I saw the collection last week," Sylvia reminded him. "Shall we forget about the past? What did you want?" She was rapidly tiring of chitchat. "I believe you called me, Zip." Only a few people who knew him before he had become important enough to have only one name — back when he was Norman Spense Fryberger, a nervous kid with post-pubescent acne taking classes at the New York School of Design — ever called Spense by his onetime nickname.

"Well, you are *coming*, aren't you?" he asked.

"To what?" Sylvia was almost irritated.

"My party for Miranda at the Sixes," Spense explained patiently.

"You mean the Vice President's wife? That sow."

"Miranda is not that bad," Spense said carefully. "She can be rather funny if she isn't drunk. The crowd is going to be a little different. She has included a bunch of Washington types."

"Sounds deadly."

"You absolutely *must* come." Spense was at his most cajoling.

"Friday evening?"

"After her performance at Lincoln Center. Can you believe that she is doing *Romeo and Juliet* readings? She should be reciting *Moby Dick*."

"Someone might harpoon her." Sylvia was enjoying herself.

"Not *that Moby Dick*. I was referring to her sex life with the Vice President. I hear that old passion pit is killing him."

Sylvia was amused by Spense's viciousness. She did not smile. She never smiled. But she was definitely amused.

"You *must* come," Spense repeated. "I have done this little number for Miranda that buries her in several square miles of taffeta. She looks like a cross between Shirley Temple and the Hindenberg."

"One of your best efforts, I'm sure."

"I feel like Christo. Wasn't he the artist who wrapped Pittsburgh in toilet paper, or something like that?"

Sylvia tapped her nails on her desk. "Christo is an artist, dear boy, which means the two of you have absolutely nothing in common."

"Oh, good, you're insulting me. That means you really love me and you will come to my party." Spense was genuinely relieved to find himself the butt of the insults.

"The Vice President will be there?" Sylvia was considering likely press coverage.

"I promise, if he can walk, he will be there."

"All right."

"Marvelous. Now I must go. Should I send a car for you?" Spense figured the gesture, though likely to be refused, would score some points.

"No, I'd rather have my own car in case I need to make an escape. I hate political conversation. I never want to hear another word about difficult times and confused economics."

"Whatever you say, love."

"Bye, Zip." Click.

On the other end, Spense was holding a line with nothing more than a drone of dial tone. *Oh, well*, he said to himself, *at least the old bag is coming with her photographers. It will be some decent publicity for Miranda and some great publicity for me.*

The intercom line linking Sylvia with Jayne's desk in the editorial department was blinking. Sylvia lifted the ivory handle of the French phone and pressed the blinking button.

"Yes, Jayne."

"Does someone by the name of Sarasota ring a bell?" she asked. "She says she is here for a job."

"I have no idea," Sylvia responded.

"She's from Texas." Jayne had long since discovered that it was always smart to prod Sylvia's memory in several ways before dismissing someone who had the look of a potential editorial assistant.

"Oh, good God! Now I remember," Sylvia said. Sarasota — that was the name of some little Texas debutant about whom Stanley Sacker had called a few months ago. While few of the department store tycoons — all of them advertisers or potential advertisers — impressed Sylvia anymore, she adored Stanley Sacker. When *Haute* was a struggling magazine in the process of editorial renovation, he had consistently placed ads for dozens of pages and run those ads nationally, not just in the Southwest edition. Although he was no longer running the department store, he would always be a power. Sylvia always was eager to do a favor for Stanley Sacker.

"A friend asked me to give her a job," Sylvia explained. "Find out if she has any noticeable talent and have her do something. If she doesn't have any talent, hire her and send her out checking store windows. Anything. I will talk to her later."

"Fine!" Jayne was used to the procedure. With luck, Miss Sarasota would soon have her fill of journalism and window shopping and return to Dallas, where she would tell her daddy and her daddy's influential friend how much fun she had working for *Haute* and being a part of the world of fashion.

"Give me strength," Jayne muttered, after hanging up the phone.

Chapter Four

Richard Barkley was not accustomed to having breakfast in the crowded and noisy confines of the Carnegie Deli. Usually he ate grapefruit and toast a few blocks away at the New York Athletic Club after his now-ritual morning workout. The mental picture of himself in his battered NYAC sweat shirt and baggy gray warm-ups doing sit-ups, push-ups, and a straining round on the Nautilus equipment every other day brought a slightly ironic smile to his soft, well-bred New Yorker face.

Only two years before, he had accepted the fact that he was nearing fifty and had decided to behave like any other overweight successful publisher and look forward to advancing years in a flood of great brandy and good cigars. Then, thanks to Sylvia Harrington, he fell in love — a heart-pounding, knee-shaking, passionate love — the kind of love he had thought was reserved only for impressionable and over-hormoned teen-agers. *Thank you, Sylvia, you old battle-ax*, he thought. *Thank you for finally doing something for me.*

A giant, affable waiter interrupted the daydream. "Whatcha want?"

"Just some coffee. Black."

"You're kidding, buddy. This is the best deli in New York. Maybe the world. Heartburn here is an art form. If you want black coffee, why don't you go to Chock Full O'Nuts? How about an omelet? A nice cheese omelet" — he looked closely at Barkley's WASP profile — "with bacon."

"Not on my diet."

"A diet yet! Who comes to a deli on a diet? Are you lost or something, buddy?" The waiter was scandalized.

"Not lost, just waiting for someone. Then I guarantee we will order something that will make you and the Carnegie Deli proud. Maybe even a blintz."

"Your mother give you permission to eat something like that?" Customer-teasing was part of the ambience of the Carnegie Deli, especially on slow mornings in January. "You look like you still got your training wheels on. All right, one cup of black coffee coming up. Here, eat a pickle." He pushed the omnipresent bowl of dill pickels at Barkley. "I shall return."

Richard Barkley had never eaten a meal in the Carnegie Deli before today. Back in his predieting days he had sometimes stopped and ordered takeout at the counter by the front window and waited while one of the beefy cooks heaped pastrami on the slab of white bread (after much complaining from the cook about his choice of bread). But that morning he had picked the place to make Sol Golden comfortable.

Sol Golden was already twenty minutes late.

Maybe this tardiness was a carefully calculated ploy designed to put Barkley on edge. But the meeting had been Golden's idea, not Barkley's. Anyway, Barkley had an idea what Golden wanted and he was excited at the possibility.

Golden himself had called Barkley at home the previous week and asked straight out, "You interested in selling *Haute*?" No pussyfooting around, no flunkies making endless arrangements, no carefully worded letters exchanged. Just a simple phone call. "Don't bother answering now. I will be in New York on Monday. Let's have breakfast. You pick the place. New York is your town, not mine."

Click.

Barkley had had five days to ponder the conversation. He *would* like to sell *Haute*. At least, he thought he might like to sell the magazine. He would certainly be interested in talking to the legendary Sol Golden about the possibility.

Haute had been his prison, and Sylvia Harrington had been his jailer. The success of *Haute*, more success than he had ever expected for himself, had tied his position in life to the position of the great magazine. Being the publisher of *Haute* gave him status. Little did the outside world know the daily belittling he tolerated from Sylvia. She had replaced his father. The old man had said Dickie was not designed for publishing, and he had been right. Barkley had almost ruined *Haute* before Sylvia gained control. Now she told him what to do and when to do it. She made him feel like shit. Rich shit, but still shit. He hated the woman but could not escape her. Finally, he might just be able to do something on his own, something that Sylvia could not dictate. Maybe he was ready to do nothing — nothing except be in love.

Richard Barkley's mind emptied of business affairs and turned to romantic affairs. He could feel a stirring in his pants. Here he was fifty years old and getting a hard-on sitting in a New York deli, just like some young kid with a fantasy, he thought, grinning happily.

Sol Golden came rolling through the revolving glass door. Although Barkley had never seen the man, he recognized him instantly. He was short, about fifty pounds overweight, bald, a cigar hanging from his thick lips. The perfect media image of the Jewish tycoon. With thirty-four newspapers, a couple of major magazines, twenty television and radio stations — complete with several FCC suits pending in an attempt to break apart his monopoly empire — a wire service, and a new cable television network under his sole ownership, he was surely a business, if not a journalistic, legend. Nobody knew how much Golden was worth. None of his companies was public, so the extent of the Golden fortune was known only to the tycoon, his wife, Marti, and the bankers of Beverly Hills. Not even his two sons, each of whom headed a different division of the Golden empire, knew how much the old man controlled and was worth. Golden liked it that way.

Only one person was really close to Sol Golden: his wife, Marti. While he delighted in revealing all details of his competitors' lives in the headlines of his newspapers, Golden demanded total privacy and secrecy for himself and his life. One of the few moments of insight into the workings of Golden Limited — it was Marti who opted for "Limited" instead of "Incorporated" because it sounded classier back in the early days of the empire — came when he bought a publicly held newspaper in the Midwest for $154,000,000. It had caused such a financial stir in the publishing industry that hundreds of newspapers were immediately reappraised following the story in *Editor and Publisher* magazine.

Richard Barkley was certainly ready to talk with this man.

"The food good here?" Golden muttered as he

wrestled with the lightweight overcoat he had purchased hastily at Mr.Guy on Rodeo Drive back in Beverly Hills. Golden hated the cold. It had to be something very special to drag him away from his Beverely Crest Drive mansion to icy Manhattan in January.

"The food's great," Barkley replied.

"Too bad."

"What?"

"I have to eat some whole-wheat toast and grapefruit," Golden griped. "I hate grapefruit, but I eat it. You see, Marti and the doctor have me on this diet. Four ounce of lean this. Two ounces of stewed that. Lots of gratefruit. I haven't been in Nate and Al's for months. Sometimes life can be difficult."

Barkley started to laugh.

Golden looked at him. "So what's so funny? My starvation cracks you up?"

"No, not at all. It is just that I'm on a diet and would be eating grapefruit and whole-wheat toast right now if I weren't meeting you."

The waiter returned, took the two orders for grapefruit, and walked away without making a joke. The food appeared instantly.

Golden attacked his grapefruit with the dexterity of an expert, slicing out every edible part of the fruit. "My wife, Marti, can eat anything and never put on a pound. Never. You married?"

"Three times."

Barkley was proud of his three marriages. While some men might have considered these marital failures as catastrophes, Barkley wore the reputations of his ex-wives as a kind of virility status symbol. All were beautiful and desirable women, the kind men would fantasize about. Yes, he was proud of them. The first, an impulsive elopement in high school, was quickly annuled. The second was to a German girl he met while attending prep school in Switzerland. The problem with attending a public high school was the fact that he had required two additional years of proper education before his father had felt he was ready to enter Yale. His third wife was a socialite type who left him and married a washer-and-dryer manufacturer in Evansville, Indiana. All in all, he had had his share of beautiful and interesting women.

But Sol Golden already knew that. His staff had prepared a detailed file on the life of Richard Barkley before the offer to buy *Haute* was made. Golden did not like surprises.

"For me, it was only Marti," Golden said. "She flew in with me on the Red Eye last night. Dropped me here and went on to the Pierre. She's meeting her best friend. Do you know Marcella Todd? She's in your business. Used to be the fashion editor of my Chicago newspaper, but I moved her to my New York office so she could write for all my newspaper. Now *there* is a beautiful girl. I bet you know her."

"I don't seem to be able to place her," Barkley said thoughtfully.

"Tall, blonde, real smart. I'm surprised you've never heard of her. She's well known in the fashion business. Her column is carried in more than a hundred newspapers and she is starting on cable television. She used to be a model."

"Sorry." Barkley shook his head.

"We'll have to introduce you. I'm sure Marti will. She is determined to get Marcella married again."

"I would like meet her." Golden was obviously very fond of the Todd woman, Barkley thought. But he did not want to meet anyone new; he had what he wanted. But he had to make the expected polite gesture.

"Shall we get down to business?" Golden said. "While I personally am not in the least interested in fashion publishing, my wife is. This might sound un-businesslike, but it isn't. My wife is just as much a part of the management team of Golden Limited as I am, and when she says a property is worth buying, she's always right. I have learned that the hard way." Golden stared at Barkley, waiting for a reaction. Barkley nodded and said nothing so Golden continued. "I want to make you an offer."

"This seems very fast," Barkley pointed out.

"Not at all. My people have been studying *Haute* magazine for months. I suspect that we already know as much or more about the fiscal side of your magazine as you do. Probably more, since it seems that you're not much interested in the magazine anymore."

Barkley tensed. He wondered just how many secrets the canny Mr. Golden had discovered.

"At first," Golden continued, "we considered starting a new magazine to compete against *Haute*. I decided this would be counterproductive. While we have the resources to make a good play for your market, the result could be two struggling magazines instead of one strong one."

Golden knew how to phrase a threat, and Barkley appreciated the fact.

"Many magazines have gone into competition against *Haute*," the urban New Yorker responded. "I can't off-hand remember any of their names right now, but there have been quite a few." Barkley knew how to answer a threat.

"Maybe it won't have to happen again." Golden had

had enough of hedging. "How does sixty-five million sound?"

That was more than twelve times the annual profit of *Haute*. It would be enough to enable him to do anything he pleased for the rest of his life. Barkley owned forty percent of the *Haute* stock; sometimes being an only child had a few advantages. Barkley tried to freeze his face. He did not want his excitement to show.

Golden charged ahead. "My people have already arranged with the other three heirs of Pendlington Publications to purchase their outstanding shares. Only your shares remain."

Another ace up Golden's sleeve, Barkley thought. He already controlled enough of *Haute* to take control of the magazine. "It sounds as if you are already my partner."

Golden shook his head. "Not quite. I want everything or nothing. I run my own show, completely. Of course, you can remain with a title and office, if you wish, but either I get everything or there's no deal."

Well, for once the family had managed to keep something secret, Barkley thought ruefully. While he was playing with his new love, the Barkley cousins had been making deals with Sol Golden. "I'll have to think about all this," he said.

"Of course."

"Would you like to have lunch at *Haute* and see the operations? It's pretty impressive."

"I'd be glad to have lunch, but not at the *Haute* offices," Golden replied. "This transaction must remain a complete secret. Only the shareholders can be told. I never make any phone calls to a publication I am negotiating to buy . . . or send any memos. I deal only with the people who own the place. Too much gossip can ruin a good deal. Do we understand each other?''

"Understood." Barkley nodded, deciding he liked the other man.

"But I would like you arrange for my wife to see the inside of *Haute*. Perhaps you could ask your editor — what's her name? Harrington, isn't it — if she could have lunch with Marti and show her around. That way I could get an inside report and nobody would realize what is happening. It would seem perfectly natural. Everyone knows that my wife is crazy about clothes. Tomorrow would be fine. Have this Harrington woman give Marti a call at the Pierre and set up a time."

"I hope that Sylvia doesn't have an appointment." Barkley did not look forward to that part of the game.

"I am sure that she can alter her plans if her publisher asks," Golden said with the authority of a man who was used to giving instantly obeyed orders.

"Of course."

Golden gulped the last sliver of grapefruit, stood up, and pulled on his overcoat. "Talk to you tomorrow evening." He turned and zigzagged through the crowded tables to the revolving door and disappeared into the midmorning throngs of New Yorkers. Barkley reached for the check and noticed a napkin on which Golden had carefully doodled "65,000,000."

As he waited in line to pay the check, he thought about the money. It was not that important. He was already rich. Escaping the success, Sylvia's success — *that* could make the deal worthwhile.

How quickly things happened, he thought. Only a week earlier, his life had been completely organized around *Haute*. He knew where he was heading and what he was going to do every minute. Perhaps he was useless, but he had a routine. Now . . .

He decided to walk to the *Haute* offices. The pros and cons of the deal went through his mind randomly. It was a lot of money. There would be taxes. He hated the place. It gave him status. The family would be irate if he queered the deal. He was never fond of his cousins, anyhow. Sylvia would go crazy. There, that was it.

Selling *Haute* would enrage *Sylvia*. Sylvia, who had made *Haute* a success. Sylvia, whose entire life was the magazine. Sylvia, who was always right. Sylvia, who belittled him and even blackmailed him. How he hated that woman. But she did introduce him — he felt that throbbing in his crotch again — at least she did something right for him, whether she intended it or not. That was the crucial point in his decision.

Selling *Haute* would destroy Sylvia. It would be his revenge.

Chapter Five

Every Monday at 10 A.M. when Sylvia was in the city, the *Haute* magazine staff of editors, the top writers, the photographers, the layout directors, the art directors, and the production chiefs were summoned to the fifty-second floor to report to the editor in chief. Since the staff was usually working on at least three issues at a time, the meetings were always problematical.

The production people wanted to discuss printing problems on the issue that was already completed as far as the editors were concerned. The writers and fashion editors needed to explain and lobby for the stories they wanted in the next issue. The editors and management wanted Miss Harrington's opinions of ideas for future assignments and themes for issues that were still in the "think" stages. At best, the Monday meetings were confusing.

It was no way to run a magazine. Most editors would have separate meetings with department heads. But Sylvia Harrington thrived on such confusion. There was to be no smaller, manageable meeting for her. Because she had the power to make instant decisions without contacting the magazine's financial and business directors, she could listen to the problems of the production people and authorize press overtime or expand the number of pages fully and more economically to utilize the capacity of the presses.

Far away in a small town in Iowa near Des Moines, the monster presses of *Haute* magazine printed and bound each issue at the rate of one hundred thousand magazines an hour. The annual printing bill was nearly seventy-five million dollars. This amounted to seventy-five cents a copy. Another seventy-five cents was absorbed for newsstand or mailing costs. The remaining dollar-fifty of the three-dollar cover price — less if the subscription was sold at a bargain promotion rate — was returned to *Haute*. *Haute* was one of very few magazines to make money from the circulation area of its empire. Most magazines had to tolerate gigantic losses for circulation expense, making up the difference from advertising revenues. Even after the editorial costs, the huge office expenditures, and travel allowances were deducted from the advertising revenues, the profit margin was huge.

The massive printing requirements of *Haute*'s average two-hundred-page issue provided the majority of the income for Midwest Printing, Inc., and supported its sprawling plant. With this ever-dependable source of monthly bucks, Midwest had, over the previous decade, installed some of the world's largest and fastest presses, capable of producing the thick magazine, with its heavy glossy cover, at a cost that was less than half the bid of the nearest competition.

Richard Barkley had negotiated the arrangement.

The negotiation did not occur during a single long give-and-take session, but over a period of years of doing profitable business. Only then did Barkley convince the executives of Midwest Printing, with their polyester suits and lunches at the Sirloin Stockade, that they should invest nearly one hundred million dollars in the new equipment that *Haute* required. It had been the best deal Barkley had ever negotiated for the future of *Haute* and Midwest Printing.

"Good boy, Dickie," Sylvia had said when she learned of the deal. The printing company now had assets in the preses far exceeding their original value. And quietly, very quietly, Richard Barkley had become a silent partner in Midwest Printing, Inc.

That was the only real contribution Richard Barkley had made to *Haute* since hiring Sylvia. Immediately after that success, Sylvia had arranged to have the production departments included in her Monday morning meetings so that she could keep her eye on them.

Before the staff meeting, Sylvia carefully removed every scrap of paper from her desk. While the staff entered the meeting lugging piles of folders and stacks of artists' layouts in the works — they had long since learned to have everything at hand to answer even the most remote question Miss Harrington might ask — Sylvia liked to give the impression that she kept everything in her head. She took no notes. She never groped for a lost file. She could remember everything. And if she could not, nobody dared notice publicly.

Her secretary buzzed. "Miss Harrington, the staff is here." Nothing infuriated Sylvia Harrington more than to be interrupted by a straggler. Jayne Caldwell had solved that problem by holding a preliminary staff meeting in the editorial department at nine-thirty and driving the entire crew cattle-style to the penthouse a half hour later.

The *Haute* staff entered with various attitudes. There

were the older ones who were no longer awed by the luxury of the offices and the grandeur of Miss Harrington; they just wanted to struggle through the meeting and get back to producing a magazine. There were the transient socialites, who looked on the meeting as a campy event, a kind of private glimpse behind the scenes. There were the young, ambitious types, who longed for the power that was represented by the lavish Georgian paneling, the antiques, and the immaculate desktop. And there were the others who were just scared.

"Good morning, Miss Harrington."

"Good morning, Sylvia."

The seating arrangement bespoke a kind of corporate body language. The artists and creative types usually chose to stand with arms folded near the long drawing board. The more secure clustered on the white couches in front of Sylvia's desk. Jayne Caldwell took her usual place, standing by the window behind Sylvia's desk, where, during particularly stressful moments, she would turn her back and face the view of New York as if she were deciding whether to say something profound or to jump. The remainder of the staff filled the outer reaches of the room, sitting on the chairs that lined the walls, clustered in a grouping around the fake fireplace, or flopping cross-legged on the floor.

"Good morning," Sylvia said, instantly quieting the faint drone of nervous conversation. "Shall we begin? Mr. Dempsey, may I have the production report?"

Donald Dempsey was one of the veterans of the *Haute* wars. He had been added to the staff by Barkley when Midwest Printing had purchased the new presses and he had been sent to school at the press factories in Japan. It was largely because of his sense of timing that his mania for efficiency that circulation had become a profit instead of a loss category.

"The majority of storyboards for the May issue have already gone to Iowa. All that's left is the sixteen-page full-color main layout, which our editorial department assures me will be completed by Wednesday," he said flatly.

A group of floor-sitters started nodding furiously in agreement.

"We have forty percent of the ads in house and positioned." There was always a minimum of one hundred thirty pages of advertising in every issue of *Haute*, at an average rate of fifteen thousand dollars per page. "All but eight pages of the advertising hole are filled. The advertising department has holds on five of those eight pages."

"Fine . . . fine." That part always bored Sylvia. "Editorial."

Jayne Caldwell turned from her view of the skyline. "The June issue is traditionally a difficult book to build." She never tired of trying to educate the newer members of the staff. "It is too late for spring coverage and too early for fall. Thus, it is a sort of summer hodgepodge of beach-and-sport looks, with some warm-weather elegance. I had hoped that this June we might experiment a little by appealing to our younger readers." Jayne was lobbying for a story that was special to her. She was also aware that one of the problems facing *Haute* was that while the readership was growing richer, the surveys proved that they were also growing older. "Bonnie, could you explain, please?"

Bonnie Vincenzo was an exception to the debutante-and-sleek-only rule at *Haute*. She was slightly overweight from a lifetime of good Italian cooking. She was highly competent as beauty and makeup editor. She also avoided all possible contact with Sylvia Harrington.

"While in most areas June is an awkward coverage month," Bonnie began, bubbling with enthusiasm, "it is a great time for my department. People are thinking about tans and skin care, going from winter climate to summer sun." She often spoke in phrases that resembled headlines. "I propose we do a section of natural skin care for summer. There is a California doctor who has concocted all kinds of lotions and salves from fruits and vegetables. We could include home recipes and —"

"Oh, good God!" Sylvia muttered.

"What?" Bonnie was not sure she had heard her editor in chief correctly.

Sylvia glared at the overweight young woman. "My dear, after we have dipped eight million women in guacamole, to whom do we sell the ads? Perhaps the Avocado Growers Association, if there is such a group? Maybe the Produce Clerks of America? Think!"

"I don't understand." The excitement had drained from Bonnie's voice.

"Obviously you don't understand. Please pick up a copy of *Haute*." Sylvia pointed a long nail toward the cocktail table between the pair of white couches. "You have actually read a copy of the magazine, have you not?"

"Yes, Miss Harrington." Tears, real Italian tears, were fighting to break loose. "I have read the magazine."

"You surprise me. Now open the magazine and look at the first ten pages. What do you see besides the masthead and the table of contents?"

"Ads."

"Oh . . . very good!" Sylvia sneered. "And what kind of ads? Read them off. Page by page."

"There's Cartier. The four pages of Revlon. Then a double spread of Estée Lauder, a page of Aramis, Sakowitz, and a section from Charles of the Ritz."

"And what are Revlon, Estée Lauder, Aramis, and Charles of the Ritz, Miss Vincenzo?" Sylvia's tones reeked of smugness and hostility.

"They are cosmetics."

"Now look through the book and see if you notice lots of expensive full-color ads from produce firms. Perhaps some company is spending thousands of dollars to advertise the wonders of mashed bananas with us and I, in my advanced age, missed it. Could you please check for me, Miss Vincenzo?"

"There are no banana ads, Miss Harrington," Bonnie said as the first tear escaped and ran down her red cheek.

"Are you positive?" Sylvia bore down relentlessly.

"Yes, I'm sure."

"Then I suppose it is safe to assume there are advertisers and readers more interested in reading about, shall we say, more conventional products. Is that safe to assume, Miss Vincenzo?"

"Yes." Bonnie's voice was hardly a whisper.

"Well, then . . . Now I have a proposal for the June issue. We will do a guide to all the most expensive and most exotic sun products available. That will keep the advertisers happy. Include a part on rating skin types, using different celebrities to illustrate everything from acne to parchment."

"All right, Sylvia," Jayne said, taking control back from the dejected Bonnie. There was a sick lump in Jayne's gut. She had been responsible for hiring Bonnie away from another magazine, and she had needled Sylvia into paying her an almost-decent salary. Now, she knew, Sylvia had made up her mind to rid the magazine of the asset. She knew the signs. Bonnie would be gone in a month. All the old-timers knew the obvious indications.

A panicked hush had enveloped the room. The plan had been to use Bonnie Vincenzo as the initial speaker in an all-out editorial assault to turn the June issue into the first completely youth-oriented edition in the history of *Haute*. Now that plan had collapsed after little more than a brief skirmish. Sylvia had destroyed it in a barrage of cutting remarks. At the same time, she had demolished Bonnie Vincenzo. Even worse, she had come up with an idea, a not unique idea, that had just enough of a new twist so that the gossip-hungry readers would probably find it more interesting than Bonnie's informative do-it-yourself-naturally version.

Since everyone else's plans were based on Bonnie's, there was a frantic mental rearranging to find stories that fit the new beauty theme and the current mood of Sylvia Harrington. Scared minds switched into high gear. The travel editor was the first to speak.

"We could adapt the celebrity concept to travel," he said. "Ask each of the celebrities where they most enjoy vacationing."

"That has possibilities." Sylvia was ready to approve of something. "Just avoid anyone who wants to take a camper through Mexico or shoot the rapids anyplace. The *Haute* reader wants elegance. You do understand what I want?"

"Yes, Miss Harrington."

The other editors soon fell into the pattern. The fashion writers selected Summer Elegance as the theme, and the art directors were again considering the posh resorts and casinos of the world as backdrops. The gaggle of social writers and editors soon were babbling about the new "in" people.

Sylvia was starting to become bored. Jayne Caldwell knew that in a matter of minutes, the meeting would be ended and the staff would be herded into a drawing room for pastries; this was the only time anything high-calorie was permitted at *Haute*. Years earlier, someone had discovered that a coffee klatch dosed with energy-producing sugar was an absolute necessity after a meeting with Sylvia Harrington.

But before Sylvia was able to dismiss everyone, Richard Barkley walked into the staff meeting, still wearing his trench coat. The feeling of January cold radiated from his layers of custom-tailored wools. "Plotting the future of *Haute*? He chuckled — and only he appreciated the inside joke. "Keep going, gang. Fill those pages."

The women in the room smiled at the dashing teddy bear of a man. There was something about Barkley that was both charming and cuddly. He seemed all the more vulnerable in contrast to Sylvia.

"Good morning, Richard," Sylvia said.

"Excuse me," Barkley added. "Got to get back to business. Keep working, gang."

What business? Sylvia thought. *That fool does not have anything to do but sit in that big office and wait for lunch. Business, indeed!*

"I believe we're finished." Sylvia stood. "Next Monday's meeting will be canceled as Miss Caldwell and I will be out of the city." In spite of the fact that the entire staff knew Miss Harrington was going to Paris for some sort of special couture showings, Sylvia tried to maintain an air of secrecy about everything, as if some other fashion magazine was lurking behind the Georgian paneling to discover the future plans of *Haute*.

The staff headed for the pastries.

Jayne Caldwell remained behind, still facing the rest of New York City outside the window. Sylvia leaned back in her chair and sighed. There was an uncomfortable silence.

"Bonnie Vincenzo is very good, you know," Jayne lobbied.

"She doesn't look much like a beauty editor. She needs to lose weight and do something about that hair," Sylvia replied.

Jayne fought the urge to scream. She wanted to turn to Sylvia and shout, "*You* don't look like a fashion editor. How dare you judge talent and potential by the way a person looks! How can you tamper with a fine career because the person — a *person* — does not meet your exact specifications of packaging? Bonnie Vincenzo is a human being." Instead, Jayne continued looking out the window. Somehow she would try to save Bonnie's career at *Haute*.

"Do you think this Paris thing will be worthwhile?" Jayne asked, changing the subject.

"It should be." Sylvia was subdued and agreeable after the meeting, almost as if she needed time to recharge her batteries. "I think the French are worried about their image."

"Probably."

"They should be." Sylvia sighed. "The last few collections have been more stage presentations than fashion shows. The clothes have been simply outrageous. Peasant for the millionth time. Harem girls. Things from outer space. And that dreadful little-girl look. The press is starting to laugh at Paris, and that could be dangerous. The French fashion industry is too important to become a joke. They have to do something to prove they are the center of world fashion because they are losing it to New York."

"But a complete special showing?" Jayne questioned. "The expense!"

"You know, this whole thing might have been my idea. Actually, it probably was," Sylvia recalled, tapping her long nails on her desk again. "About two years ago I saw this coming. You remember that silly Saint Laurent collection? I told Pierre Cardin that I thought Yves's costume fad was going to make the business into a joke. Cardin agreed. You know how incredibly promotion- and public-image-oriented Pierre is. A few months later, I heard he had talked to the top designers and convinced them to do a special collection of their concepts for the future of fashion. This way they'd get the spectacular publicity they want and still continue to keep Paris the place where the innovation and future of the fashion industry are rooted."

"Do you think it will work?" Jayne continued to sound doubtful.

Sylvia nodded. "For some, yes. Others still will insist on putting silly things in their collections to attract the press. But the French are not going to concede this industry without a fight. It should be interesting."

"It's costing them enough," Jayne repeated.

That was true enough. The French government and the French fashion industry had chartered Concordes to take the most influential members of the world fashion press to Paris. The supersonic jets would arrive from New York, Rio, Tokyo, and Johannesburg. Individual luxury transportation was being provided for the significant European editors. Two floors of the Hotel Georges V had been reserved, complete with unlimited champagne in every room. Only the best restaurants were selected for luncheons and dinners. The showings were scheduled for the Hall of Mirrors at the Palace of Versailles. There were to be elaborate gifts and private functions for the ladies of the press.

The entire plan was very French. First, the designers would insult the intelligence of the public to the point where even the editors who most enjoyed their frequent trips to Paris had to admit publicly that the clothing was becoming cartoonlike. Then they would mount a spectacular comeback event, spreading the goodies around, to convince those same editors that they should not desert Paris for the practical fashion centers of New York and Hong Kong.

It was sheer journalistic bribery.

"Do you think we will get a decent story from the trip?" Jayne asked.

"I do. I think it will be one of the biggest stories in fashion history. That is why I have decided to hold thirty-two pages open in June for the Paris preview of our future." Sylvia's voice was calm.

Jayne was shocked. *"Thirty-two pages!"*

"Yes."

"That's so risky. By the time we photograph and design those pages, we will be right at deadline. Couldn't we go for fewer pages? Maybe we could run more in the July issue." Jayne's very practical mind was whirling.

"It could save June."

Jayne stared out the window again. The idea of thirty-two pages of designer fantasies worried her. *June is a summer issue,* she thought, *and women want to know what is available for the beach. Haute* would be featuring looks planned for chic space travel. She had always hated the impractical gimmicks designers used to garner publicity.

Jayne pondered the potential for mistakes. If the layout ran into overtime, millions of dollars could be lost each day. She was the person who was in charge of that part of the magazine. She was the managing editor. She would be blamed.

But there was a worse fear.

The clothing in Paris would, most probably, be fantasy stuff. The editorial climate in the United States seemed all wrong for it. Some instinct, deep inside, flashed a warning. The layout could be dangerous, very damaging to *Haute.*

"Why don't we shoot a backup layout? Just in case this Paris thing does not pan out," Jayne suggested, looking for some protection from the potential disaster.

Sylvia glared at her managing editor. "There will be no backup layout. The Paris story will be excellent. I don't want it, or me, undermined in any way. I want *this* story."

"No one is trying to undermine you." Jayne's voice was becoming shrill. "It is just sensible to be protected."

"And I'm not being sensible? Is that what you're saying?" Sylvia was getting back into stride.

"No, of course not."

"Jayne, I think I have had quite enough of this conversation. You must have duties elsewhere. I will hold you up no longer." Sylvia motioned toward the door.

"Yes, I have." Jayne hesitated a moment.

"Then go do them."

Jayne turned, walked across the Oriental rug, and stopped at the doorway. She turned again toward Sylvia and started to say, "I wish . . ." Then, seeming to think better of it, she said, "Never mind." In a moment she was gone by the back stairway to the editorial department, where she would sit at her desk staring at the piles of raw copy and stacks of unculled photographs. Seeing nothing. Thinking nothing. Just trying to clear her mind.

In the penthouse office, Sylvia Harrington was also pondering the conversation. For some time tiny bits of self-doubt had been sparking in the fringes of her mind. She knew she did not comprehend *Haute*'s younger readers and their attitudes. But she rationalized those attitudes as being just fads. They would fade. She would be right, as she had always been right. But maybe the combination of expensive elegance and whimsy that had always personified fashion to Sylvia, maybe . . . Sylvia *was* worried. No, the new concepts that Jayne supported and other magazines were repeating in one form or another in every issue — they were the fads. Sylvia was sure she was right.

"Natural makeup . . . bullshit!"

Sylvia smiled as she restored her own self-confidence. She was right. By God, she *had* to be right.

Chapter Six

Richard Barkley sat at his grandfather's desk and worried about Sol Golden's words. Not the words about selling the magazine. That question did not have to be faced immediately. What worried him was how he was going to tell Sylvia Harrington that she was scheduled to have lunch with Marti Golden. "I'm sure she can alter her plans when her publisher asks," Barkley recalled Golden saying. Maybe none of Golden's editors would dare to balk at a request from the tycoon, but Sylvia Harrington would not hesitate to tell God Himself — to say nothing of Barkley — to go straight to hell for tampering with her schedule.

Barkley cursed his own weakness.

"How the fuck did I get into this one?" he said to himself. "Oh, well, I might as well get it over with."

He stood, leaned against the massive oak desk that had been his father's and grandfather's, then walked the sixty feet from his office to Sylvia's.

Without knocking, he opened the double doors and strode into the room. Sylvia was not alone. She was sitting in her huge silk-upholstered executive chair. One hand was brushing her forehead as if she were fighting off a migraine. On the other side of the desk, lounging on one of the white couches, was one of the most beautiful red-haired creatures Barkley had ever seen. Sylvia looked annoyed.

"Excuse me." Barkley could feel an attack of intimidation approaching. "If I'm interrupting, I can come back later."

"Not at all, Dickie." While the sound of Sylvia's voice was overtly affectionate, she used the nickname, something she seldom did in front of outsiders. Evidently, this vision was someone she had to tolerate. "Do come in."

"Sure, come on in, honey." The redhead bubbled, smiling at him.

"Richard Barkley" — Sylvia was being positively courtly — "I'd like you to meet a new addition to our staff, Buffy Sarasota. Miss Sarasota just arrived from Texas."

"Dallas," Buffy said.

"Yes, of course — Dallas," Sylvia echoed. "Mr. Barkley is the publisher of *Haute* magazine. His grandfather founded Pendlington Publications at the turn of the century."

"Oh, my, which century?" Buffy batted her huge green eyes.

"This one, dear," Sylvia said, raising her eyes toward the Waterford crystal chandelier. A momentary look of exasperation passed across her face. "We hope to put this charming child to good use at *Haute*."

Barkley realized instantly that the beautiful but less-than-brilliant person had to have friends in high places. The idea that a Buffy Sarasota could serve any purpose at *Haute* other than as, perhaps, a model was an idea that would normally send Sylvia either into hysterical laugher or a screaming rage.

"Have you been in New York long?" Barkley asked, trying to make conversation.

"Why, I came up on Daddy's jet last night. I didn't really want to come. I was doing right fine in Dallas. I had a career there, a real career." She did not pause for anyone to ask the nature of the career that was right for Miss Buffy Sarasota of Dallas. "I even just got elected chief cheerleader — well, one of the chief cheerleaders. I was the 'D.' Do you like football, Mr. Barkley?"

"Not really." He smiled. "I never seem to have time to watch."

"I don't understand the game a hoot, but I love football players." Buffy paused and looked hard at Richard Barkley, as if she were measuring his assets by gridiron standards. "Football players — that's why Daddy sent me to New York City. He said I liked football players too much," she continued, staring at Barkley's crotch, "if you get what I mean." Buffy gave Barkley a broad wink.

Sylvia kept staring at the chandelier.

"I think I catch the drift, ma'am." Barkley blushed, feeling very uncomfortable.

"Fascinating," Sylvia muttered.

Buffy turned to Sylvia, a huge, warm smile on her face. "I think you are going to be just like a momma to me. I feel like giving you a great big hug."

"Try to restrain yourself, dear." Sylvia seemed truly alarmed at the possibility.

"I just can't communicate with my family. They don't understand me. I guess no one's family ever understands them. They are all so talented. My brothers are at

Vanderbilt and the University of Oklahoma studying the oil business. My little sister is in Paris studying the piano. And here I am, just a little old cheerleader with a crush on the whole team. My daddy was just damned embarrassed." Buffy hardly paused for breath. "He said if I wasn't going to go to college — shit, I never really made it through high school — I might as well go to work and make a future for myself. Then he got the idea that I would be perfect for a magazine like *Haute*."

"I would be interested in his reasoning," Sylvia said blandly.

"I just dearly love clothes," Buffy explained enthusiastically. "I know it's terrible, but I spent nearly a hundred thousand dollars just at Neiman-Marcus last year. Well, Daddy said with that much invested, I should have a real education in clothing and that I should come to New York."

Sylvia nearly choked. "But with such a background, surely you could have opened a store in Dallas or perhaps done a little modeling. Do you know Kim Dawson? She runs a fine modeling agency there. I could call her for you." Sylvia was extremely eager to help send Miss Buffy Sarasota back to Dallas and her favorite football players.

"I said that very same thing to Daddy." Buffy pouted, watching Barkley from beneath lowered eyelids. "He said he wanted me away from Dallas because I would meet the kind of men he thinks I should be associating with here in New York. He wants me to dump my football players. He is afraid I might get into trouble or something. I told him, 'Daddy, I won't get into trouble. I take the pill.' "

"You can get into that trouble here, too." Barkley

smiled. "What kind of young men does your daddy want you to associate with?"

"Gay boys!"

At the unexpected reply, Barkley burst into laughter. Even Sylvia was rubbing her eyes as if, for the first time in a decade or so, she might actually smile. She resisted the impulse successfully.

"My daddy says gay boys are better than the pill. I told him some guys go both ways, but he doesn't understand that at all. With my daddy, either you are or you aren't. After all, Daddy's gotten born again."

The conversation was starting to embarrass Richard Barkley.

"Daddy says that the fashion industry is just full of boys who . . . uh . . . well . . . wouldn't have no need to take advantage of a girl like me. I told him there were plenty of those types right at home in Dallas. Even a couple of the football players. But he said I had a much better chance of being unsoiled working in the fashion industry in New York than back home."

"I think you might be surprised," Barkley commented.

"Do you really think so?" Buffy perked up considerably at the prospect. "I mean, it doesn't matter if they are a *little* gay. That way it could make both Daddy and me happy."

"Oh, dear God," Sylvia mumbled.

"I'm sure something will work out." Barkley was surprised that he suddenly wanted to reassure this strange and beautiful girl about the future of her sex life.

"Hot damn! I'm so glad. Here I've been in New York only a few hours, and I have me some fine new friends who really care. You don't know how good that makes me feel. One of you is going to be just like my momma, and the other . . . well . . . Mr. Barkley, maybe you could find it in your heart to help this little girl from Texas find an apartment in big old New York City. Daddy has a corporate apartment at the Sovereign, but I want a place of my very own. I would be most obliged."

"I have rather a hectic schedule," Barkley explained, "but we might arrange something."

"Why, thank you, Mr. Barkley." She batted her long lashes at him automatically.

"If he can't find the time, there is someone I think would be perfect to show you around town." Sylvia was suddenly interested. "He is a model who used to be a baseball player. Very good-looking. Do you like baseball players, too?"

"I bet I would," Buffy said, carefully mulling over the idea. "What team did he play for? What's his name? He isn't black, is he? I don't think Daddy would like that."

"His name is Andrews, I believe, and he is blond. I really can't remember the team."

"You are just so sweet." Buffy was bubbling again. "When do I meet my new baseball player?"

"I will have to see if he's in town," Sylvia said. "Richard, you know Tom Andrews, don't you?"

"Yes," Barkley responded, instantly on guard.

"Is he in town?"

Barkley managed to hold Sylvia's stare without breaking. "I have no idea."

"Really? This has been ever so charming." Sylvia turned the conversation back toward Buffy. "But we do have a magazine to run, and there are only so many hours in a day. Why don't you run along and find Miss Caldwell and get started?"

"Yes, ma'am." Buffy stood to her almost six feet, in

heels, turned with the grace of a dancer, and flowed out the door. Her thick rich red hair caught the rush of air from the hall and gave her the look of a lioness. "Bye-bye," she said behind her before disappearing.

Barkley started to laugh again. "I don't know who is going to be learning what from whom down there in editorial. She will be a real education to that collection of Junior Leaguers."

"Ghastly." Sylvia was totally back to normal. "Absolutely ghastly. A whore, certainly a rich whore from an important family, but still a whore. Working for *Haute* magazine. Ghastly!"

"It wouldn't be the first time, Sylvia." Barkley clearly was amused by the entire scene.

"What would you know about it? Obviously you came here with some purpose in mind. I somehow doubt that you just had to meet the shy Miss Sarasota. What is it, Dickie?"

"There is a favor I need, a kind of professional courtesy. Have you ever heard of Marti Golden? Her husband owns a bunch of newspapers." Barkley wanted to assure Sylvia that the Goldens were important.

"I believe I've seen the woman. She goes to the Paris collections and buys a lot, somebody said. Blonde hair. Jewish. From Beverly Hills. Very Californian. Yes, I remember her. We've never run her photo in *Haute*."

Sylvia most certainly had heard of the rich Mrs. Golden, and she guessed that Mrs. Golden had an urge to be published on the social pages of *Haute*. It might be possible at that. She was attractive enough, and all the couture designers in Paris and Milan hoped to see Mrs. Golden and her hefty checkbook prominently displayed at the opening of their collections. "I've never really met the woman," Sylvia added.

"Then you're going to have the chance."

"Really? Do tell." Suddenly Sylvia was curious about Barkley's strange attitude. "You are not going to invite her to one of our parties, I hope. Californians always talk about their cars and avocados. I've had quite enough of avocados for one day, thank you."

Barkley did not understand the reference, but then he often did not understand Sylvia. "No, I'm not inviting her to one of our parties," he said.

"Thank God."

"I invited her to have lunch with you in the dining room. Tomorrow. Then I said you would show her around the offices. Let her see how a fashion magazine operates."

"You *what?*" Any slight hint of affability drained from Sylvia Harrington's voice. She was furious. Something was happening here, with Dickie trying to give her orders. "Impossible. Totally impossible. I have an interview preview with Spense tomorrow." She was lying. "There is no way I could or would cancel."

Sylvia glared fiercely at Barkley, but he did not flinch. Something unexpected was changing the attitude of the always subservient Richard Barkley. Sylvia did a few seconds of instant calculating. There must be a reason for the outrageous defiance. She needed time to think. "Have you promised this Golden person?"

"Yes."

"Does she expect me? Or does she just plan to gossip with you?"

"Actually, just you. I won't be there," Barkley said.

Sylvia was holding the side of her desk to keep her hands from shaking with rage. Her voice was a controlled monotone. "All right. I will give you your fucking professional courtesy. But let me tell you something, Dickie, *dear*, don't *ever* pull a trick like this on me again. Don't ever!''

"I told her to expect a call from you," Barkley said in an attempt to finish the conversation.

"How lovely." Sylvia fumed at the added insult of having to make the call. "And where is she staying?"

"She has an apartment at the Pierre."

"How lovely for her," she replied sarcastically. "Now get out, Dickie. Get away from me." As Barkley closed the door, she muttered to herself, "He shouldn't own *Haute*. I created *Haute*. It's mine. It wouldn't be here without me. He would be nothing — *nothing* — without me. Richard Barkley, you will never give me an order again."

On the other side of the door, Richard Barkley was smiling. He had won. It was hard to believe, but he had faced Sylvia Harrington and for the first time had *won*. Sure, it was a small victory, but it *was* a victory. It was a step toward freedom. He broke into a run across to his office. Richard Barkley had an important call to make.

Chapter Seven

Marcella Todd always awoke early. From her youngest childhood days back in Ohio, she was instantly wide awake as soon as the sun started pouring through the windows.

In Manhattan, the towering apartment buildings that encircled her Grammercy Park town house floor-through apartment usually blocked whatever morning sun might have reached her bedroom. But sometimes a few rays would filter through the undraped fan windows above her pair of French doors, even on a cold Tuesday in January.

Marcella loved her second-floor apartment, overlooking Grammercy Park. It was possible to pretend there, to look out the windows and see only the tops of the aging trees in the tiny locked park — only residents of the immediate area around the park had keys — which made the area an oasis of greenery in the midst of all the concrete of the city. No junkies or winos ever monopolized the benches in Grammercy Park. Even in January, when the sound-deadening leaves were gone from the trees, the din of jackhammers and outraged horns could not drown out the sound of birds. It reminded her of the town square back in Canfield, Ohio. Grammercy Park did not have the carefully restored bandstand, but it did have daffodils in the spring and colored leaves in the fall. It made her feel as if she had some roots in this hard, rootless city.

Marcella decided to take a walk around the iron fence of the park. Fresh snow had fallen, so for a few early morning hours everything would look clean.

There was plenty of time. She did not have to meet Marti Golden at the Pierre Hotel until eleven. Then they were having lunch with Sylvia Harrington. Marcella was very curious about the reasons for the luncheon. When Marti had called the evening before to tell her not to bother going to the office today "because we are lunching at *Haute* magazine with that Harrington woman," Marcella immediately started asking questions. She was, after all, a newspaper reporter. Marti called her the fashion editor of the Golden Syndicate, but Marcella preferred the term "reporter." Most fashion editors were thought of as extensions of the advertising departments. When she had gotten her first reporting job on the *Chicago Herald*, the staff had resented her as a shill for the advertising department.

Maybe that was what she was supposed to be. But it was not what she became. Getting the job was just lucky. It was her first newspaper job, and the *Herald* was a big newspaper. She had never tried to fool herself about how she landed that job. She was a friend, a close friend — "a very close friend," according to some members of the staff — of Kevin O'Hara, the boy-wonder editor of the somewhat raunchy tabloid newspaper. The first days at the *Herald* had not been so easy. Half the staff thought she bedded her way into the job, and the other half hated her guts.

But all that had changed.

Marcella had become a real reporter. She wrote well-documented stories about price-fixing and shoddy quality. For her there were no sacred cows. She made fun of the fashion industry when it was being pretentious and silly. She attacked mighty designers for making junk and charging too much for it.

The readers loved her, even though a few of the advertisers went into shock. Most important, she won the respect of her coworkers. Those years in Chicago had been good years.

New York was not so bad, either.

She did miss the fellowship of a city room filled with strange individual personalities. At the Golden offices, she had a private nook with three walls that discouraged yelling across desks. The easy camaraderie of a newsroom was not there at the Golden offices. Since most of the syndicated columnists were usually traveling somewhere, the place seemed empty and lonely.

The morning off was a welcome change. Before exploring the very limited confines of Grammercy Park, Marcella had to go through her daily ritual. She slipped off her flannel bathrobe — warm, if not exactly stylish — and stood naked in front of her three-way mirror. It was a ritual suggested by Shirley Hamilton back in Chicago when Marcella started as a model over a decade ago. "Keep looking for those bones," Shirley would say. "You girls will get asked out to dinner a lot. Going to dinner is fine. Just don't eat. The bones. Remember the bones."

At thirty-four years old, Marcella Todd's bones still looked great. The same one hundred eighteen pounds she had weighed since she was sixteen were still distributed in the same places. It had been unusual when she was sixteen. It was even more amazing nearly two decades later. The cheekbones were always tight, the skin flawless. The hair was not only the same light blonde it had been when she was a teen-ager, but it was still easy to manage. One minute it would be the lioness look; then, with a few twists of a brush and some pins, it was ready for a formal evening. Marcella had never had to worry about her looks. They had always just been there.

Her clothes were simple. With perfect legs — she had been the star of a national pantyhose commercial that ran for two years — and surprisingly impressive breasts for a mannequin, she had no flaws to be covered or minimized by clothes.

But she still checked every morning. It was a matter of habit. Was the skin behind the elbows, at the heels, or inside the thighs starting to wrinkle or sag? No, nothing had happened since yesterday's inspection. She had no idea what she would do if she ever did detect some drooping. She hated nonproductive exercise. While walking thirty blocks to work might be classified as fun to Marcella Todd — she often did exactly that in order to look at the people on the street and see what they were wearing — she would never consider going to a gym or starting a day with fifty agonizing sit-ups.

She was not the type to have plastic surgery; Marcella was not afraid of aging. Maybe she was immune to beauty. She had known too many beautiful women who were stupid or self-centered or — worse — boring. Sometimes she even resented her own natural beauty. Maybe her marriage might have been different if she had not been so beautiful and her husband had not been so jealous. She would never be impressed with beauty unless it was part of a total package that included personality and ambition.

Ambition — that could be very impressive and attractive in a person. Marcella's life had been a spring-board of ambition. No sooner would she achieve one goal than she would discover another goal worth pursuing. She liked ambition both in herself and in the people around her.

She pulled on a bulky sweater with a massive turtleneck, a straight skirt with a slit to make walking easier, brown boots since it was still snowing a little, and her lynx coat. Fur coats in New York, with its cruel climate, were more a necessity than a luxury. She glanced at her watch. It was just nine.

There was still a touch of the rural Ohio tomboy in her. The long strides she took down so many fashion-show runways were the result of her girls' basketball training back at Canfield High. She was, after all, the tallest girl in the class; for years she had been the tallest anything in her class. As she bounded down the stairs from her second-floor apartment she took the steps two at a time.

The air outside the heavy wooden door of the old town house was clean and very biting. *Clean air*, she thought gaily. *I'm going to enjoy it while it lasts.*

Marcella hated killing time. She thought of just making a quick circle around the park and going into the office anyhow, day off or no day off. Then she rejected the idea. If she went to the office, there would be a thousand things to do, invitations to answer, and chatty telephone calls. She might be late for Marti's lunch, and Marcella hated tardiness. In an industry where people prided themselves on being late — it was considered a sign of their importance to keep someone waiting for interminable periods of time — she was usually early for an appointment. In the early period of her writing career, she had startled many a haughty designer by leaving if she had to wait more than ten minutes past a set appointment time. More than once, a designer who was very anxious for the publicity of a nationally syndicated newspaper story would miscalculate and find an empty waiting room and a public relations director in a state of nervous collapse.

How to spend the two hours?

She decided to walk to the Pierre Hotel, about fifty blocks away. It would be a ten-minute trip by subway — at the most — or a cab ride that could last forever, especially in the snow. Buses, of course, were too frustratingly slow.

She crossed Park Avenue, with its steaming manholes, then headed along Nineteenth Street toward Fifth Avenue. Fifth Avenue in the mid-Twenties was a nondescript street. It did not radiate the trendiness and excitement that could be found a little farther down in the Washington Square area, and there was none of the glamour of Fifth Avenue's midtown segment. In the Twenties there were blocks of loft buildings filled with garment manufacturers and photographers, importers and wholesalers. Traffic on the street, even in the snow, was moving at a bustling pace, quite unlike the pace of Fifth Avenue in the Forties, Fifties, and Sixties, where the pace slowed to a leisurely window-shopping stroll.

On and near lower Fifth Avenue Marcella could see the results of the fashion industry. On the streets were the shop girls, the employees of the loft designer showrooms, and the people who bought clothing — usually wholesale — and made very careful decisions on what new fad they wanted to spend their three-hundred-dollar-a-week salaries, *before* taxes. Shoppers could see and touch and feel and price everthing that was available in the world. What these girls and women chose was what was going to make it out to Davenport and Sioux City, where the woman would never be offered the wide selection that was carefully boxed or hung on portable racks in the dingy lofts. Everything was there. That was where Marcella found much of the inspiration for her informative, provoking newspaper columns.

People glanced quickly at Marcella as she sped up Fifth Avenue. Because of her bearing and height, most thought she was a model. But she was not carrying one of those huge duffel bags filled with extra pairs of shoes, pantyhose, jewelry, and her portfolio of eleven-by-fourteen-inch photos of her previous work. No, she was not a model, they decided. She did not fall into any of the standard categories. She was too manicured and perfect to be a shop girl or an assistant to a designer. She might have been somebody's wife. She was definitely too classy to be one of the street hookers scrounging around for some morning trade in the middle-Thirties, one of their favorite locations. She didn't fit any category.

At Thirty-fourth Street, the first of the big department stores appeared. With the shadow of the Empire State Building looming and reflecting in its windows, B. Altman was already promoting spring clothes. The new merchandise was a welcome change for Marcella after enduring two weeks of windows filled with after-Christmas sale merchandise.

"I just don't understand those lace bathing suits," she said softly to herself. "All those little holes will make a person tan like a speckled trout. It doesn't make sense." She made a mental note to write a column about selecting practical bathing suits.

The usual mixture of humanity had gathered on the steps of the massive New York Public Library building at Forty-second Street. The library personnel were always efficient in cleaning the snow from the flights of steps so that, immediately after a storm, students, vagrants, housewives, business types, and passersby naturally gathered there. Vendors sold roasted chestnuts, steaming hot dogs, and hot pretzels doused with mustard. Drug pushers offered everyone low-grade cocaine, oregano-spiced marijuana, and big promises.

They are already wearing T-shirts, Marcella thought. *The temperature is not even thirty degrees, and both sexes are opening their heavy winter coats to show bright-colored T-shirts. Everyone is sick of the drabness of winter.* She made another mental note.

After the snakepit of Forty-second Street came what was supposed to pass for chic Fifth Avenue. In fact, many of the once-plush boutiques and elaborate stores had been replaced by Oriental rug bazaars, discount video-equipment outlets, and airline agencies. But there were still Saks, Bergdorf's, Bonwit's, Tiffany's, Cartier's, and the mass of concrete that was Rockefeller Center.

Better than almost anyone, Marcella knew the treasures to be found in credit-card heavens. She was advised of the slightest movement of a trend by enthusiastic public relations people over hundreds of lunches of poached salmon at the Four Seasons or quiche at Sign of the Dove.

"Dammit, it's not even ten-thirty yet," she said, checking her watch. She decided to check out the ice skaters at Rockefeller Center. One overweight girl in a too-short skirt was doing dramatic turns and leg lifts, monopolizing the ice. Only a few people had gathered around the walkway that looked down twenty feet to the ice rink. In an hour the space would be packed with people seeking lunch-hour freedom, and the show would be better quality.

Marcella felt a pang for the lumpy girl in the tacky outfit who was pouring her frustrations out onto the ice. It was like so many people's reality in New York City, she thought. They came to the city to be the center of attention and to try to grab a piece of the spotlight. But they did not have the talent or the brains or the personality or the money or the luck to be anything more than another member of the crowd waiting to cross every street. So they grabbed at an instant of imitation glamour. For a moment they would convince themselves that they were really talented and famous and desirable. Marcella watched the heavy girl on the ice with sympathy.

"Hey, whale, want to see my harpoon?" a teen-aged boy yelled from the railing to the girl below on the ice. His voice echoed between the skyscrapers, intensified in the unexpected mid-morning stillness.

The girl stopped skating and froze, not knowing how to respond.

Marcella turned and walked to the teen-aged taunter. "Hey, little boy, you don't look as if your harpoon could handle it. I bet it's nowhere as big as your mouth."

The kid looked at Marcella, stunned. Normally, he would have returned a volley of foul-mouthed comments, but he was not used to having his insults returned by a beautiful woman. Worse, his buddies were laughing at him. "Ah, shove it!" he muttered before slinking off.

Marcella turned to the girl on the ice. "You were doing beautifully. Don't stop." With that, she started clapping and was joined instantly by a elderly couple nearby and a tour group that seemed to be German.

The girl on the ice smiled. She raced around the rink, gaining speed. Then she flung herself into a corkscrew twist. Everyone applauded again. The girl on the ice had her moment of stardom.

Marcella watched for a few moments before deciding it was time to meet Marti at the Pierre.

Chapter Eight

Marti Golden disliked New York City. She would have pushed her husband into buying *Haute* magazine years earlier if *Haute*'s offices had been located in Los Angeles or, better yet, Beverly Hills.

Long ago her journalistic instincts had told her *Haute* would be a great addition to Sol's empire. There were those who said, "Whatever makes Marti Golden think she has journalistic instinct? She has never worked for a newspaper or magazine. The only thing she has ever written is a check. Other than being the boss's wife, what does she know?"

For Sol Golden, it was enough that Marti was the boss's wife. But the behind-the-back indictment of Marti Golden was not really fair. While it was true that she knew nothing about the day-to-day operations of a publishing empire, she had all the best instincts of the consuming public. The food and fashion sections of her husband's bigger newspapers had been expanded at her insistence. The result was an increase in readership and a far more attractive advertising buy. This also meant millions of dollars in added profits for Golden Limited. She had suggested that a cable network start producing fifteen-minute life-style segments, and those ultimately helped to fill awkward time slots between movies and, in fact, became so popular that they led to the launching by Golden Limited of its own news and feature departments. Now she wanted *Haute* to give Golden Limited a veneer of elitism. Golden had immense success; now all it needed was a class image.

Today was going to be quite a day.

Marti had started preparing for her scouting expedition immediately after Sylvia Harrington had called early the previous evening, right after five. Normally, Marti would not have been in the suite, since she usually met Sol for a drink at that time. But she waited for the call. Sylvia Harrington had waited, too, thinking that she would get no answer if she called during the cocktail hour. Then she would merely leave a message and be unavailable, as usual, when the call was returned, thus escaping the lunch.

The call had been arrogant. It started with a snippy voice asking, "Is this Mrs. Golden?"

"Yes."

"Hold for Miss Harrington."

Click. The phone went dead for several carefully planned minutes while Sylvia Harrington kept the wife of the publishing magnate waiting.

But Marti Golden had hung up.

The phone rang again.

"We must have been cut off, Mrs. Golden." The secretary sounded even more haughty.

"No. I hung up," Marti said.

There was a startled gasp at the other end of the phone, then silence. The secretary debated whether to become ruder or more respectful to this courageous voice. Luckily for her, she opted for respect.

"I'm sorry. She will be with you in a moment. She got a call from our Paris office as she was about to pick up the line."

"Oh, Parisians must be changing." Marti decided to give the secretary a politely rough time. "The ones I know would never work this late. It must be past eleven o'clock there."

"Just a moment," said the secretary, completely flustered.

A second later the throaty tones of Sylvia Harrington cut into the line. "Yes, this is Sylvia Harrington," she announced.

"And this is Mrs. Golden." Marti almost laughed. The conversation was starting to amuse her.

The bitch one-upped me, Sylvia thought. Most women were eager to be on a first-name basis with her — at least, most women she cared to know. "I understand your husband is a friend of our Mr. Barkley."

"He knows Richard. I believe they had breakfast the other morning." Marti was playing it close to the vest.

"I was so hoping that you could lunch with us tomorrow. I can assure you that the lunches at *Haute* magazine are most interesting," purred Sylvia.

"I'm sure," Marti returned. "I should be delighted to have lunch. But tell the chef that I eat very lightly. Just a salad will be fine."

She's giving orders to my chef, Sylvia noted mentally. *this woman will have to be put in her place.*

"About twelve-fifteen, then?"

"That will be fine."

Marti hung up the receiver without saying good-bye, leaving Sylvia Harrington holding a disconnected receiver. Normally, Marti was almost overly courteous, but she had taken an immediate dislike — another thing she normally never did — to the imperial Sylvia Harrington.

Marti would probably have been late for the *Haute* luncheon, except that she had invited Marcella, and Marcella refused ever to be late for anything.

"Let her wait," Marti said to her friend as she pushed through the overstuffed closet of the suite looking for something suitable for a slushy day in New York City. "It will do her good. God, how I hate dressing for New York," Marti bellowed from the depths of the closet. "This horrible climate. How can anyone look good in this disgusting weather? No wonder we never use this apartment."

It was entirely characteristic for the Goldens to keep a six-room suite year-round in one of the most expensive hotels in the world to use it maybe one or two weeks a year.

"Damn, everything I bought is too lightweight," Marti complained.

"The sable should be adequate," Marcella teased.

"Oh, what a clever, clever girl you are. The perfect solution. I will wear my sable and my suntan. Then I will tell Sylvia, darling, that the Baroness de Rothschild does that same thing simply all the time. By mid-summer it will be a new trend."

"How about the Dior suit?" Marcella suggested.

"Maybe Sylvia will wear the same thing."

"A Dior suit?"

"No, a suntan. She might decide that my suntan idea is something she should personally adopt. You know what that makes me think of? Remember that television commercial where the prune gets a suntan and becomes a raisin? Suddenly I can see Sylvia with a tan. A raisin. A skinny raisin."

"That's terrible." Marcella laughed.

"That's always safe," Marti said reasonably.

"What *are* you talking about?" Marcella asked.

"The Dior suit. That was what you were talking about, wasn't it? I said that it's always safe. Please try to keep your mind on the conversation. I hate having to explain things over and over again. You *are* a trifle dense, you know. Attractive, but dense."

Marti never dressed fast except when she was with her best friend, Marcella. Even then she was reluctant to speed up what had become a ritual with her. Appearance was an obsession with Marti Golden. She was a wonder of modern plastic surgery. The face had been the first body part to be rearranged, then lifted; it was a ritual she repeated almost every seven years. She dieted and exercised away every hint of flabbiness from her body. Her breasts had been reduced and slightly relocated when they started to sag. The result was that she looked twenty years younger than her true sixty years. "Forty and holding — desperately," she often commented to her friends.

She had been married to Sol Golden for forty years. During that time, she had watched him turn from a muscular boy with bushy hair into a pudgy old man with no hair. In the same period, she had managed to go from a gangling wallflower to a matronly beauty. She loved it when some new acquaintance asked if she was Sol's daughter. He loved it, too. While many people thought the hundreds of thousands of dollars she spent on surgery, beauty treatments, clothes, and diets were for her own vanity, they were not. She would have been perfectly happy to eat herself into half sizes and wear crow's feet like battle stripes, but Sol wanted her always to be young and beautiful. He loved her but wanted her to be a goddess. She loved him enough to do it for him.

"The Dior, you say?" Marti asked.

With Marcella's encouragment, Marti managed to get dressed and ready more than a half hour before her scheduled arrival in *Haute*'s private dining room. "Shall I have them bring the car around?" she asked, reaching for the house phone to call the hotel garage.

"Let's walk," Marcella suggested.

"Walk! Are you crazy? Remember, dear, I'm from California. We don't walk out there. Jog, maybe. But walk, never. It might even be illegal, probably un-American, and definitely un-Californian." Marti looked out the window to the street far below. "There is a blizzard out there. We could get stuck in a glacier and not be found until spring, if this God-awful place ever actually has a spring.

"You'll love walking. You can look at the windows."

"We could have the driver go very slowly and use binoculars to look at the windows," Marti suggested.

"Let's go, Mrs. Golden."

Marti knew she was going to walk. Ever since she and Marcella had become close friends, she had found herself doing things like that. Marcella always treated her as if they both had the energy of teen-agers, which they both usually did.

"There is one good thing about New York," Marti teased. "At least I don't have to worry about the sunlight showing all my carefully hidden wrinkles when I'm standing beside you. This place hasn't seen the light of days for months."

"In every cloud there is a —"

"Don't say it," Marti interrupted.

In spite of the continuous barrage of complaints, Marti enjoyed a brisk walk to the *Haute* building. She listened when Marcella pointed to someone wearing a particularly well-put-together outfit. Marti was very proud of the fashion sense she had developed under Marcella's guidance.

The receptionist seemed impressed when Marti gave her their names. She recognized not only the Golden name, but also Marcella's. "Oh, Mrs. Golden, I didn't know there were two of you. Just a moment. I will have someone show you to the penthouse."

"She didn't know I was coming?" Marcella sounded concerned.

"Perhaps I neglected to mention I was bringing a guest. The phone call was brief." Marti did not sound at all concerned.

"Dammit, Marti . . ." Marcella began.

"Forget it. I'll tell her I thought the place served cafeteria style. So we send out for an extra pizza and order an extra plastic fork." Marti laughed. "Big deal."

The copyboy assigned to usher the pair to the penthouse overheard the remark and burst into laughter. So did Marcella and Marti. "What's your name?" Marti asked the copyboy.

"Frank, ma'am."

"Hmm! Polite, as well as having a sense of humor. Maybe I'll buy this place and make you a vice-president. Would you like that, Frank?"

"That would be great, ma'am."

"See you around, kid." Marti pinched his cheek.

The dining room was empty. All the tables had been cleared except for a small one at the window that was covered with layers of pink linen. The executive staff had been given orders to eat out.

"There were only two places set." Marcella sounded apprehensive.

"Maybe Miss Harrington isn't hungry," Marti suggested. "Perhaps she had her fill of virgin blood last night. It was a full moon, I think."

"What in heaven's name happened on the phone between you and that woman?" Marcella demanded. "I've never heard you sound so bitchy."

"Nothing, really. She just affected me badly for some reason. I guess I'm acting more on a gut instinct than actual firsthand knowledge. I'll try to be nicer," Marti promised without much enthusiasm.

"Please."

A waiter entered the room. "Will there be three for luncheon? I didn't know. Miss Harrington said to expect only two."

"There will be three," Martin said with her usual tone of authority. She was used to directing servants.

"Very good, madam."

The waiter disappeared, and the two women walked to the window that seemed to overlook everything expensive in New York City. He reappeared in less than a minute with an additional gold Spode place setting and a service of antique Georgian silver. A place marker with the name "Marcella Todd" in perfect script was set at the top of the dinner place.

"That was efficient," Marcella said.

"There is probably a monk with a quill pen in the basement," Marti said. "Shall we be seated?"

The waiter returned with a bottle of Roederer Cristal. Mrs. Golden studied the bottle and approved. Then the waiter poured the champagne into delicate Waterford fluted glasses.

"It's showtime." Marti was starting to enjoy herself.

Sylvia Harrington was precisely fifteen minutes late. "I'm terribly sorry. It seems there are always last-minute decisions to be made just before lunch. You see, we have this story on the Duchess of Ashburn, and she had been promised a final okay, but some silly twit of a writer neglected to get it. I had no choice but to ring up Mary Ellen myself and read it to her. A bother, but you know how she can be."

"Yes, I know exactly what you mean." Marti smiled. "She has always been a very exacting person. She plays cards the same way."

"Of course." Sylvia decided to change the subject. She had been bested still another time by this woman from California. Dickie would pay dearly for the luncheon, she vowed.

"I understand that your husband is a friend of our Mr. Barkley. In newspapers or something like that. And you, Miss . . . uh . . . ?"

"Todd."

"Of course. You look very familiar. Have we met?" She remembered Marcella very well. She had noticed her five years ago at a Lagerfeld ready-to-wear showing in Paris. They both were sitting in the front row. Sylvia had asked Jayne to find out who she was and to tell one of the photographers to take a few shots of her in case she was the new wife of a somebody important enough to rate a mention in the social section of *Haute*. Jayne returned to say that she was only the fashion editor of the *Chicago Herald*. A seedy tabloid rating a front-row seat! Sylvia had a difficult enough time tolerating the woman from *The New York Times* and the Californian from the *Los Angeles Times* being given seats of honor in the front rows. But a Chicago tabloid? After the show, Sylvia had had a talk with Karl Lagerfeld and gently suggested he be more selective in his seating. He seemed to understand. It had not really been worth being concerned about.

"No, we haven't really ever met," Marcella answered. "We cover most of the same openings, and I have seen you at parties; but we were never really introduced."

"How unfortunate, dear," Sylvia cooed.

Maybe that is what this meeting is all about, Sylvia thought. *Sol Golden wants me to take his nubile fashion editor under my wing. Maybe I will. Then he would owe me something.*

"Are you going to the special February showings?" Sylvia had added a sudden blast of calculated warmth to every syllable. "Perhaps we can spend some time together. That should be nice."

"Perhaps," Marcella agreed.

"We must promise to try. Really try," Sylvia urged. "You know how hectic things are. We make promises, and then with all those crowds and deadlines, we just never seem to do what we really mean to do. But we will try, won't we, dear?"

"Of course," Marcella assured her hostess.

"Tell me, what is it like to run a huge magazine like *Haute?*" Marti interrupted. "How do you find enough time to oversee everything?"

"It was impossible in the beginning." Sylvia was almost enthusiastic at the turn in the conversation. "The magazine was nothing when I came."

"When was that?" Marti asked.

"About 1952. It was almost broke. I started in the advertising department. You probably don't remember, but this used to be one of those housewife books with lots of recipes."

"*I* didn't remember," Marcella added.

"It was just about broke, and I begged Dickie — Mr. Barkley — to let me put together a little fashion section to wrap around some of the advertising I had sold. Actually, I hadn't sold the advertising at all, but I had promised free promotion in the magazine for anyone who bought an ad."

"Was the section a success?" Marcella asked.

"Not much of a success, but it did add enough money to keep the magazine going. I became head of advertising, mostly because so many of the men in the advertising department had decided that the magazine was folding and they were jumping to more secure publications."

Sylvia suddenly froze. She realized she was being interviewed. Maybe this Todd woman was more than an ornament. She might be a reporter, a real reporter. Sylvia was always very careful about granting interviews.

"Is this an interview?" Sylvia demanded.

"Maybe," Marcella answered.

"I suppose it can't hurt. I'm careful about giving interviews. So many of them seem, well, you understand. Should I have the public relations department send over a photo?"

"I'll call if I need one. Please continue. I am enjoying this." Marcella glanced at Marti, finally realizing why she had been included in the strange luncheon. She was supposed to use her instinctive reporting ability to probe Sylvia Harrington. By why?

Sylvia relaxed. "The big turnaround came when we did our first Paris coverage. At the same time, I took over as editor and changed the entire book. Pictures were enlarged to fill entire pages. Before that they had always been tiny, really postage-stamp-sized. We couldn't afford it, but we started using color. I also discovered some fine photographers at that time."

"Like Franco Brenelli?" Marcella named the most

famous and successful fashion photographer in the world, a man who had produced more than one hundred *Haute* covers.

"I *created* Franco. He had to rent a Hasselblad for the first shooting with *Haute*. We had to advance him the money. There was just something different about his work that really attracted me to Franco. He could also follow orders. I dislike prima donnas."

Marti chuckled.

"His work is often so violent," Marcella said. "Then sometimes it is so aloof and cold."

"That is part of the attraction," Sylvia answered, "the glamour."

"He is considered somewhat of a prima donna now," Marcella said carefully.

"Not with me," Sylvia retorted. "Never with me."

The luncheon was served. Prawns on a bed of spinach with a wonderful light dressing. No bread. No extras. It was the kind of lunch being eaten by the rich and the slim all over the world.

"More champagne?" the waiter offered.

"The effect of that redesigned issue was immediate," Sylvia continued, waving to the waiter her silent instructions to refill the glasses. "Newsstand sales tripled, and I had already increased the price by fifty cents, which was a lot of money in the fifties. We went from less than a million to three million subscribers overnight — that is, overnight after three years of careful planning and effort."

"You were very innovative for that time," Marcella said.

"*Haute* is still innovative!" Sylvia replied a little sharply.

"Critics of *Haute* have said that the magazine is preoccupied with elaborate photographs of unrealistic, expensive clothing. That the magazine has no meaningful copy. That all the editorial content is supposed to do is provide a limited amount of space between ads. How do you respond to such criticism?" Marcella had dropped a bomb of a question.

How dare that damned little bitch ask me a question like that? Sylvia thought. *How dare she question my managing of* Haute? *Cunt! Fucking little blond cunt! I would like to scratch her eyes out!* Sylvia's face froze into a practiced noncommunicative expression.

"I haven't really heard such criticism. But, just saying there was, I would answer these nameless critics by pointing to our eight million readers and record revenues."

"I understand that your readership has been dropping and that the average age of your readers now is in the mid-forties," Marti interjected. Both Marcella and Sylvia looked startled by this "inside" statement.

How did she find out about that? Sylvia wondered, realizing that somewhere inside the *Haute* organization somebody was leaking secrets. That survey had come out only a few months before and was top secret. Dickie had been mildly concerned that the readership seemed to be growing older. He seemed to accept the rationalization that this was just a period of adjustment, that it was the fault of the fashion industry for not setting any interesting new trends that season. The thought of that conversation brought back a nagging sensation of worry to Sylvia.

"As you know, Miss Todd — it is *Miss* Todd, isn't it? — the entire population is aging. The baby boomers of the fifties are already in their mid-thirties. I think the shifts in *Haute* readership are just a reflection of our changing times."

"Perhaps," Marti again entered the conversation. "My husband has a lot of success in gearing his newspapers more toward younger readers."

"A newspaper is not a magazine. Younger readers cannot buy furs, designer clothing, and jewelry," Sylvia said.

"Some of us do," Marcella added.

"We have found that many of them can," Marti said.

"Then I guess we are at editorial odds. I can only hope that there is room enough in publishing for both economic theories to be successful," Sylvia continued. "*Haute* certainly has been." She was trying hard to be diplomatic. Some inner instinct was warning her it was not the time to explode; it was a time for caution.

"Where will you be staying in Paris?" Marcella asked, changing the subject.

"We always stay at the Georges *V*," Sylvia responded.

"That is where we will be located this time," Marti said. "The apartment is being redone, and since it is just Marcella and myself, well, the hotel is nice."

Marcella looked at Marti with curiosity. Marti had taken the apartment off the Place de la Concorde years ago to avoid hotels. Marti disliked hotels. Her apartment in the Pierre was her least favorite residence. That was why the Goldens owned their own home almost everywhere they traveled. The town house in Mayfair. The casita at Las Brisas. The villa at St. Tropez. And the Paris apartment, which was *not* being renovated. Marti was lying. Something definitely was happening.

"Do you have enough for your little story?" Sylvia asked.

"I'm not sure I'm going to do the story yet," Marcella said, covering herself. "Perhaps we can talk again."

"Certainly, although I usually don't give interviews. But enough of this shop talk. I'm sure we will see each other at the showings." Sylvia had had enough of the conversation.

"I'm sure we will," Marti agreed.

"Now, if you will excuse me, I have a long afternoon ahead." Sylvia stood in preparation to show her guests to the door.

"It's been delightful." Marti smiled, a smile that had detectable hints of practiced insincerity. "You were everything I had heard and more."

"We must do this again sometime." Sylvia returned the identical smile. "Of course, we are all going into a hectic time of the year."

Sylvia used her special key to summon the elevator. As her guests entered, she turned the key in the lock to whisk the occupants of the elevator to the main floor without having to stop.

Both Marti and Marcella waited until they were away from the building to exchange impressions of the luncheon and Sylvia Harrington. Elevators, especially private elevators in big corporations, tend to be bugged. Marti considered commenting on Sylvia's vulturelike appearance, just in case the elevator did have a listening device. But she decided against the bit of fun since she was playing for bigger stakes. Up in the penthouse, Sylvia Harrington heard nothing.

"Do you mind telling me what was happening there?" Marcella paused at the curb of Park Avenue. "That was hardly a nice social lunch. Are you and Sol planning something?" Marcella had always been smart. That was what was always so attractive about her — the alertness, the keenness.

"Sorry, honey, I have to keep this to myself for

now. You'll know soon enough. Since we are in the neighborhood, let's do some people-watching at Bloomingdale's.''

"You mean you're willing to walk all the way to Bloomingdale's? You might lose your rating as a truly motorized Californian. Something is happening here.''

"It's just that I feel so full of energy. Let's see if you can catch this old lady.'' With that, Marti started up Park Avenue.

Chapter Nine

A winter rain in Manhattan intensified the sounds of the island. At night, it was even more so. The sound of a siren ringing somewhere on First Avenue carried for blocks. The relentless splashing of the rain against the sidewalks had an almost bell tone, while that same raindrop sinking into dissolving slush was muted. The voices of New York were even harsher and shriller: the mad bag woman who circled Grammercy Park wailing insults at some blurred but not forgotten memory; the slick couple clicking along the pavement with voices dramatically emphasizing that they were New Yorkers living in New York; the garbage men complaining about the rain or the cold or the heat or the smell of the city; the taxi driver conducting Brooklynese business with still another late-night fare.

Usually the sounds were symphonic to Marcella Todd. They were reassuring signs that she was in the most exciting city in the world . . . at the top of the heap . . . exactly where she had always wanted to be.

Tonight was different.

Something was going to happen. Marcella had an instinctive inner warning device that anticipated problems. Not that she could not handle any sort of high-pressure problem. A work problem never interrupted her sleep. Even romantic difficulties could not trigger the inner panic. She was the capable Marcella Todd who thrived on pressure and demands.

This feeling came when something was about to happen that she could not control. She had had the pounding-in-the-chest-hard-to-breath-heat-and-chill feeling before, the afternoon at Dr. Asbaugh's office when he told her she was pregnant with Diane; and the night Randy tried to strangle her.

Marcella lay in bed and shuddered.

There was a crash somewhere on Park Avenue. In New York, it was possible to tell how many vehicles were involved in a crash by the sounds. A car had hit one of the iron light poles. Crews would be replacing the pole in the morning when Marcella walked to work, and by the time evening arrived, all signs of the crash would be gone. There was a deep airhorn blast of a firetruck echoing down Park; the car must have burned, or the gas tank leaked all over the lumpy pavement. A shrill wail of a siren told of ambulances racing to compete for a customer. Doors slammed. A deep voice yelped in pain. More sirens.

Marcella tossed and buried her head in the pile of pillows that she clustered at the head of her bed. She rubbed her hand along the satin sleekness of her night-gown, feeling the tight muscles of her thigh and leg. It was reassuring after a cry of pain in New York City to find oneself intact. It was so very reassuring to know that cry of pain was not your own.

This is crazy, Marcella thought. *Too much imagination. That's it.* She concentrated returning her heartbeat to its regular rate; after all, she was not some hysterical woman who would drive herself in a frenzy for absolutely no reason.

Deep breaths. In-two-three-four. Out-two-three-four. Better, better. It's nothing. Nothing. Get some sleep. Close the eyes. Sleep. The satin is so smooth and cool and perfect. That's right. Marcella's mind cleared and the mental void that had been filled with nervousness drifted toward more pleasant thoughts, warm thoughts, warm arms. Burt's warm arms around . . .

The phone rang.

Her breathing stopped. Every muscle in her body stiffened. She reached for the receiver.

"Yes," she said.

"Marcella." The strong, accusing voice on the other end of the line had never changed over the decades. It was the same when Marcella was a child. The same when she was a teen-ager. The same when she was a housewife — housewife . . . that was the correct word, alright — the same when she was a success. Accusing!

"Mother!"

"Diane is gone!"

"Gone! Gone where?" Marcella fought down panic.

"If I knew that, I wouldn't be bothering you about your own daughter." Yes, accusing. Still accusing. "I called the police but they said it was too soon for them to get involved."

"Why, Mother?"

"How should I know? She is just like you. She doesn't listen. She does exactly what she wants. I am too old for all this. My doctors said . . ."

"Please, Mother." Marcella was regaining self-control. "There must be some reason."

"You know about my blood pressure . . ."

"I want to know about Diane!" Marcella was firm.

"Of course."

"When did she leave?"

"Sometime around six last night. She stormed out of the house."

"You argued."

"I was just trying to raise your daughter properly, the only way I know how."

"What did you argue about?"

"You wouldn't approve, but then you aren't the one who has to watch over her every day."

Marcella knew that her mother was right. She did neglect her daughter emotionally. Yes, the money she earned kept that idyllic setting back in Canfield, the white clapboard house on Court Street, the picket fence; all that was jeopardized, almost lost, but she had saved it all with the monthly fifteen-hundred-dollar checks. She kept the roof in place over her mother's head, and, in turn, her mother kept Diane. If Marcella had raised her daughter, there would not be the time for her job, that high-paying job. That job that was her life.

"Please, Mother, just tell me what happened!"

"It was about that boy, Jud James."

"Who is that?" Marcella searched mentally for some connection to the name.

"She has been seeing him for the last *year*."

Marcella winced. She did not know. Something had happened that was traumatic enough to make her daughter run away. Something to do with a boy named Jud James. And she did not even know who he was.

"What about this boy?"

"I think they have been sleeping together."

Sleeping together. Marcella considered the phrase. It was normally a funny phrase to her. The last thing a pair of sixteen-year-olds would be doing together in bed would be sleeping. Her mother's verbal ignorance of the situation would be funny, but Diane was somewhere unsafe. Somewhere far away, perhaps, from the fifteen-hundred-dollar-a-month Rockwellian environment provided by her glamorous mother.

"I can't go through that again," Marcella's mother whined. "I told her that I couldn't go through that again."

Marcella's hand was shaking as she listened to her mother's voice.

"I want to know about my daughter. I don't want to rehash the past." Marcella replaced the tone of fear in her voice with a practiced cold business tone. She felt cold. She had not spoken to her mother in that way for years, not since she took control of her own life.

Silence.

"Mother, did you tell her about what happened to me?"

"Yes."

"Oh, God, Mother, why?"

"I didn't want her to get into trouble. The same trouble."

Marcella felt the guilt again. She knew what her mother had done. She knew how Diane must have felt.

"Damn!" Marcella had no other words at the moment. There was only a churning in her stomach that swelled to a ball of tightness. She was wrong. She knew it. She did not want to be wrong. She had not done anything. That was wrong. "What are the police doing?" she finally asked her mother.

"Nothing officially. Not for twenty-four hours. That is the law. They have to wait twenty-four hours."

"Can't they do *something*?"

"The chief said that they would watch for her, but if

she doesn't return in twenty-four hours, that is a bad sign."

"A bad sign!"

"Well, you certainly have read about young girls who run away from home. You know as well as . . ."

"Yes, I do." Marcella had not only read about teen-aged runaways, she had written about them. Her name appeared prominently on the letterhead of a national association to assist parents of runaways. She had agreed to endorse this program following a series of articles she had written on the subject. She had a letter of commendation from the President's wife lauding her insight into "what has become one of the most serious problems facing young women and their mothers in today's complex and demanding environment." What pretentious words, she had thought. But she agreed to let the committee use her name on the letterhead.

"All we can do is wait," Marcella's mother said.

Marcella realized that the old woman was worried. She knew she should tell her mother she realized that she was just trying to do her best at raising a teenaged girl. She wanted to use words to form some sort of bond between the two of them.

"Mother . . ."

"Yes . . . ?"

"Mother?"

"What?"

"We had better hang up. We had better keep the line open. Someone might . . ." Marcella's voice trailed off.

"I'll call you if anything happens. Good-bye, Marcella."

Click. The drone of the dial tone mixed with the sirens. Still another ingredient of the sounds of Manhattan on the rainy winter night. It was the most threatening sound in the city to Marcella Todd.

Chapter Ten

The mercury-vapor-lighted night was evolving into dawn. Marcella noticed the dawn. It meant the night — the horrible, fearful night — was over. Night usually was a time she did not have to organize. Instead, she slept, and her magnificent body gathered the energy for the next day. She could not fill these unexpected hours that she lay in her brass bed with anything but fear, panic, and guilt.

But she had control of the mornings.

Every minute of the morning was part of a routine. Wake without an alarm at exactly seven. But that night she had not slept. Turn on the instant-coffee machine. Check her answering service — a machine — at the office by calling the business number and beeping a code on her push-button phone. But she had called the office every hour since that phone call from her mother to see if Diane or the police might have tried to contact her at Golden Limited.

Her careful routine was falling apart.

Even the light seeping in uninspired grayness through the sheer undercurtains of her bedroom seemed different.

Seven A.M. Everything should be normal. Everything

would be normal. She reached for the phone but did not dial her office line. Her manicured fingers tapped out a number she had been given, but a number she had never used — Burt Rance's private home line. She remembered when he gave it to her, saying, "This rings right by my bed and only by my bed."

He had smiled menacingly when he told her that number.

But she had not forgotten the number. While the thousands of numbers that she needed to run her business affairs had to be carefully recorded in a Rolodex on her secretary's desk, Burt Rance's very private number was instantly part of her intimate memories.

The phone rang. One . . . two . . . three . . . four . . . five . . . times.

Suddenly, a deep voice thundered, "Hello!" He sounded abrupt. She could hear the shower still flowing in the background. Her index finger slipped to the shut-off button. "Who's there!"

"Burt . . ." Marcella's voice broke.

"Marcella, is that you?" His voice became instantly gentle and worried. She was a very different woman from the confident Marcella Todd he had always known. "Are you all right?"

"I'm all right . . . yes," she managed to say.

Burt let out a sigh of relief. But something was wrong and she needed him.

"Are you at your place?" he asked.

"Yes."

"I will be right over." The phone went to dial tone. Marcella held the receiver in both hands for a moment, then put it back in its cradle and walked to the bathroom to get her bathrobe.

She needed Burt Rance. She was realizing that she needed somebody, and that somebody was Burt.

A few moments later Marcella automatically pressed the release button when the buzzer announced that Burt was in the foyer of the town house. She undid the three security locks on the door as he bounded the stairs, two at a time.

Suddenly, she felt foolish.

"I'm here," Burt said softly. "Now tell me what is wrong."

"I shouldn't have called you," she began.

"But you did and I am here."

Marcella couldn't suppress a slight smile when she looked at the Burt Rance who was filling her doorway. This was not the immaculate tycoon in his one-thousand-dollar Dimitri suits. He was wearing jogging shorts, his New York Athletic Club sweat shirt, and his Reeboks. He must have pulled on the first clothes he saw. Even in the coldest weather, he would wear shorts for his morning run.

He does have great legs, Marcella thought, looking at his thigh muscles. Then she felt guilty. She should not be thinking about Burt Rance's muscular legs. She should not be thinking about Burt Rance.

And Burt was looking at her. This was not the Marcella Todd he knew. This was not the gleaming and self-assured woman who skillfully deflected his every pass. There was no makeup. The hair was tangled and unruly. She was wrapped in an aging corduroy bathrobe. Her feet were bare. Her clear blue eyes were red and puffy from lack of sleep.

But, by God, she was still beautiful, Burt thought. The women in Burt Rance's life were always careful to be beautiful around him. Even those who visited his bed, and most did, were careful to sleep with appropriate makeup. In New York City, most women with enough money, enough time, enough willpower, and enough pride could seem beautiful. But Marcella Todd, looking as destroyed as Marcella Todd had ever looked, was still beautiful to him.

"It's my daugther," Marcella said simply.

Burt raced through his memory for details about the daughter. There were not many. She lived in Ohio with her grandmother. She was a teen-ager. That was all he knew.

"She's run away."

Burt walked across the small black-and-white tiled entrance hall and placed his arms around Marcella. He wanted to say the right words to lessen her fears. But the elegant and eloquent Burt Rance, for once, did not have those perfect words. All he could do was hold her and feel helpless. "Everything will be fine. Your daughter will be fine. I'll stay here."

"No . . . you don't have . . ." Marcella began to say.

"I'll stay here!"

Marcella was too tired and too alone to resist. While she feared being dependent on a man again, she needed Burt's strength more.

"You get some rest," Burt said, taking control. "Go get back in bed and I will stay by the phone. Go on!"

"No, I . . ."

"You won't be any good to anyone acting like a zombie. Get some rest. I'll wake you if there is anything you need to know."

Marcella knew he was right. She turned and climbed the spiral staircase to her bedroom. Seconds after she placed her head on the pillow, she was asleep. She could sleep because there was someone sharing her responsibility. Burt was there.

It was afternoon when she awoke. She could hear Burt talking on the phone downstairs.

"Look . . . I don't want to tie up this line. I don't know when I will be back in the office. You run the place for a while. I gotta get off. The daughter might be trying to call."

Marcella walked down the stairs. She hadn't removed the corduroy bathrobe before getting back into bed.

"Nothing. No word," Burt said as he saw her coming into the room.

"I'm sorry. I should not have bothered you." There was real embarrassment in Marcella's voice.

"Why *did* you call me?" Burt asked.

"There was no one else."

"Oh . . ." Burt was pleased at the admission.

"No one else I wanted to be here."

In that instant Marcella realized how very alone she was. She was beautiful. She was rich. She had thousands of . . . friends . . . numbers in a phone book . . . invitations to posh parties. But all were merely names and faces and glib conversations. She had demanded independance and she had got it. She looked at herself in the Adam mirror in her living room. "Good God, I am really a mess."

"Me, too."

He stood there in his shorts, unshaven and . . .

"What's wrong with your hair?" Marcella asked.

Burt Rance's curly blond hair was matted into lighter-than-usual ringlets.

"If you remember, I was in the shower when you called. I was washing my hair."

"You mean that's soap?"

"Yeah, soap."

She could not hold back a small laugh. The meticulous tycoon had rushed to her side without even rinsing the soap from his seventy-five-dollar haircut.

"Maybe I could finish my shower upstairs," Burt suggested, slightly embarrassed. "It does itch . . . the soap, I mean."

"I'm sorry. Of course," Marcella agreed. "I should dress, too. You use the bath while I get dressed."

Marcella pulled on a pair of jeans and a huge turtleneck sweater and listened to the sound of the water in the shower hitting Burt's body. The sound of the water stopped. Burt emerged from the bathroom wearing only his shorts.

"You got an extra towel?" he asked.

She handed him a towel. And she looked at the man. She knew that he spent twelve hours a day running his empires. But his waistline was not thickening. There were no signs of successful middle age. He was almost too muscular. Too tan. Too blond. Too perfect. He looked like one of the ads in his own magazines.

"You approve?" he asked.

"When do you find the time to go to the gym?"

"You think this body isn't genetic"

"No . . . you have to work at that."

"Just like you do yours?"

"Just like I do mine."

Marcella was gripped by another of those stomach-twisting pains of guilt. Here her daughter was . . . missing . . . and she was thinking about the beautiful body of a handsome man. She was a rotten mother. She had always been a rotten mother.

Her shoulders started to shake.

"Hey, don't do that." Burt came to her side and held her. She buried her face in the hairs of his chest. She could feel the dampness. Smell the soap.

"I want you to need me," Burt said softly. His powerful hand gently ran across her cheek, through her hair, and down her neck. "You have a right to need someone. I want that someone to be me. I have wanted that since the first day I ever saw you." He pulled her toward him.

The phone rang.

Marcella jumped away and grabbed the phone. "It's for you." She handed the receiver to Burt.

It was Burt's driver. "Yeah . . . bring the clothes over and get some sandwiches."

"You should go," Marcella said. But before she could continue, Burt had taken her in his arms once again and was kissing her. It was a kiss that was more than the lips. It was a kiss of strength and power. But it was a kiss without controls. Neither of them could end the kiss that was more the uniting of two spirits than the kindling of mere physical passions.

The door buzzer sounded.

That will be my clothes and the food. I'll get it," Burt said. He went down the winding metal stairway to the entrance hall and pressed the admittance buzzer.

Seconds later there was a knock on the door, which Burt immediately opened.

"Is my mother here?" a girl asked.

Chapter Eleven

Diane Todd just looked at Burt Rance standing in front of her wearing his all-too-brief nylon jogging shorts.

Burt Rance instantly felt embarrassed. *How much she looks like her mother,* he thought. That same height. That same blonde hair. The same insolent set to the chin and demanding blue eyes.

"Mother!" Dianne stepped past Burt into the hallway. She looked around the layout of the apartment as if she did not know exactly where her mother might be. It was then that Burt realized Marcella Todd's daughter had never before been in her mother's apartment.

"Diane!" Marcella clattered down the staircase and grabbed her daughter.

"I know you're angry," Diane said.

"Right now I am just relieved. We will talk about anger later."

Burt suddenly felt out of place. "Look," he said, "if everything is all right here, I guess I'll be going to my office."

"Like that?" Diane asked softly but accusingly.

Burt felt embarrassed again. "No, I plan to change. I did come over here in a bit of a hurry."

"Evidently." Diane had no mercy.

Burt turned and went up the stairs to get the rest of his clothes.

"You've grown up," Marcella said, appraising her daughter.

"You noticed."

"Why did you do what you did?"

"And just what did I do?" Diane asked defensively.

"You ran away."

"I came to see my mother. Is that running away? You are my mother, aren't you? Or am I misguided there, too? Maybe I am a total bastard. No mother. No father."

"Please, Diane." Marcella shook her head.

"Granmama says I am going to be just like you, so I thought I would come and see my future." Diane looked around the beautiful apartment. "Not bad." She picked up a clear crystal globe from the mantelpiece and held it in front of her clear blue eyes so that the image her mother saw through the leaded crystal was distorted but penetrating. "Is this my future? It looks a lot better than Canfield to me. I'll take it; I take the future of a whore."

Marcella slapped her daughter.

Diane returned the slap.

Both women stared at each other, breathing heavily. Diane still clutched the crystal globe in her hand. She raised the globe slowly, then hurled it at the marble fireplace. The globe smashed into thousands of crystal facets that sparkled on the hearth and in the pile of the pale blue carpeting.

"Don't *ever* call me a whore." Marcella's voice was cold and businesslike.

"I wasn't calling you a whore. I was the whore. Granmama said I was a whore. She somehow found out about Randy. I thought, I think I love him. Granmama didn't understand. It isn't like when she was a girl. I know about the pill. I'm not going to get into trouble or anything. She called me a whore, Mommy. What did I do that was so wrong?"

"I'm sorry." Marcella hugged her daughter. "I am so very sorry for everything. What else did your grandmother say?"

"She said I was going to end up just like you. She said she was too old to go through all that again. She said I was going to be ruined just like you were."

Marcella felt a flash of hate for her mother and the rigid moralistic world in which her mother fit so very perfectly.

"Mommy . . . I want to be like you." Diane's voice was small and pleading.

Marcella realized that though she had given life to this beautiful young woman, she had never shared her life. Certainly, she had provided financially, but what her money had bought for Diane was a repeat of the life she had fled seventeen years ago. It was not really her mother's fault that this child — no, she thought, this young woman — was so very miserable.

"I'm happy you are here," Marcella said, almost surprised at how glad she honestly was.

"Really?"

"Yes, really. I don't approve of what you did, running away. But we will talk about that later. Right now I want to talk about us."

Diane looked interested but said nothing.

"I should have told you about what happened, but . . . I didn't. It's my fault. Your grandmother never understood that. She was probably right. I am sure that she doesn't understand now." Marcella took her daughter's hand and led her over to the white couch piled with pillows. "I should have told you, but there are a lot of things I should have done. But I will tell you now."

"Mother . . ."

"What, darling?"

"I just want someone to love me."

Marcella understood her daughter. She had been the same age when she had wanted Randy Williams to love her enough that she would never need anyone else's love. And her daughter, who was so much like her, was making the same mistakes in her search for love.

"We are a lot alike," Marcella began. "I know that your grandmother has not told you much about when your father and I were first married. She doesn't like to think about it. First, your father and I were married when you were born, so you were not a bastard. Not that anyone would have cared at that time anyhow. A lot of people were living together and having children then, except not in Canfield and not around your grandmother."

"Did you love him?"

"I did once. Not when we were married, though. I might have even hated him then. He did love me, though, and your grandmother wanted us married. So I did it."

"Was I an accident?" Diane asked.

"Most definitely." Both women sat silent. For a few minutes both seemed to be searching for the right words, reassuring words, but the words did not come.

Finally, Marcella took a deep breath and continued. "You see, I grew up in the swinging sixties, but it was still the fifties in Canfield. I knew nothing about sex.

Oh, I knew how to do it, and I certainly knew that it felt good, but I didn't understand sex. Randy, your father, was everything a high-school girl could want. He was handsome and strong and he seemed so caring. But he was still a boy who was lost in a man's body.''

"You made love," Diane said.

"Oh, yes, we made love. We had gone steady since my freshman year. He was a junior. Randy turned down a scholarship to Ohio State to attend Youngstown University because he wanted to stay near me. I loved him for that. I loved him for a lot of reasons then: his decision to stay close to home, the attention he gave to me, his always being available. I loved him for all the things he did. I just did not love *him*, although I did not realize it at the time. I thought what we had was what love was supposed to be.

"Randy seemed so very strong and in control. Part of me liked having him make all the decisions, so when he said we should make love, I was ready. Sex was fine with him, but what I really wanted was the holding and the caring. He used to say, 'I want to be the only person in your life, and you are the only person in my life.' "

"That sounds beautiful," Diane said wistfully.

"Yes, it did then." Marcella sighed. "While I was experienced at sex, I knew very little about it," Marcella continued.

Diane looked confused.

"You might be an expert on the pill, but that subject was never mentioned in your grandmother's house. Randy said not to worry. He always took precautions. It just wasn't my problem.

"In my senior year I was offered several scholarships. The one I wanted was to the Northwestern School of

Journalism in Chicago. I was so excited when the letter came offering me the scholarship. I wrote back that same day accepting."

Diane frowned thoughtfully. "But you never went to college after high school. You got married. You only went to Northwestern after the divorce." She was already starting to put together what happened to her mother.

"Yes, when I told Randy, he was furious. He said I was selfish and that he had turned down his scholarship to stay near me. He was right, of course. But I had decided to go to Chicago."

"But . . ."

"Randy seemed to accept that fact. He talked about transferring to Northwestern, but Northwestern would not accept many of his credits from Youngstown University, and it was very expensive. So we decided to do what we each had to do, but we continued making love . . . having sex. I could not refuse him that when I was about to leave him."

"Didn't you want to make love?" Diane asked.

"No. By that time I didn't. Then I was pregnant. Later Randy told me he had purposely gotten me pregnant. It was my fault, too, but I just didn't know much, except how it felt. Your grandmother was furious. I was so confused. Randy wanted to get married. He said everything would be all right if we were only married. We spent the entire night driving to Winchester, Virginia, and the following morning I was Mrs. Randall Williams. I never used my scholarship to Northwestern."

"Couldn't you have had an abortion?"

Marcella shrugged. "I didn't know about abortions. By the time I told Randy I was pregnant, I had already missed two periods. He said to leave it all to him, and I did. I was four months pregnant when I finally considered an abortion and . . ." Her voice trailed away.

"You would have had an abortion, wouldn't you?" Diane demanded.

"If I could have . . . then . . . yes."

"Then what you really mean" — Diane sobbed — "is I should have been aborted. You didn't want me. I ruined your life."

"Whatever happened to my life, I caused," Marcella continued. "You didn't exist at that time. You were not a person. Maybe I didn't want you then, but I am so very glad to have you now."

Diane continued to cry and Marcella took her daughter into her arms, rocking her.

"You were a mistake, my darling, but the most wonderful mistake of my life. If you had not been born, I would never have had a child at all. And I do love you. Maybe I have not shown it the way I should, but you are wanted. You are the best part of my life. I want to be a mother, a real mother. I just don't know how."

Then Marcella, too, was crying, crying in the arms of her daughter.

Chapter Twelve

Diane seemed to have sunk deep into the pillows of the huge white couch. Her quick mind was collecting and sorting the pieces of the story her mother had told her and deciding how those long-buried events must have affected her own life.

"Why have I never heard from my father?" she asked.

"The decision to move out of our — your — life was his. I suppose it was because he was terrified that the people he worked for would learn that he seduced little girls or was a wife beater. My lawyer has a complete record of everything that happened. It still could damage him."

"But not to try to find me in all these years," Diane said. "Don't you realize what that can do to a person?"

"I didn't know what else to do. I still don't know what I should have done."

"But what about now?" Diane was becoming angry.

"Maybe it's the money. I was awarded alimony and child support, but Randy never paid a dime and I never asked him, or forced him."

"You counted on Granmama," Diane pointed out.

"Yes, I did that. I gave you to her. Then I went to

Chicago. I suppose I had always wanted to go to Chicago ever since I was offered the scholarship to Northwestern. I had a girlfriend, not a particularly close girlfriend, but I wrote to her and she said I could stay with her until I could get a place of my own. It was my chance to make a life for myself. I had no training or any abilities that I could see. I didn't know what kind of work I could do."

"So you couldn't have a kid hanging around . . ." There was a harsh chill in Diane's voice.

"No, I couldn't. I was a kid myself. Being capable of reproducing is not an instant ticket to adulthood. Can you understand that?"

"I'm starting to."

"What would have happened if I hadn't left you with your grandmother and gone to Chicago? It has been the money I made all these years that kept you and your grandmother secure in Ohio. Did you know that when your grandfather died, there was almost no estate? It was fortunate that I started earning the kind of money I did so quickly. Back in Canfield we would have been poor or I might have had to marry someone else just for financial security. I was little more than twenty years old, with no education and both a child and mother to support."

"So you became a famous model." There was more than a tinge of sarcastic humor in Diane's remark.

"I suppose you will always have a right to be bitter." Marcella thought about those Chicago days. It all must seem so wonderful and glamorous to Diane: the modeling, the career, the adoration, and even Kevin O'Hara. No, she could not tell her daughter about the dashing Kevin O'Hara.

Both women were exhausted and absorbed in their

own thoughts. Diane was thinking about the reasons for her mother's neglect. But Marcella was remembering Kevin O'Hara.

She became a model completely by accident. Her friend Barbara Black was a stylist for one of Chicago's top photographers, Hector Rothstein. After a week in Chicago, Marcella had had no luck in getting a job, but then she was only looking for work in the exciting Michigan Avenue area. She had no secretarial skills. She had no previous employment. Barbara was worrying about whether Marcella would ever find employment and be able, at least, to pay her share of the food and rent. Marcella wasn't that good a friend.

One afternoon Barbara got an emergency call from Rothstein's secretary. His regular stylist, a person who pressed and ironed and pinned the garments on the models and was sometimes permitted to select some accessories, had canceled. Rothstein was the big time in Chicago. Barbara wanted to look her most professional, so she asked Marcella to pretend to be her assistant. Both women wore matching smocks when they arrived at the double doors of Rothstein's marble-faced town house on Astor Street, the most exclusive residential street in downtown Chicago.

Marcella was curious about the new environment. Inside, everything was white marble. Vases were filled with lilies. Starkly lit photographs of the beautiful and famous people captured by the photographer's lens loomed from the walls four times larger than life. All the prints were in dramatic black-and-white. A tape played harpsichord rock through tiny expensive speakers hidden in huge freeze-dried plants.

That was the first time Marcella had entered a glamour factory.

Marcella smiled to herself now at the memory. The model who was scheduled that day had not arrived for the shooting. Rothstein ranted through the marble halls. Then he noticed Marcella.

"Are you a model, my dear?" he asked.

"No . . ." But she wanted to try. God, how she wanted to try.

"Come under the light." Rothstein led her into a white high-ceilinged room filled with cameras, lights, and reflectors. "Stand there," he ordered. "Hold it. Try to smile. Look elegant." Lights were flashing. Cameras were clicking. A small group of Rothsteinites was studying some preliminary Polaroid photos that were always taken before the actual shooting began.

"What do you think, Hector?"

"Hmm . . ."

"Exactly."

"You know."

"Yes! I think this girl will do. Look at the way the skin absorbs the light."

"Certainly does, Hector."

"Well, my dear, if you were not a model when you came in here, you will be a model when you leave," Rothstein declared.

And she was. As Hector Rothstein's newest discovery, Marcella immediately had a choice position as a number-one girl at the Shirley Hamilton Modeling Agency. That position improved when she was selected to be a national spokesperson for Corlean Cosmetics, an honor that was usually reserved only for the $3,500-a-day top models of the exclusive New York agencies. Certainly, Marcella had every opportunity to leave Chicago for New York. Every agency wanted her. But she had enrolled in night school, studying journalism at Northwestern University, and she would not depart. Even this seeming loyalty to Chicago helped her career. Many national companies with home offices in the Midwest would request Marcella for their commercials and ad campaigns. She was one of them. She was a Midwestern girl who stayed where she belonged and they loved her for it.

She was the most glamorous woman in Chicago café society when she first met Kevin O'Hara. Odds were immediately offered on how long it would take the ever-so-confident Kevin O'Hara to bed the ever-so-beautiful Marcella Todd. O'Hara was the youthful and handsome editor of the *Chicago Herald*. He worked at being a golden boy. His first marriage to an heiress — he didn't have money then — had ended when she tired of his carefully nurtured Gatsby image and ran away with an aging media hippie who devoted his life to protesting in front of national television cameras and drinking eighty-dollar-a-bottle champagne. Of course, everyone said that she was a fool to dump the gorgeous Kevin O'Hara for that hairy unbathed creature. He was just too good for that rich piece of trash.

Kevin, of course, agreed.

Yes, Kevin O'Hara did have the image. He kept his body sleek by doing a very visible run every morning from his apartment at the Carlyle down Michigan Avenue, giving the early arriving sales girls a thrill because he looked just as good in the flesh as he did on his three-minute spot on the evening news station owned by the *Chicago Herald*. His hair was streaked blond by the sun: Aspen in the winter and southern France in the summer. His features were chiseled; he had had a little plastic surgery. His teeth were perfect: porcelain crowns over gold.

He was even a good editor. His personal glamour rubbed off on the staff of the *Chicago Herald*, which had been a not particularly important tabloid before the arrival of the golden boy. A straphanger's paper. "Now we will give them a little excitement and glamour to hang onto, too," O'Hara said. Kevin O'Hara wanted only the best. He lived at the right address. He knew the right people. He was invited to the right parties. And he was seen with the right women.

One of those women was Marcella Todd.

To the present day, Kevin O'Hara still believed that he had been responsible for transforming Marcella Todd from star model into star journalist. But it was Marcella who had arranged it all. She had learned to admire really powerful men during her time in Chicago. While Kevin was showy and definitely did have influence, a powerful man was someone who was behind, quietly behind, a Kevin O'Hara. But Marcella did have just as much a need for Kevin O'Hara as he did to be seen with the top beauty available in his Midwestern world.

It all was so easy.

"You don't mean that you are studying journalism," O'Hara said, already thinking of the publicity and attention that would be focused on the *Chicago Herald* if Marcella Todd were to join the staff.

"What could I do at the *Herald?*" Marcella asked carefully.

"Fashion editor, what else? You certainly are an expert on fashion."

"What about salary?"

"About fifty grand." O'Hara thought she would jump at it.

"I'm making a quarter of a million now," Marcella said, smiling.

"How about fifty thousand, and I will give you the complete rights to the syndication of your column." This was a costly mistake that he later regretted. "That could add another hundred grand or so if you get in a few hundred newspapers."

"Can I still do some modeling?" Marcella asked.

"Sure. Why not?"

"You're wonderful, Kevin. I will have my lawyer draw the papers." She gave her lover-boss a kiss, a very public kiss, since the deal was made in the main room of Arnie's, Chicago's Art Deco extravaganza and watering hole for the beautiful. Everyone noticed. Kevin was pleased. The contract was sealed with a kiss.

If it was a simple task to convince Kevin O'Hara that Marcella Todd should be one of his highest-paid staffers, it was not quite so easy for Marcella to impress the professional newshounds at the *Chicago Herald*.

Most despised her immediately.

The highly paid people in the newsroom of the *Herald* had struggled through years of low wages on small- and medium-size newspapers to get to the large daily. It might be a trite phrase, but they had paid their dues. Marcella's dues had been a donation.

"Maybe I should try sleeping with the boss," said one sportswriter who had been a professional hockey player.

"He might like that," one of his co-workers added.

"Maybe I would be better off sleeping with the boss's lady," the hockey player-turned-reporter continued. "She might give me a raise."

"The only raise she can give you is in your little tiny prick!"

But Marcella did not waste any typewriter ribbon on the usual puff stories that filled the spaces around the lucrative fashion ads of the *Herald*. Immediately she started comparison shopping, naming a fashion item and discussing what it cost at different stores. The advertising department demanded that she be fired, but the public loved the informative yet witty columns that punctured many of the pretensions of the fashion industry.

Her gossip was not superficial, even the time when she explained that one of the city's leading female fashion plates was definitely not involved with another woman . . . not as long as she could teach her white German shepherd some new tricks. The story was true, and for months that celebrated canine was walked only on the twentieth-floor penthouse terrace of the Lake Shore Drive co-op, rather than being seen on the streets with its . . . mistress.

When the readership surveys showed that just as many people read Marcella Todd's column buried deep inside the *Herald* as the sports editor's comments, which were prominently displayed on the back page of the tabloid newspaper, the staff threw a party for her at the Billygoat, a revolting little bar buried deep beneath the streets of Chicago and frequented only by established newspaper types. She was easily the first fashion writer ever to enter the Billygoat. Kevin O'Hara, of course, never went there. Marcella started to like the place.

There was a rift developing between Marcella and Kevin. He had created her, he told himself, and she was becoming more famous and more sought after than he. She was traveling a lot: Paris, London, New York, Milan, and Rome, covering the fashion and glamour whirl. He was trying other women . . . black-haired this time . . . South American . . . money.

The relationship ended when Spenser Cohen, the owner of the *Chicago Herald* and the real power behind

Kevin O'Hara, sold the paper to the chain of Golden Limited.

Marcella continued as fashion columnist. Kevin was fired. To the outside, it seemed that O'Hara had chosen not to remain under the new management — but he was canned. Sol Golden had little use for glamour-boy editors.

Marti Golden admired Marcella. The day following the surprise announcement of the purchase of the *Chicago Herald*, Mrs. Golden, complete with Lhasa Apso tucked under one arm, strolled into the features department of the newspaper.

"There you are!" she bellowed, plunging toward Marcella's cluttered corner.

"How do you do? I'm Mar ——"

"I know who you are. I am your biggest fan. One of the reasons I wanted my husband to buy this newspaper in this miserably cold icebox of a city was the fact that you are part of the staff."

"Well, thank you —"

"I want you to come to California, or New York if you insist. You are going to be a big part of Golden Limited, my dear. Fashion is going to be a big part of Golden Limited. Now, no arguments. I am going to head all fashion projects, and I refuse to do it in this horrible city. You will rush right home and pack. No arguments . . . understand?"

"Of course." Marcella smiled at the brash woman who could seem so coarse but was wearing an understated Channel suit instead of that symbol of the pushy Beverly Hills matron: the Halston Ultrasuede suit. There was class there.

"No excuses . . . uh . . . what did you say?"

"Of course I will go to New York. I don't want a life full of red-eye flights, so it has to be New York."

"Done." Marti Golden liked the beautiful woman who could write so well and could make a decision. "Let's have lunch."

Those memories seemed so close to Marcella as she sat silently in her Grammercy Park living room. Yet years had passed.

Diane was sleeping on the white couch. Even while she slept she retained her beauty, her mother thought. That was one of her tests of true beauty, whether it was a woman or a man. Sleep stripped everyone of all accumulated attitude. People who projected great beauty while they were awake might seem hollow and drawn and tight when asleep. Handsome men, with their jaws agape instead of set, lost their calculated aura of power when asleep. Double chins appeared. Hair that was not carefully tended could become rumpled or suddenly seem too thin. Only the truly beautiful could be admired while asleep.

Diane was truly beautiful.

"What do I do, my darling?" Marcella whispered softly to her sleeping daughter. "What do I do?"

Chapter Thirteen

It had been three days since Diane Todd arrived at her mother's door wearing jeans and a sweater and carrying a backpack. It was the first three-day period the two women had ever spent entirely together. The morning following Diane's appearance, Marcella called her office and said she would not be coming to work and asked not to be disturbed . . . for *anything!* So for seventy-two hours, Marcella showed her daughter New York City and saw both the city and her daughter afresh. They climbed to the top of the Statue of Liberty. They had lunch at Windows on the World atop the World Trade Center. They rode a horse-drawn carriage from the Plaza Hotel through Central Park and ate crab salad in the crystal room of Tavern on the Green. There was shopping in Chinatown and on upper Lexington Avenue. Diane had her hair styled at Suga's and everything else done at Elizabeth Arden.

"You know, Mother," Diane said, "I don't want to go back to Canfield."

"You have to finish school. You are already behind."

"I wouldn't be behind if I never went back. I am just as good a student as you were. I haven't really learned anything new since my sophomore year. School is boring."

"Boring or not, you have to graduate," Marcella insisted.

"I know that."

"And go to college."

"You didn't," Diane pointed out.

"I was lucky."

"You were smart."

"So I was lucky and smart. You might be smart and not so lucky. You are going to school."

"I'll think about it," Diane compromised.

"I really want you to go to college," Marcella urged.

"Maybe for a while."

"There was so much I needed to know when I started. I had to fake a lot."

"You did all right, Mother."

Marcella decided to change the subject. "Tonight I have to go back to work."

Diane was disappointed but she understood. "Sure, you have to make a buck."

"I'm covering the Spense party. You know him, don't you — the designer?"

"Yes, I know him. You write about him all the time."

"Do I?" Marcella made a mental note not to devote quite so much space to Spense in future columns. ."Well, I have to go to the party and — guess what! — you are going, too."

"You mean it, Mom?" Diane was genuinely excited at the prospect.

"It will give you a place to wear some of those clothes we have been clearing out of the showrooms this week." It was nice that Diane was a perfect size eight and could wear the models' samples. She would be the only girl in

Ohio, probably the world, wearing one-of-a-kind designer originals bought at a fraction of the cost after they were used for runway showings or photography sessions.

More like girlfriends than mother and daughter, Marcella and Diane dove into the piles of clothes and accessories that filled the apartment. Marcella chose a black silk cocktail dress by de la Renta, while Diane decided on a very tight black strapless Cardin sheath with a red flower at the hip.

"Just perfect for a sixteen-year-old girl who is about to turn thirty," Marcella said rather disapprovingly.

"You mean it, Mother? That's exactly the effect I want. I want to look New York."

"You look New York all right. You also look Rio and Paris and Rome."

"Do you think so? Really?"

"Yes, really." Mother and daughter hugged. "Diane, I missed being close to you when you were a child, but I am going to enjoy knowing you as a woman," Marcella said sincerely. "I am not sure whether I have a daughter or a friend."

"How about both?" Diane asked seriously. "I have plenty of friends. What I want is a mother, and the way I see it, you will do just fine."

As the address 666 Fifth loomed on the top floor of still another skyscraper, Marcella said to her daughter, "Those numbers are supposed to have something to do with deviltry or Satan worship or something. It is just like Spense always to use that place. Every time I mention it in print, I get the strangest letters from ladies in the South. The place does give me the creeps."

The Sixes was a passion pit of interior design as seen through the eyes of a eunuch. There was far more concern paid to the Middle Eastern interior design — carefully raked sand dunes in the entry — than to the passion. Diane commented, "More pits than passion," a line Marcella used in her story describing the evening.

Spense was standing next to the stuffed camel. "I'd walk a mile for a hump," he bubbled.

"Did you stay up all night thinking of that line?" Marcella returned.

"What an optimist you are, darling," Spense dripped. "Wouldst that I could stay up all night, but emotionally and physically I am just a worn-out old queen."

"You aren't so old,'. Marcella volleyed.

"And *who* is this ravishing creature?" Spense asked, pointing to Diane. "Tell me you haven't given up men. Tell me."

"I won't give up men until you do, Spense." Marcella's tone was noticeably chilly. "I would like to introduce you to my daughter, Diane."

"Oh, God, I fucked up that time, didn't I?" Spense was attempting to be cavalier, but he knew he had made a monumental mistake.

"Yes, but don't worry. I am forgetting everything about all this," Marcella added, "including your name."

"No, not that. Anything but that. I would rather suffer the fate of a thousand deaths than have you forget my name."

"In my column."

"In your column."

"Spense, darling," Marcella cooed.

"What, my dearest?"

"Your camel is calling you," Marcella said, grabbing

her daughter's arm and sweeping into the restaurant proper.

The main room of the Sixes was a dark place; it had been designed that way so the stains on the heavy silk-padded walls and furniture would not show. Famous faces seemed to float out of the haze of smoke, appear instantly, then disappear as if they were ghosts.

Miranda Dante, wife of the Vice-President of the United States, did not disappear so easily. Always larger in life, usually from twenty to one hundred twenty pounds larger, she was in the midst of a lightning storm of flashbulbs.

"They have to fire them all off simultaneously to light the entire carcass properly." The voice of Sylvia Harrington cut through the animated din of the smoke like a cleaver slashing through raw flesh.

"Actually, she seems to have lost quite a bit of weight," Marcella noticed. Sylvia had seemed to appear out of nowhere at her side.

"She should lose some more by having her tongue cut out," Sylvia added.

Marcella wondered why the opportunistic Sylvia Harrington would be so openly hostile to someone as powerful as Miranda Dante. Something must have happened.

Marcella felt a famliar nudge in her back. Marti Golden, who seemed to be surrounded by a nest of feathers, flapped by her side. "Damn if this joint isn't dark! Where is a waiter? I need a drink," Marti complained.

A waiter appeared instantly.

Marti ordered a martini. "Then the waiter turned toward Diane.

"I'll have some chardonnay," Diane ordered.

"Some what?" her mother asked, startled.

"Chardonnay."

"Since when do you drink chardonnay?" Marcella demanded.

"Since I read that's what you drink. Remember the interview in *People* magazine?"

Marcella was startled to think her daughter had to learn about her by reading a magazine. "I suppose you can make that two chardonnays," she told the waiter.

"You haven't commented on my dress," Marti teased, making even more of an effort to animate the feathers.

"It looks a little like Big Bird went punk. All those colors, Marti. Where do you find these things?"

"On Brighton Way in Beverly Hills. A friend of mine by the name of Brigeta creates them. She is German, I think, and *very* decadent. I decided Spense deserved this; he is so very Ultrasuede. I just won't let the boy hog all the feathers for himself . . . Oh, hello, Sylvia. I didn't see you roosting there. Really, dear, you should try not to blend into the shadows so. Be assertive, dear, you might get somewhere," Marti advised.

Sylvia Harrington stalked away toward the Vice-President, but was stopped by an exquisite hand clutching her arm. It was the hand of supermodel Melissa Fenton.

The high-paid fashion figure was drunk or stoned, probably both. "Why are you trying to ruin me?" Melissa whispered in the same husky voice that had sold millions of bottles of perfume.

"You're drunk," Sylvia said, starting to pull away.

"I want an answer." Mellisa's voice was rising and several people turned toward the confrontation. "What have I ever done to you that would make you say what you did to my agency?"

So word has gotten back to the little tramp, Sylvia thought, pleased with herself. *That will teach the ungrateful little bitch something about appreciation and loyalty.*

Melissa was becoming more and more excited as Sylvia tried to struggle free of her grasp. "Why hurt me? Don't you know how much you can hurt me?"

Sylvia started to feel uncomfortably warm. She wanted to be far away from the beautiful but drunken and rather hysterical creature. "You are making a fool of yourself. Let me go," she demanded.

"I love you!" Melissa shouted.

The group around Sylvia and Melissa Fenton quieted. "Oh, shut up," Sylvia ordered.

Instead, the girl threw her arms around Sylvia's neck and sobbed. "I love —"

Sylvia slapped the girl. "You are drunk. Somebody had better take you home." Two doormen appeared instantly and gently ushered the frenzied model from the room.

"Well, I'll be damned," Marti said.

"Marti." Marcella tapped her friend's arm in a way that said, *This is not the time for witty remarks.* Marcella genuinely felt compassion for the devastated woman being escorted from the room. She could not conceive of the emotions that motivated Melissa Fenton's outbreak, but she understood that this girl, who the world thought had everything there was to offer, was lacking something, and that emptiness was making her miserable.

The Vice-President was speaking to Sylvia but motioning for Marcella to join the conversation. Diane was impressed that the Vice-President called her mother by her first name.

"I want to tell the two most powerful women in the fashion world about a plan I had to create a museum of the fashion arts right here in Manhattan." The Vice-President's voice was approaching oratory.

"And what am I, chopped liver — no, I take that back; *pâté de fois gras* — Donny Parker?" Marti Golden thrust herself into the conversation. She had known Vice-President Donald Hartley Parker since he was a junior congressman from Pennsylvania.

"I stand corrected — the *three* most powerful women in the fashion world," he said charmingly. "I am hoping to woo one of you away to head the Museum of American Fashion —"

"I'm not ready for a museum yet," Marti interrupted. "Talk to Sylvia."

"I have all I can handle at *Haute*," Sylvia snapped.

"That's true," Marti agreed. "You probably have *more* than you can handle. But a government job is so secure, and I bet there is a nice pension," Marti said gently. "You really should think about it."

"Why don't you go to hell or Beverly Hills, whichever is worse?" Sylvia snarled at Marti.

"Darling, have I said something to upset you?' Marti was enjoying herself. "And we all came here to have fun and enjoy one another's company, didn't we? What a shame. I'm devastated."

As Sylvia stormed away, Miranda Dante leaned toward Marti and said, "You were particularly hard on that harpy, weren't you?"

"I was. Yes, I was." Marti smiled wickedly.

"She seems to be having a difficult night," the Vice-President's wife observed. "What was the scene all about with the beautiful young thing? I don't know her name."

"Melissa Fenton."

"I heard a snatch of the conversation."

"Everybody in the building heard a snatch of the conversation, Miranda. Evidently, Melissa, as difficult as it might be to imagine, is the one person on this planet who is actually attracted to Sylvia Harrington."

"Good god, the poor child!" Miranda laughed.

"Too bad all women can't have great men in their lives like my Sol and your Donny. Sol is the only man for me. Donny, on the other hand . . ."

"Is number six," Miranda said.

"But he *is* the Vice-President," Marti added.

"My very first Vice-President."

Both women turned toward Marcella. "How about you? We have heard that there might be someone tall, blond, and handsome in your life," Miranda said.

"They must mean me," said Burt Rance, joining the conversation. "Hello, Marcella. Hello, Diane. Do you remember me?"

"This is the first time I'm seeing you with your clothes on," Diane said smugly. Her mother gave her a warning look.

"Oooh! Tell me more," Marti cooed.

"There really isn't anything more to tell. It wasn't much," Diane answered.

"Ouch!" Burt grimaced.

"Diane!" Marcella put a strong warning tone in her voice.

"Excuse me, Mother. I want to go over and meet Mick Jagger. I never have, you know." The young version of her mother was radiant as she crossed the floor toward the rock star, who was entertaining his own group in a far corner of the Sixes.

"What did I do to her?" Burt asked.

"It's not you. It's me," Marcella explained. "She's jealous of you. I've neglected her so much for so long that now she is afraid we might become something."

"Can we?" Burt asked.

"No . . ." Marcella said rather hesitantly.

"Why?"

"I owe her, Burt. I never took the time to be a mother. She wants to have me to herself, and she is going to have whatever of me is left after my work."

"No time for me, then," he said sadly.

"No time for you." Marcella shook her head.

"We will *see* about that," Burt challenged, raising his glass in a mock salute.

Chapter Fourteen

A few days after the Spense party, Marcella and Diane were in a cab headed toward Kennedy International Airport with destinations a world apart. Diane had agreed to return to Ohio and had her ticket to Cleveland, where her grandmother would meet her. She would return to New York City forever the following summer, after she finished school.

Marcella was going to Paris.

"Mother," Diane said as the cab bumped over the pothole-ridden highway, "it seems as if I have been here all my life."

"You have. New York does that to a person. It is either the cruelist city in the world, or it takes you into its soul immediately, making it seem as if you always belonged here."

"That sounds like something you would write."

"It will be." Marcella smiled at her daughter.

The cab stopped at the American Airlines terminal and Diane jumped from the battered yellow cab. It had been only a few days more than a week, but she was completely different from the blue-jeaned girl who had arrived at her mother's door. Marcella looked at her daughter and thought, *She is chic. What an overused word, but she really is chic.* The backpack had been disgarded and replaced with four pieces of Marcella's Hermès leather luggage.

"What are you going to do with a wardrobe of evening clothes and suits in Canfield?" Marcella questioned.

"I'm going to wear them and let everyone be jealous." Diane flashed a smile that Marcella realized was soon going to be seen by millions of people. Her daughter was going to, indeed, be a model. That was obvious.

"Clotheshorse."

"Mother clotheshorse," Diane retorted before turning away.

"Lady." The driver knew the police would soon be ordering his departure from the busy ramp.

Marcella watched for glimpses of her daughter in the crowd of people headed for places such as Cleveland, Pittsburgh, and Detroit.

"Lady, I gotta get going," the cab driver complained.

"Go ahead . . . I'm sorry."

"Where to, lady?"

"Air France," Marcella said.

The Concorde: the fastest and most expensive aircraft on earth. For a few thousand dollars extra, a person avoided jet lag by cutting the trip to Europe to only a few hours. Marcella would not have spent the money, but Marti Golden insisted. She said it enhanced the status of Golden Limited to have its fashion columnist fly on the Concorde. Anyway, the wine, the chardonnay, was excellent and the cuisine was delicious, though the plane was small and claustrophobic.

After the necessary passport and security checks, Marcella settled into the plush Air France private waiting room. Then she noticed Jayne Caldwell standing nervously by the window.

She walked over to Jayne. "Are we on the same flight?" Marcella asked. "You are going to Paris, aren't you?"

"On the Concorde," Jayne said. "I have to admit I'm excited. I am writing a story for *Haute* on the flight so Air France agreed to let me fly free."

"You will be impressed," Marcella said, remembering her first Concorde flight.

"I hope so. I have to like it. Sylvia would never permit an unfavorable story about Air France. The line takes very good care of her."

"That can be a fact of life, taking care of those who take care of you."

Jayne said nothing. She knew she probably would like the flight, but it would be nice if she could consider the alternative of not having to rave about the plane. "I hope I like it," she said again.

The announcement to board the aircraft began, first in English, then French, German, Spanish, and finally Italian. Marcella and Jayne had arranged to sit together.

The stewardess recognized Marcella and began to chitchat in her heavily accented English. "We will be a few minutes detained to wait for someone very important. I apologize."

"Who is this person?" Marcella asked.

"I do not know . . . most distinguished," the stewardess said.

"Hello, ladies," Burt Rance said as he bounded through the airplane door. "Were you by any chance waiting for me?"

Marcella laughed. "The fastest plane in the world has to wait for you. Now, that *is* power."

"Jayne, I'm glad to see you," Burt lied. He liked the capable Jayne Caldwell, but he did not approve of her sitting in the seat he wanted next to Marcella. "There are a lot of rumors flying about *Haute*."

"What kind of rumors?" Jayne asked carefully.

"There's talk the magazine is about to be sold. It would be a pretty big deal. Only a few could handle it. Maybe Hearst, or maybe Sol Golden."

He looked pointedly at Marcella. She had honestly heard nothing of such a possibility, but she had been busy with her daughter for the last week. It was amazing how quickly a person could be out of touch with day-to-day affairs. Marti had purposely left her alone with Diane, so they had not discussed Golden Limited. She was interested in the possibility of Sol's buying *Haute*. Marcella realized that Burt Rance did not waste his time on mere rumors. When a man of his power became interested in a deal, there was something happening.

"Maybe you are making an offer," Jayne said, voicing one of the rumors that had been mentioned around the office.

"Not interested," Burt said flatly. "I publish business magazines. You ladies want too many pictures and not enough facts for my journalistic tastes," he added.

"Then why are you accepting this free trip to see some frivolous fashion-magazine-type stuff?" Marcella asked teasingly.

"Maybe I just wanted to fly the Concorde. I don't have a rich boss like you do who always lets me use the most expensive plane in the world," Burt returned.

"I had heard the guy who runs *The Business* is a real skinflint," Marcella said with a grin.

"This show had better be good," Jayne interrupted.

"Does it really matter that much?" To Marcella the special French showing did not seem to be very important. It was, in her mind, just another publicity ploy.

"We have held thirty-two pages open for the June issue." Jayne did not have to say anything more.

"Thirty-two *pages*!" Marcella was genuinely shocked. "Jayne, you know that a lot of the clothes they are going to be showing are nothing more than photo opportunities. There won't be much that's wearable. It's all merely an extravaganza to attract the press. You just can't devote a whole issue of *Haute* to something that the reader will never be able to own or even want. It will be things like Rudee du Beck's helicopter blades. Remember two years ago when he showed hats with four-foot revolving rotors covered with sequins? They weighed a ton. There were a lot of pictures taken, but nobody ever seriously considered wearing them."

Jayne Caldwell was silent.

"My guess is this is the inspiration of Sylvia," Burt suggested.

Jayne nodded.

Rance immediately understood what was happening. His June issue was going to examine the business reasons the French seemed to be losing much of the leadership in fashion to New York and even Hong Kong. New York was really more functionally creative and Hong Kong was cheaper. Someone in the French fashion industry had gotten to Sylvia Harrington, probably with a bribe, and she was going to test to see if even all-powerful *Haute* had enough influence to convince the fashion-buying public that Paris was, indeed, still the only place to find real fashion.

"Your boss is going to make the magazine look ridiculous," Burt said to Jayne. "Too many good magazines are not following the 'Paris is the only place' line anymore. One of these days, the public is going to start laughing at *Haute* for its 'more exclusive than thou' attitude. All that worked in the fifties, but the public knows when it's being had.''

Jayne Caldwell was a company person. But she believed every word that Burt was saying. She understood if he did business stories making fun of the special French showings and *Haute* swooned over those same outrageous designs, it would be *Haute* that would seem foolish, especially to the store buyers who read both magazines. But she would not criticize her boss openly. She had done everything she could to convince Sylvia to have some backup stories to fill all those pages if the French show was a dud. Her boss had decided otherwise. Jayne could only do her best.

Marcella was impressed with Jayne. She understood Jayne hated the thirty-two-page special-insert concept but was too loyal or too businesslike to be critical of her boss.

The Concorde flight to Paris had the advantage of being so speedy that there was no real time for the kind of probing conversations that could transpire on the longer transatlantic flights.

The French, being so unpredictably snobby, gave special customs attention to those traveling on their Concordes, but even with *tout* service, Jayne had a lot to do making sure the crates of photographers' equipment — which had been sent days earlier and stored at the airport — were actually in France and not in Morocco, one of the French government's favorite places to send anything with an American return address.

Marcella found herself walking through the corridors of the international jetport with Burt Rance.

"You staying at the Georges Cinq?" Burt asked. Marcella nodded. "I suppose instead of taking one of the free rooms, Golden Limited is paying."

Again Marcella nodded.

The journalistic integrity amazed Burt. Some four thousand dollars for an airline ticket, another two hundred fifty a day for a room in one of the most expensive hotels in the world. At a time when the usually cheap French government and fashion industry were willing — no, anxious — to pay the bills.

He estimated the budget for Marcella Todd in Paris would be about twelve grand, plus photographers — and Marti Golden was coming, too. God only knew what that woman would cost. Sol Golden was a great businessman, but where these two women were concerned, he forgot business and gave them the world.

Chapter Fifteen

Thousands of miles across the ocean from Paris, a silver Mercedes roadster glided along the steaming pavement of the causeway from Key Biscayne to Miami.

Richard Barkley could feel the relentless south Florida sun starting to affect the New York paleness of his complexion. But he had decided when he arrived in Miami that he wanted to rent an open car. He wanted, for once in his life, to feel free and young and ready to live.

Barkley was glad to escape from New York City and *Haute* magazine and especially from Sylvia Harrington. True, his choice of warm-weather places would not usually be Miami. Maybe Palm Beach. More likely Bermuda or somebody's private island.

But right then there was no place on earth that Richard Barkley wanted to be more than the fading yet exciting city that was somehow more South American than a part of the U.S.A.

The plane from Rio is due at 3 P.M., Barkley thought happily to himself. It was only noon, but he had decided to leave early for the airport.

He was feeling and acting like an excited teen-ager

because for the first time ever Richard Barkley was alive and in love. And the object of his love was arriving on a 3 P.M. flight from Rio.

That was why he had borrowed a friend's mansion and pool in Key Biscayne for the week. He could have used some luxurious condo on Collins, but Barkley had opted for the seclusion and privacy of Key Biscayne.

The mansion was an extravaganza. The period was pink Hollywood Spanish with covered walkways, fountains, an indoor pool, tennis courts, and a thousand feet of ocean frontage. If the place were for sale, it would be in the twenty-million range, but it would never be for sale as long as the capitalistic system survived. Barkley had given all but one of the ten servants the week off. The one servant he kept on duty, the houseman, Raul, would be understanding and discreet.

He turned into the short-term parking area of Miami International Airport. Checking himself in the rearview mirror, he saw the humidity was making his thinning hair look soggy and beaten down after he had spent an hour blow-drying and spraying it. Still, he looked pretty good. In the last three weeks he had dropped fifteen pounds and been to the health club every day. His white shirt and triple-pleated slacks would have been shown to better advantage if he had a tan, but . . .

Damn! I should have used the tanning room at the gym, he thought.

The coolness of the airport's interior hit the perspiration forming on Barkley's forehead. *Good*, he thought, *there will be plenty of time for the sweat to dissipate. I want to look cool and — young — when the plane arrives.*

He had more than two hours to wait.

He strolled down the concourse, stopping at every

magazine stand. Of course, *Haute* was displayed prominently at each station.

How I hate that magazine, Barkley thought, looking at the shiny cover and the beautiful woman who was smiling across the high-gloss paper that month.

The more successful *Haute* became, the more Richard Barkley found himself trapped in that success. He had money and prestige and some power, but he was also subjected to the eternal belittling of Sylvia Harrington. She, who would always remind him that *Haute* — and Richard Barkley — would have been nothing if she had not saved them both. She, who called him "Dickie, dearest," as if he were a silly, fat little boy who was not very good at anything.

No, I don't want to think about Sylvia Harrington, Barkley thought. He resumed his previous fantasy about what was going to happen the rest of the week.

Miami was another world. At the airport, English did not even seem to be the main language. It was an easy place for Barkley to lose himself and adopt a new identity. He was going to be the assured, attractive, and loved man he had always wanted to be. No more fear. No more insecurity. He took a deep breath and looked at the arrivals board.

"Christ!" he said aloud. The plane had arrived almost an hour early. The passengers should be almost through customs. He rushed to the greeting area at the exit to the out-of-the-country arrivals location and pushed through the mob of humanity waiting there.

Hundreds of people were walking past. Some were met by throngs of squealing relatives. Others were alone.

The stewardess on Flight 311 from Rio, Diebre Malaga, was practicing her English on the tall, extremely handsome young man who had been traveling in the first-class section. She had paid special attention to this American throughout the trip because it was a rarity for someone so young and so handsome to be able to afford to travel first class; he was wearing an eight-thousand-dollar Rolex President's watch, he had said he was not married, and he had smiled at her.

"You stay in Miami long?" she asked.

"A few days. How about you?" He smiled again. His teeth were perfect.

"Me, too," she added. "Where you stay?"

"I don't know. With friends. Why don't you give me the number of where you will be and I will call you."

"What do you do in Miami?"

"Actually, I am headed to Orlando," he lied. "I am a baseball player down here for spring training." Another lie. Tom Andrews had not been to Florida for spring training since he had been cut.

"Basabool," Diebre said huskily. "I bet you a famous player."

"Not so famous," he said modestly.

"What you in Rio for?" she asked.

"I was shooting a television commercial. I do a lot of television commercials."

"Wait." Diebre pulled away from the crush of people to a telephone station. "I write down where I am. You call me."

"Sure," Tom Andrews lied again. He was feeling good about that lie. He liked the way women reacted to him. They always made a fuss about his looks. Very tall and very blond with a deep tan and what he was very satisfied to say was one of the best bodies in the modeling business. He was six-two and one hundred ninety pounds of perfection. He worked at it. He knew it.

Richard Barkley noticed Tom Andrews's head towering over the mostly Brazilian and Mexican crowd.

"Tom, over here," Barkley said, waving.

"Hey, Dick. Are you picking me up? Damned nice of you, buddy."

Of course Richard Barkley was picking up Tom Andrews. He was in love with Tom Andrews. He would do anything for the blond man.

"I want you to meet someone from my flight." Tom had already forgotten the stewardess's name. But Richard Barkley was used to such situations in which names were not worth remembering, and he extended his hand.

"I work for Dick a lot," Tom said to the girl.

She pressed the piece of paper on which she had written her address into Tom's hand and whispered in his ear, "I hear from you soon . . . no?"

"Sure . . . you bet."

The two men walked down the concourse together. "Now don't go getting jealous or anything," Tom said. "She just latched on to me on the plane. You know how it is."

"Sure," Barkley said. He did know how it was — always was.

Tom was becoming more defensive. "Look, I happen to like women, too. You know that. Don't go getting your feathers all ruffled. It doesn't mean a damned thing."

"Do we need to get any more luggage?" Richard asked.

"No, I got everything in this bag." Tom waved a small carry-on. "What you see is what you get. Is that all right, buddy?" He made a fist and playfully tapped the older man's shoulder.

"Yeah . . . that's all right," Barkley agreed.

The two men strided across the parking lot to the Mercedes. The seats of the car were black leather and blazing hot.

"You approve of the car?" Barkley asked.

"It's an old man's car." Tom spoke before he thought. He could see that Richard had put special thought into the selection of the car.

"What kind of car would you have wanted?" Richard asked caustically.

"Maybe a Jeep," Tom improvised quickly to placate Barkley. "Yeah . . . something we could drive out to some remote little piece of beach together in and really be alone."

"We could still rent a Jeep," Richard said enthusiastically.

"Nah . . . this is fine. Great. I love this car. It is the best car in the whole world." Tom threw a muscular, tanned arm around Barkley's shoulder. "You gonna take me for a ride, buddy?"

Handsome Tom Andrews was the only nice thing Sylvia Harrington had ever done for Richard Barkley. He hated to admit they would not be together if she had not hired Tom for some layouts at *Haute* and arranged repeatedly for them to be alone together. Richard was very nervous about Tom. He was attracted from the first time they met — Sylvia had counted on that — but he never intended for anything to happen. He had always been straight. Tom Andrews was his first affair, and that would never have happened if they had not had a foul-up on hotels during the photography of the special Moroccan issue and the two men had been forced to share a room. Tom, who was far more experienced than the older man, had moved into Richard's bed in the middle of the first night. Richard could not believe it. Tom Andrews — jock, handsome, the All-American kind of guy Richard Barkley always wanted to be — had wanted Richard Barkley. What he did not know was that Sylvia had told Tom part of the reason he was being used so much by *Haute* — which was also the reason his career was flourishing — was Richard Barkley was attracted to him. "I hope you understand," she had said pointedly.

Tom Andrews did, indeed, understand.

But Tom did not regret hustling Barkley. He liked the man. He liked him more than he even wanted to admit. He might have gone after Barkley on his own, but it was good the old hag made the deal. He would much rather think of what he was doing as a means of furthering his career than to accept the fact he was actually in love with Richard Barkley.

Tom was impressed with the pink mansion in Key Biscayne. "Are we all alone in this joint?" he yelled as they walked into the massive white marble entrance hall. His deep voice echoed and he liked the sound.

"I kept the houseman on duty to cook for us," Richard said. "I told all the rest of the staff to take the week off."

"Where is he now?"

"Out somewhere." Barkley grinned shyly.

Tom Andrews smiled; he knew a hint when he heard one. He pulled off his T-shirt and hung it on the bottom of the banister. "See anything you like?" he growled suggestively.

Richard saw something he liked . . . a lot.

The young man walked to his older lover and put a

strong hand on each shoulder. Then he leaned forward and kissed him. "You know in my own way I *do* care about you."

"I know." Barkley had trouble talking.

"Come on, buddy, let's go upstairs."

Tom bounded up the stairs removing his T-shirt. Richard Barkley looked at the muscular tanned skin of Tom's back. There was an easy kind of animal perfection about Tom's body. A perfection that was appreciated by Barkley because, in spite of hundreds of trips to the gym, he would never . . . could never . . . be so perfect.

At the bedroom door, Barkley caught Tom by the shoulder and pulled him around. The two men faced each other. Then Barkley grabbed each of Tom's powerful arms in his commanding grip and slowly backed the young man into the bedroom.

When Richard Barkley, the soft, some said weak, publisher made love to Tom Andrews, Barkley was a forceful man. There were no other words for the act. Barkley raped this young man who could have easily broken the older man into pieces. He pushed Tom onto the huge bed and pulled his jeans down past his knees.

"Let me take off my shoes . . ." Tom started to say.

"Shut up!"

Silence.

Barkley placed his hand over Tom's mouth and inserted his erect penis into Tom's anus. Tom took quick short breaths as Barkley repeated his thrust again and again.

The lovemaking proceeded in almost total silence except for an occasional wince of pain from Tom.

Yes . . . pain!

Barkley's mind was flashing back through his life and

to the boys in his high school and prep school gym who laughed at his lack of ability in sports. How like Tom they were. They made him feel so inferior. But he was not inferior now. He was in control.

Roughly Barkley pulled free of Tom. Then he grabbed his lover's neck and pulled him toward his still erect penis. Tom wanted that penis. He wanted it in his mouth. Tom Andrews was having his own fantasy — it was a fantasy of security. He wanted to be controlled. He had been told that he had to be leader. But he never wanted any of it. He wanted this.

Maybe he did love Richard Barkley.

Barkley both loved and hated Tom Andrews. He loved possessing his perfect body and his defiant attitude. Or was that lust? Whatever it was, it was what Barkley wanted.

Barkley laid back on the satin sheets as Tom Andews, the former king of the sports pages, sucked his cock dry. There would be time later when he was alone again to ponder whether this was love or lust.

Richard Barkley laughed.

The next twenty-four hours were the happiest time of Richard Barkley's life. The two men made love. They swam naked in the indoor pool. They jogged along the beach. They ate dinner at midnight on a terrace balcony off the ornate second-floor bedroom. And late at night when Tom Andrews slept beside him, Richard Barkley looked at the perfect face and wondered whether he was in love with Tom or just wanted to be the younger man.

He worried about the impermanence of their lives in the magazine fashion world. There was always someone attempting to interfere, someone trying to change things, someone trying to take everything away.

We need to get away from all those people, Barkley thought.

The following evening, Tom was running on the beach — Richard could not really keep up with Tom when he did his serious running — when the phone rang. Only one other person in the entire world knew where Richard Barkley was that week, and that person wanted him to make a decision.

Tom bounded into the room wearing only his Nikes and nylon jogging shorts. Sweat glistened on his perfect body. Barkley wondered why sweat looked so great on Tom, but when he perspired, he looked tired and bedraggled.

"You look serious, Dick. Come on, buddy, loosen up a little," Tom teased, perching on the arm of Barkley's chair. Richard could smell the mixture of sweat and soap and salt air on his body.

"We have something to talk about," Barkley began.

"Good, I hope," Tom said with a generous smile. The smile was practiced and perfected in front of cameras. A smile that could look natural even though calculated.

"Somebody made me an offer to buy *Haute.*"

"Holy shit!" Tom was impressed.

"Sol Golden has been talking to me secretly for months about selling the magazine. My family wants me to accept the deal. It's a lot of money," Barkley said.

"How much?"

"Four hundred million."

"Double holy shit!" Tom yelped. "Looks like I have got me a rich one."

"Not that rich. I have to divide it with the family and there will be taxes. In the end I figure I should net about . . ." His voice suddenly trailed away.

"How much?" Tom prodded.

"About twenty-five million," Barkley admitted finally.

Tom moved from the arm of the chair and walked to the bar, pouring himself a triple shot of Russian vodka that was kept in the bar freezer. "Are you going to take it?"

"What would you do?"

"I would take the money and run." Tom turned his back on Richard and looked at his face in the mirror that surrounded the bar.

"Would you run with me?" Barkley asked very seriously.

"Dick —"

"We could go someplace away from New York," Barkley interrupted, afraid of the answer. "I have thought it all through. The Riviera could be the perfect place. If you are worried about giving up your career, I will arrange a trust to take care of you, and when I die you'd get everything."

Tom was silent.

"You were going to say something," Barkley prompted.

"Do you think you could be happy with me?" Tom realized that he really meant those words. Barkley might get tired of a big dumb jock with a bad knee, and then where would he be?

"It's a chance we will have to take."

"Then do it," Tom said.

"Do what?"

"Sell the thing," Tom said firmly.

While Barkley made the call to Sol Golden's house in Beverly Hills, Tom showered, changed, and thought about his commitment. Had he made a commitment to Richard Barkley? He liked the guy. Maybe he more than liked the guy. There was all that money. Walking from the Spanish-tiled bath, Tom grabbed his suitcase and fished through the contents for his passport case. In the back of the case was a folded slip of paper that he had been thinking about — a check.

A check for twenty-five thousand dollars drawn on Sol Golden's private account at Crocker National Bank. For a few minutes Tom stared at the check, then carefully refolded it and slid the valuable piece of paper back into the leather pocket of the passport case.

Chapter Sixteen

Sol Golden slowly replaced the telephone receiver in the cradle. His hand was shaking. It was not because he had again gotten what he wanted — *Haute* magazine — but simply that he was tired.

Being tired was a new feeling for him. He had always had more energy than those around him. Since he took over his father's newspaper sixty years ago, he had always been the perfect example of the strong energetic Jew who thrived on his success and worked eighteen-hour days day-in and day-out.

He grabbed the wrist to still the shaking in his hand. No, he was not so excited about buying *Haute*. He was not even concerned about the four hundred million dollars. Sol was buying the magazine for Marti, his beloved Marti.

"I wish you were here, my Marti," he said aloud. It made him feel better to say words aimed at the woman he loved so much in the house that was so much her. It seemed that she could almost be standing in the mirrored dressing room that stretched sixty feet off one side of the peach-silk-filled bedroom where Sol sat at the ornate French desk attempting to steady his hand.

Sol Golden knew all was not right with his body. He had hidden the problem from Marti. At his age, physical ailments were to be expected. She was so excited over the possiblity of owning *Haute* magazine that she had been postively radiant the last few weeks. If she knew he had health problems, she would devote herself to that and he would miss seeing her so very happy. *What good is it to be worth two billion dollars if you can't make sure the woman you love never has to worry or be unhappy?* he thought.

And, by God, this would make her happy!

There was work to do. Golden had been prepared for Richard Barkley's decision and already had started the paper work. He had purchased hundreds of publications, television stations, and businesses for his empire and his Marti, so his platoons of lawyers and executives were ready for the *Haute* takeover. The secret was to do everything as quickly as possible before someone changed his mind or too many people became aware of what was happening.

He pressed a button of the redialer that was connected to the telephone. The strange black box could not only instantly dial the coded phone numbers of the generals of Sol Golden's business empire, but it also functioned as a sophisticated way to block, as much as possible, the Golden phones from wiretapping.

"Hello, Ogden." Ogden Livingston was Sol Golden's chief lawyer, with a two-million-dollar annual retainer. "Tell them to get the plane ready. The deal is made. Are the papers in order?"

"Yes, Mr. Golden."

"I am on my way to Van Nuys Airport," Sol said. "I should be there in forty minutes."

"Yes, Mr. Golden."

"Have everyone necessary on the plane and we will complete everything between here and New York."

"Yes, Mr. Golden."

Sol liked doing business in the privacy of the black-and-gold Golden Limited jet. Only there would the exact figures of the purchase be revealed. Legal secretaries would feed the data into a computer, and a word processer would belch out a contract that would give *Haute* to Marti.

Sol took a deep breath. Then another. And another. It was as if he could not pull enough oxygen from the Beverly Hills air into his system. There must be a third-stage smog alert today, he decided.

He reached for a hand-knit woollen sweater that Marti had custom-ordered for him in Ireland. It would be cold in New York. Certainly the sweater would not be enough, but someone from his New York apartment would meet him at JFK with a heavy jacket. Maybe that was the problem. He was catching a slight cold.

He pressed a button alerting his staff that he was ready to leave. Outside, his chauffeur straightened to attention, got out of the car, and opened the rear door just as Sol walked through the great double doors of the mansion he had bought for Marti.

In the car, he poured himself a brandy and smiled. *Why not call her?* he thought. He picked up the phone as the great gold Rolls-Royce maneuvered toward the private airport.

"Get me the overseas operator," he said as he clutched the Baccarat snifter. "The Hotel Georges Cinq . . . Mrs. Golden." Sol did not bother attempting to speak French. In his world, people spoke the language of Sol Golden.

Ring . . . ring . . . ring. Those strange old-fashioned

rings were as a much a part of the French phone system as was inefficiency.

"Hello."

"Hi-ya, honey," Golden boomed into the receiver. "Just thought I would give you a call."

"Are you all right?" Marti asked, instantly concerned.

"Sure. What could be wrong with me? I'm like a bull, ya know."

"My big bull." Marti chuckled affectionately.

"Just wanted you to know I bought you a little something that you wanted while you have been over in France spending all my money on clothes."

She knew what it was. But after decades she also knew that Sol wanted to play his favorite giving-guessing game.

"Oh, tell me! What?" she begged.

"Guess."

"Is it jewelry?"

"Hell, no. You own all the jewelry in the world."

"Then it must be clothes."

"No clothes. This house has only thirty-five rooms. There isn't space for another dress. You know I prefer you naked."

"Oh . . . I wish I were there," Marti purred.

"I wish you were here, too." Golden meant the words with every emotion in his heart.

"I give in, Sol. What is it?" Marti bubbled.

"You remember that silly little magazine you took such a shine to . . . what was its name?"

"Haute!!!"

"Yeah, I think that's it. Well, there was this fire sale, so I said, what the heck, if she wants her own magazine, why the hell not?"

"Oh, Sol!"

"It's yours, my darling."

"Sol?"

"What?"

"I love you."

"I love you, too. Come back to your old Sol soon . . . okay, honey? Your old Sol misses you."

Marti Golden was crying. After all these years, only one man in the world could make her cry, and that was the man she loved so passionately. The man she married. Never for an instant had she wanted another, and she knew he felt the same way about her. Neither Sol nor Marti Golden could hang up the phone. They did not talk. They just listened to each other breathing.

Chapter Seventeen

The two women in the front-row seats of the special French showings were thinking very different thoughts. Marti Golden was repeatedly looking at her watch and calculating the time in New York, where the contract to purchase *Haute* was being signed by her husband and the Barkley family.

Sylvia Harrington was watching the runway. No, she was not watching the clothing. Just as Marcella Todd had predicted, the showings at the Palace of Versailles were nothing more than another French publicity stunt with lots of five-thousand-dollar peasant looks, outer-space looks, little-girl looks, and even a less-than-tongue-in-cheek clown collection that, according to the English program, "is designed to bring out the whimsical little person in every woman."

"Oh, shit!" Marti Golden exclaimed as the chic clowns paraded past the fashion press wearing shoes that curled at the toes and polka-dotted pantalones. "Paris is really a circus this year, all right."

But Sylvia Harrington was not interested in the clown suits. What caught her attention was the auburn-haired beauty, Melissa Fenton, who might have been a pill-swallowing mess away from the runway, but, there in her kingdom, she was the princess. In collection after collection she was elegant or carefree or enticing, whatever the designs or the designers demanded. Clothes that looked baggy and shapeless on some of the other girls adapted to her long and graceful limbs and gathered strength from her elegance. Sylvia watched the way the muscles in Melissa's long legs moved as she strided along the runway. Inevitably, the best designs of every collection were saved for the supermodel.

I wonder what she meant. Sylvia remembered what Melissa had cried out at the Spense party back in New York. *Could she have been serious?* Sylvia wondered.

The possibility that a creature as perfect and exquisite as Melissa Fenton could love her was confusing to Sylvia. No one ever had loved her. No family. No man. No woman. She had built a life and a personal philosophy on not giving or needing love. All she cared about was *Haute* and her power. At least that was all she *thought* she cared about.

But . . . Melissa.

Between shows Sylvia had ventured back to the chaos behind the stage. There, among the jumble of naked women, racks of clothing, and screeching groups of dressers and designers, sat Melissa Fenton eating a banana as if she were back in her Third Avenue apartment.

"Melissa." Sylvia looked at the girl.

Melissa stopped in mid-bite and looked at Sylvia with her huge green eyes, which spoke volumes when she was saying nothing.

"Melissa, I feel I owe you an apology." Sylvia had never before apologized for anything. "You've been wonderful today. I would love to have you for the cover of the June issue.''

"Do you want to see me back in New York?" Melissa asked, then took another bite of the banana as if she had said nothing.

"Yes," Sylvia said in little more than a whisper.

"What did you say, Sylvia?"

"I said yes."

A liveried stagehand walked past, striking a muted mallet against a small gong, indicating that the show was about to continue. Out front the fashion press were carrying champagne glasses back to their seats. At that moment the alarm on Marti Golden's watch started beeping. *It's done*, she thought. *The deal has been made.* She signaled to her photographer, Zackery Jones, and he scooted over to her side.

"I don't think this is the best vantage point for my photos," she said to Zack. "We are going to move to those seats."

She pointed to the seats at the very end of the runway — seats that were reserved for the editor and staff of *Haute* magazine.

"Those are *Haute*'s seats," Zack warned.

"Yes, they are, aren't they?" Marti smiled. She stood, straightened the perfect line of her Piero Dimitri suit, then walked to the end of the runway and sat in the center seat — Sylvia Harrington's seat.

She was still sitting there when Sylvia returned from backstage.

"Oh, good God!" Sylvia roared. "This is nervy — even for a pushy Beverly Hills Jew." Marti looked into Sylvia's flaming eyes while maintaining an expression of innocence. "Listen, you jackass!" Sylvia roared as the entire room became silent. "Are you deaf as well as dumb, you kosher contessa? You are sitting in the *Haute* magazine seats, and I demand you get out!"

"I know exactly where I am sitting," Marti said in a clear voice that filled the room. Marcella watched in confused amazement. A few savvy photographers moved to position themselves for photos of what was later called the fashion-world fight of the century. Notebooks and pencils were poised. Something big was happening. The news people were doing something that would make news.

"If you are so very aware of where you are sitting, then you should be equally aware of the fact that you do not belong in these seats." Sylvia was attempting to control her voice as she realized that others were taking notes. For political reasons, she regretted the anti-Semitic remark and the bad publicity it might cause.

"But I do belong here. I belong here more than you do, my dear Sylvia," Marti said.

Sylvia stared.

"In fact, Sylvia, you may not belong in these seats at all anymore. You see . . . wait, I want everyone to hear this."

Marti Golden climbed to the runway and took the microphone in her gloved hand. "Listen, all my friends, I have something to say that I am sure will interest you all. Approximately five minutes ago, my husband, Sol Golden, chairman of the board of Golden Limited, completed his bid to purchase *Haute* magazine."

The entire room faded before Sylvia Harrington's eyes. Her hand jumped uncontrolled to her throat and she hissed in a deathlike whisper, "No, it can't be true. It isn't true."

"But it *is* true, Sylvia." Pencils and flashbulbs were

in action throughout the room. "If my delightful French hosts might indulge me, I would like to make a brief announcement at this time. I am delighted to be the new owner and publisher of *Haute*, and I . . . intend to make it an even more exciting and provocative magazine then it has been."

Dozens of editors started firing off questions. "What did you pay for the magazine?" asked a squat little woman from a Cleveland newspaper.

"Four hundred million for the ensemble," Marti joked.

"Are you going to make any staff changes?" questioned the woman from the *Los Angeles Times*.

"I am creating a new position of executive director of all Golden Limited fashion publications and asking Marcella Todd to be in charge of the entire editorial and business management. That will incude *Haute*."

Marcella gasped.

"What about Sylvia Harrington?" commented a young reporter from *Time*. "There seems to be ill feeling [there were twitters throughout the audience] between you two. Is she out?"

"Miss Harrington's future with the new *Haute* is yet to be discussed. I must take this opportunity to say that although we have had our differences, in the historical sense I do respect what she was able to do for the magazine at one time."

That bitch, thought Sylvia.

That is *bitchy,* thought Marcella.

"Are these going to be major changes in *Haute?*" This question came from a CBS television correspondent.

"I would think so," replied Marti. "Like any great success, *Haute* has developed a tendency to rest on its previous accomplishments while the world grows. With some new ideas and new blood, I hope to restore this great magazine to the highest standard of fashion and journalism.''

Sylvia Harrington felt more hatred for Marti Golden than she had ever felt in her life. Her face looking ashen, she stared across the room and saw too many people relishing her downfall. She was a woman without friends, with only power — and in the signing of a check that power was now disappearing.

''Now, please, I have interrupted this showing far too long with my little announcement,'' Marti said. ''Shall we return to the clothes?''

As the music started up once again, more than one hundred internationally based journalists fled the room in a stampede for telephones, much to the chagrin of Pierre de Tête, the next designer who was to be presented, and who was introducing his new fur: collie.

''It looks as if there are plenty of seats for all of us now,'' Marti said to Sylvia.

''I don't believe a word of this.'' Sylvia ground out the words. ''There is no way that Richard would sell *Haute* without discussing it with me.''

''Oh, you can be sure he did.''

''We will see about that!'' Sylvia turned and walked toward the door. Then she realized that her assistants were still half sitting in their seats and looking confused.

''Well, are you coming?'' she ordered.

''No, Sylvia, they have a show to cover,'' Marti interjected, ''but you can have the rest of the afternoon off, Sylvia. Why don't you go back to the hotel and make a few phone calls?''

Sylvia turned and stomped through the Hall of Mirrors, the grandest area of the palace, breaking a heel on her shoe as she exited.

"That certainly was dramatic," Marti remarked gleefully.

"And perhaps a little cruel?" Marcella added.

"I hope so," Marti said with a chuckle. "I sincerely hope so."

In her suite at the Georges V, Sylvia Harrington was frantically dialing every number she had for Dickie Barkley, Dickie-the-Bastard Barkley, Dickie-the-Faggot Barkley, Dickie-may-he-go-to-hell Barkley. But there was no answer. Dickie Barkley was gone.

Chapter Eighteen

Three days had passed since Marti Golden had made her perhaps overly dramatic announcement of the sale of *Haute*. She had left Paris that same day for New York. Sylvia realized that Marti was eager to begin the physical takeover, and when she would return to the magazine she had built, everything would be different. For that reason, Sylvia had lingered in France. But the time had come to go home, home to *Haute* . . . if there was a home there for her anymore.

Marti had ideas about that.

"The first thing I want to do is see that woman leave the building, preferably through the window," Marti said to Marcella as they entered the *Haute* offices.

"No, we can't do that," Marcella said firmly.

"You don't like her any more than I do. How many times have you said that her thinking is dated and the magazine is too elitist? You have told me she should go, but now, suddenly, you are saying that banshee should be permitted to hang from the rafters for a while longer."

"Just for a while, Marti," Marcella said. "We need her for the transition period. A lot of the readers and the advertisers consider her to *be Haute*. They might become alarmed and uneasy. I would prefer that the changing of the guard be as smooth as possible."

"I get your point." Then Marti brightened. "Maybe she will quit. You know, even if she doesn't quit, it will be fun subjecting her to a living hell."

"Marti —" Marcella stopped and looked at her closest friend. "I have never seen you so vindictive. You actually *hate* Sylvia Harrington. You hate her so much that it isn't good for you. I think you even convinced Sol to buy the magazine just for revenge."

Marti was very quiet for a moment. "I did," she said finally.

"A lot of people have fought with you. Why this vendetta against Sylvia Harrington?"

"It wasn't just our personal relationship; it was what she did with the magazine. She set a tone that was anti-Semitic. If she had a story about plastic surgery, she would comment that a certain doctor might have built a practice on reshaping ethnic noses. She meant Jews. If she did a story on the right places to live, her 'elite' places would be areas that were either closet-restricted or known to have few Jews. There isn't a single Jew on the staff, and every few Italians or Middle Europeans. She has never used a black model in the fashion-layout pages; they appear only in ads, which she cannot control. The only blacks on the staff are the errand boys. Yet, thousands of blacks and Jews and people of Slavic ancestry buy *Haute* and read that bilge that puts us all in our place. The big Jewish-owned department stores and the Jewish-owned clothing firms bought the ad space that made *Haute* rich and Sylvia Harrington a success. We supported her and she insulted us. We made fools of ourselves while that ugly, nasty, and hateful bitch twisted the way people think."

"You have been thinking about this a lot." Marcella looked straight into Marti's eyes.

"I have been planning to buy *Haute* for more than ten years. When I met you and realized that you had the brains to change this magazine and manage it," Marti continued, "I insisted that Sol buy it. It was really the only time we have disagreed. He didn't want *Haute*. He said it did not fit in with the other investments and would demand too much of our efforts. But I insisted."

"And he spent four hundred million dollars for you," Marcella added.

"It took him a year of concentrated effort," Marti said. "He had to contact all of the owners secretly. Then he had to win over Richard Barkley. He worked almost twenty hours a day during the last week with lawyers to do the deal."

"Isn't that hard on him?"

"He does look tired. He used to thrive on this kind of action, but he never really had his heart in the purchase of *Haute*. I told him that as soon as I have finished getting you settled here, we would take a nice long vacation."

The arrival of Marti Golden and Marcella Todd at *Haute* magazine had been anticipated by the staff. As the two women walked through the offices, most of the employees came out to introduce themselves.

"It's always like this," Marti said to Marcella as they shook hand after hand and listened carefully to each name. "Taking over a magazine or a television station is like a change in political administrations. A lot of handshaking and smiling."

Jayne Caldwell joined them. "Welcome to *Haute*," she said. And she did mean her words.

"Where are our offices?" Marti asked. "I forget the exact layout of this place."

"I suppose Mr. Barkley's office is available," Jayne explained. "He left very quickly and had everything of his crated and moved."

"That is fine," Marti said. "I will use his office and Miss Todd will use Harrington's office."

Jayne Caldwell paused for a moment. "Miss Harrington forbids anyone to use her office when she is not here. She has a special lock on the door and she has the only key. She has very strict rules about her office."

"Her rules don't count for much anymore. Call maintenance and have the lock drilled. Miss Todd will use that office. Find another place for Sylvia Harrington."

"Marti," Marcella said warningly.

"That is my decision."

Both women were in Richard Barkley's office reading the piles of congratulatory telegrams that had arrived. Every designer and fashion house in the world was professing his or her or its eternal support and devotion. Photographers hoping finally to work for the magazine issued enough lunch invitations to feed both women for a decade or so. Some of Marcella's coworkers at the *Chicago Herald* had sent a huge horseshoe-styled flower extravaganza, the kind that was usually wrapped around the neck of a winning Thoroughbred. Sol had seen to it that the room was filled with bowls of floating white orchids, his wife's favorite flower. There was a nice note from Cecil Fine, the man who owned a store back in Illinois that Marcella had once mentioned in a story. Beverly Boxard send a wordy letter of encouragement on *Architecture Now* stationery. A piece of pink WHILE YOU WERE OUT memo paper said that Diane had called to wish her mother luck.

In the background the sound of drilling filled the reception area as the maintenance men battered the bronze locks of Sylvia Harrington's office.

"All done, Mrs. Golden," one of the workmen said.

"Come with me, Marcella and Jayne. Let's take another look at the throne room." Marti walked to the sacred office. "We are going to change everything. This is all so staid. All these antiques. It's more like a museum than an office."

"It's beautiful," Marcella said.

"It may be, but it is going to go. Jayne, don't let those workmen leave. Why don't you oversee them while they pack all of Harrington's personal stuff and put it in storage?"

"You are trying to make her quit." Marcella sighed.

"You'd better believe it." Marti was moving fast. She looked at one of the secretaries and said, "Dear, there is an interior designer in Beverly Hills by the name of Phyllis Morris. She did our offices there, and they are very plush and very contemporary. I want the same feeling here. Tell Phyllis to send a crew to New York immediately and get started. I will call her myself later. I want this place changed, fast."

Marti Golden had been in the office less than an hour.

A few days after Marti's takeover, Sylvia Harrington arrived back in New York. Not even the inner security of her cloistered bedroom was able to ease her anguish.

She hated Richard Barkley.

She hated Marcella Todd.

But most of all, she hated Marti Golden for taking

away her magazine. There was little doubt things would be different. She just did not realize how different.

She dialed her private number.

"Miss Todd's office," a voice answer brightly.

A wave of nausea passed through Sylvia Harrington. "This is Miss Harrington. Tell Sandy I am ready for the car."

"Oh, Miss Harrington . . ." the voice dropped from a cheery tone to one of distress.

"Oh . . . what?"

"Mrs. Golden has ordered that Sandy keep the car here all morning in case she needs it."

"*I* need it," Sylvia insisted.

"I will have to check with Mrs. Golden." There was panic in the voice. The line was put on hold and Sylvia found herself listening to Barry Manilow. She would never be able to tolerate Manilow's voice again. Then the receptionist returned: "Mrs. Golden said to take a cab."

"Tell Sandy I want the car *now*." Sylvia slammed down the receiver. She took deep breaths. She had to do something. As she reached the street level of her building, she knew the car would not be waiting. She knew it would never be waiting again.

Sylvia Harrington hailed a cab.

When Sylvia entered the lobby of *Haute*, one of the guards dialed the number of the executive offices. "She is in the elevator." By the time Sylvia reached the fifty-second floor, Marcella Todd was waiting for her.

"We have to talk, Sylvia," Marcella said.

Sylvia said nothing. Marcella led her into the conference room and closed the door. Outside the room every telephone in the building was in use as employees conjectured about what was transpiring behind the double doors.

"This is not easy," Marcella began.

"Are you firing me?" Sylvia mustered every bit of arrogance she could to embellish the words.

"No," Marcella said. "I will begin by emphasizing that I would like you to stay."

"And does Marti Golden agree?"

"She has placed me in charge of the magazine."

"Oh, she has, has she? Isn't that just wonderful! If you remember, I used to be in charge of *Haute*. If I am not running things, just what is it you want me to do?"

"The title I have selected is 'associate publisher.' " Marcella's voice was hardening.

"And I suppose it is just a title," Sylvia said bitterly. "No authority. Just a title to keep my name on the masthead so that the advertisers do not become nervous and the public does not think there is a revolution going on here."

"That is about it," Marcella said calmly.

"Perhaps I choose not to play."

"That would be your choice, but I think *Haute* would survive. Frankly, this arrangement is favorable to both of us. I get to keep your name and reputation as an asset to the magazine, and you get a thirty-thousand-dollar raise to stay."

"Thirty thousand dollars," Sylvia said slowly as she thought about her small bank account and her apartment, the only place remaining in the world where she had complete control.

"Well . . ." Marcella waited.

"I will cooperate for now. I want a press release issued about my promotion." The word "promotion" stayed formed on her lips after the sound had faded. "I will write the announcement myself."

"That will be fine," Marcella said.

"Now, if you don't mind, *madame* editor" — Sylvia seemed almost too controlled — "I would like to be alone in my office to —"

"Sylvia, I *am* sorry." Marcella was embarrassed to have to tell the woman about Marti's actions. "Your office is gone. Everything has been moved to the floor below. I feel the need to apologize for that. It was not my idea."

"I know whose idea it was." Sylvia could feel the hatred as she thought of Marti Golden. "The Jewess."

"I will have someone show you to your office," Marcella said coldly. "You know, you do not even have to come to work. We can have the checks mailed to your house."

"Then have them mailed." Sylvia turned and walked unblinking out of the room and out of *Haute*.

Marcella watched her go. "I wonder, what made her become the way she is?" she asked herself softly.

"I don't know," responded another voice. It was Bonnie Vincenzo, the makeup and beauty editor, holding a pile of page layouts.

Chapter Nineteen

Cabs were a fact of life Sylvia Harrington despised. She disliked especially the battered yellow cab that turned on to East Fifty-ninth Street, taking her back to her apartment from the *Haute* offices.

"Thatilbe four-ten, lady," the cabbie said in the usual New York matter-of-fact tone.

Sylvia reached for her purse and realized she had not used a cab in almost two decades. *Four dollars and ten cents,* she thought to herself. *What a lot of money for a few blocks' ride.* She overlooked the fact that her limousine had cost the magazine several hundred dollars a week. Sylvia had long ago grown accustomed to the perks of her position: the limos, the private dining rooms, the free clothes and trips, the gifts, and the lavish expense account. She started to rethink her budget without these perks.

It was not a pleasant thought.

She paid the fare with the exact change and tipped a quarter.

"Oh, thank you, generous person," the cabbie said with a mock courtly reverence.

"Drop dead," Sylvia retorted.

"See if I ever pick up another bag lady," the cab driver snarled.

Sylvia was already out of the cab and sweeping through the doors of her apartment building. *Bag lady . . . that son-of-a-bitch.* Bag lady. The thought worried her. The possibility of her becoming one of those pathetic pushcart creatures cut deeply into her rapidly developing sense of insecurity.

Cabs cost so much. Clothes cost so much. Her apartment cost so much. Dinners out were so expensive. She had always been of the belief that power was as good as money, and she had been right. Only now she questioned whether she had much power anymore.

The elevator rose to her floor.

Once inside the privacy of her apartment, she felt safer. She checked the mail but there were no sympathy notes. Her friends — her if-not-friends-her-whatevers — had not sent notes of condolence. They were waiting to see what was going to happen and whether she had any power left. There were no welcome-home bouquets of flowers that had always arrived previously from pandering American designers upon her return from Europe. Her mind did a quick estimation of what all those arrangements must have cost each time: a thousand dollars . . . maybe more. It would be better if they sent checks instead of calla lilies. She had never been that fond of flowers.

She settled down on the living room couch and looked out the huge windows at the Fifty-ninth Street Bridge, which went someplace she had never cared to investigate. The huge collection of girders and rivets seemed so close through the windows. The bridge was so intimate. So was the red tramway car that bobbed back and forth to Roosevelt Island and its condominiums. She had never had the time before to look at the world through her living room window. A group of tourists seemed to be looking directly at her from the dangling tramway car. They had no idea who she was, she thought. Then she restructured her mental sentences . . . who she *is*.

"I still *am*," she said aloud. Then she repeated the sentence again. "I still *am*!" And again. "I STILL AM!"

She smiled.

There would be some surprises for Marcella Todd when she tried to reorganize *Haute*. One of the reasons Sylvia had lingered in Paris instead of racing back to New York to defend her territory was that she was arranging "difficulties" for Marcella. First, she had contracted with Franco Brenelli, one of the few people she thought she might be able to trust, to take all the photos for the special thirty-two-page section. And she had agreed to pay him his regular fee — one hundred thousand dollars — instead of the editorial cost she could have so easily negotiated. Franco had been shocked when she insisted that he charge full rate. But that was not all. She had also arranged to fly all the French models, plus Melissa Fenton, back to the States to recreate the photos in New York. All in all, the cost of that thirty-two-page section would approach the four-hundred-thousand-dollar mark. It would be impossible for Marcella Todd to change what she had done. It would be far too costly. Perhaps she could alter the July issue into whatever she wanted it to be, but June would be a momument to Sylvia Harrington and the Sylvia Harrington philosophy. Let the designers compare the issues. See what the advertisers thought. There would be no gentle transition period. Let Marcella Todd fall on her beautiful face.

At that very moment Marcella was realizing what had been done. She had just finished talking to Franco Brenelli, who said — lied — that he had already completed the shooting and that the photos were being printed and retouched. She could see the transparencies in three days.

"Three days," Marcella told Bonnie Vincenzo, who had just happily agreed to do a complete remake of her beauty pages for the June issue. "What he is trying to say is that I had better like the pictures because I will have no choice but to use them."

Sylvia Harrington was dialing Franco Brenelli's number at the same time Marcella was worrying about what Brenelli's photos would be like.

"Franco . . . Sylvia Harrington."

Brenelli was curious to know what the woman had on her mind. He had heard rumors that she was out at *Haute* magazine and had been dealing with Marcella Todd in a series of phone calls all morning.

"Franco, I am calling in my markers." Sylvia wasted no time making small talk.

"For you, Sylvia, darling, anything."

"I will be at your studio in fifteen minutes, and I want to see every photo you have for the June issue. Every proof sheet. Nothing is to be culled before I arrive. Am I understood?"

"Of course, but there are more than two thousand photos, and some of them are unusable."

"You heard what I said!" Sylvia snapped.

Brenelli was amazed. Not only was the imperial Sylvia Harrington coming to his studio to make her selections — he had always shown her only the top choices in the luxury of her private viewing room — but she wanted to see everything: the out-of-focus; the test shots; the photos in which the models or the clothes were awkward or hanging strangely.

Sylvia arrived exactly fifteen minutes after she had hung up the telephone. It had been another four-dollar cab ride through the park to West Seventy-second Street, where Brenelli had his high-ceilinged penthouse loft studio.

"What is happening?" he asked Sylvia.

"Just let me see the proof sheets." Sylvia took a small magnifying viewing lens and pressed it to her eye to better scrutinize the small-scale proof pictures. With a red marking pen she placed small marks at the corners of her selections.

Anxiously, Brenelli took the sheets from her to examine her choices.

"Oh, no!" he exclaimed. "I don't understand. This is all wrong. What are you doing, Sylvia?"

"I am making the selections for Marcella Todd's first major layout in *Haute*," Sylvia remarked in an almost inaudible voice.

"But you are picking the worst!" Brenelli wailed. "I will be made to look foolish. People will laugh."

"I hope so."

"I cannot let you ruin my reputation. Give me those proof sheets."

Sylvia Harrington looked sternly at Franco Brenelli and carefully arranged her words. "I *created* you. You were nothing and you would have been nothing but a second-rate catalog photographer if it had not been for me. Everything you are you owe to me. Now you are going to pay me back."

"But . . . my reputation . . ." Franco stammered. Brenelli knew that if the photos Sylvia was selecting were run in the magazine, some of the criticism would fall on him.

"You once said that if I ever wanted anything from you — *anything* — all I had to do was ask. I am asking." Sylvia knew Brenelli's weak point; he did have a sense of honor that had been instilled in him by his immigrant Italian parents. He had leanred to give his word rarely so that he would not have to worry about having to keep rashly made promises. But he had been much younger and much more hungry when he had so profusely and eloquently thanked Sylvia Harrington for handing him success.

He had promised.

"You don't need to look so bad," Sylvia continued. "I want you to send only the photos I selected for the issue, but the others will still be around later for people to see what was available for the issue. The people who count will not blame you."

"They will think Marcella Todd selected only the worst choices." Brenelli understood. "For you I will do it."

"To make sure, I will keep all the negatives, until you need them later." Sylvia did not want the artistic Franco to have second thoughts and include some of the better photographs.

"If you insist," Franco said. "You know, Sylvia, you are the only woman in the world who could do something like this to me."

"Smart boy." She patted his cheek. "By the way, include this photo."

"But it is a good one. Melissa looks radiant." Brenelli did not understand.

"Yes, she does, doesn't she?"

Two days later the slim packet of photos arrived at Marcella Todd's office.

Anxiously, Marcella started to sift through the pile of proof photos and transparencies. Then she dialed Franco's number. "Franco, these stink."

"What stinks?" Brenelli asked.

"Your photos of the Paris showings. Send over all the proof sheets and all the transparencies. I will make my own decisions."

"That is all there is," Brenelli said.

"Look, we are paying you a hundred thousand bucks, and you have given me crap." Marcella was angry, very angry, and frustrated. "If you ever want to see that money, you had better do something more professional than this."

"I can, of course, reshoot, if you insist." Brenelli liked the idea of having another more closely watched opportunity to redo the photos.

"Actually, I would like to scrap the whole layout, but there is not enough time to reshoot and the budget is gone." Marcella realized that Sylvia somehow was behind the mess. "I hope *all* our reputations will survive what you have decided to do."

Franco felt sick. He understood all too well the implications of what Marcella was saying. There were few secrets in the fashion industry. People would find out about what Sylvia had done. And what Franco had permitted her to do. His reputation would suffer. His honor was very costly. Too costly. If Sylvia had not taken possession of the negatives and outtakes, he would have rushed them to Marcella.

"I am sorry," Brenelli said.

Marcella hung up the phone without saying good-bye. It would be a long time, if ever, before the name Franco Brenelli would appear in *Haute*.

The private phone line that had been used only by Sylvia Harrington rang on Marcella Todd's new desk.

"Hello," Marcella said.

"Hello, Sylvia, my darling. I had to talk to you. The few days since our naked bodies have clung to each other seem like centuries to me. How I long to caress your budlike breasts. How my body quivers at the memories of my fingers in your hair. How I pine for the feel of our flesh pressing together and that exquisite moment when our juices mingle in a moment of the purest ecstacy —"

"Oh, shut up, Burt!" Marcella snapped.

"This does not sound like my tender and gentle little Sylvia."

"No, she is out right now having her broom tuned up."

"Oops . . . this couldn't be Marcella Todd on the other end of the phone. The voice sounds like that of Marcella Todd; she was a person I knew a long, long time ago in a country far, far away. We were lovers, but she was stolen away from me by a seducer by the name of *Haute*." Burt continued his clowning.

"I am not in the mood for this."

"*Haute* shit!"

"Burt, stop it!" Marcella was almost screaming. "I don't want to hear your jokes right now." She was almost crying, but she refused to permit the tears to begin.

"Has my little girl had a hard time at her nasty old magazine today? Then Burt has the perfect answer. How about my picking you up and taking you to a nice dinner at . . ."

He had said the wrong thing. It was obvious to Marcella that Burt Rance would never take her seriously. She had had a bad day and he was acting as if she were some flighty housewife who was hysterical because the permanent-press cycle on her dryer did not work.

"Stop it, Burt."

"Okay . . . okay . . . I am sorry. I understand you are having a bad day. Let me try to help you feel better. I will be there in an hour and we'll—"

"No, Burt."

"No, what?"

"No dinner. No making me feel better. No anything. The only way to say this is just to say it straight out. I care about you, but you don't have any respect for my work. Right now there are two things that are important in my life — my daughter and *Haute*. I just do not have time for anything else."

"Or anyone else." Suddenly, Burt's voice was very serious.

"Or anyone else," Marcella echoed firmly.

"I guess you can't make it any clearer than that. Look, Marcella, if you ever decide that you might want to be something else, like, say, a woman, give me a call. You know I was joking when I made this call, but maybe I was wrong, maybe I got Sylvia Harrington after all . . . the *new* Sylvia Harrington."

Chapter Twenty

Failure was a word that appalled Marcella Todd. She had been a failure in her marriage. She was probably a failure as a mother. But she had never been a failure in her career. As a model, she had been the very best. When she decided to become a writer, she became the top fashion writer in the country. Now she was the editor of the world's most important fashion magazine, but the very first issue that would have her name at the top of the masthead would probably be the most unprofessional-looking book in the history of *Haute*.

For two days after she received the photos of the Paris showings from Franco Brenelli, she had not left the *Haute* offices. She had slept on the couch in her office. She had showered in her private bath. All her meals were prepared by the *Haute* chef, who was already dismayed because she wanted only simple salads and just nibbled at those.

She had considered calling Marti and asking for a new budget to reshoot the entire issue. Marti had returned to Beverly Hills to be with Sol. Marti would have understood that Sylvia had booby-trapped the issue and would have authorized the expenditure. Actually, Marcella had the authority to authorize the new budget herself. But it seemed so wasteful, so unprofessional. When in trouble, just spend money.

Several times she had decided to ask Burt for his advice. His magazines were run on fractions of the budget available to *Haute*, and quite often they were great issues. Something stopped her from asking Burt for help: pride. She wanted — no, needed — to solve the mess herself.

If there was a way to solve it.

The buzzer hummed gently on Marcella's desk, indicating a guest was waiting in the outer reception area.

"Yes," Marcella said, still lost in her own contemplations.

"Mr. Spense is out here," the secretary said in an all-too-cheerful voice. "He says he knows he does not have an appointment, but he is wondering if he might take you to lunch."

Marcella had accepted no luncheon invitations since arriving at *Haute*. Obviously, Spense was attempting to bribe her in an effort to retain his high reputation in the pages of *Haute*.

"Tell him I can't," Marcella said as she hung up the phone.

A moment later the phone rang again. The secretary seemed alarmed. "Mr. Spense says that he is going to stay out here for the rest of his life, or until you see him."

"Oh, all right, send him in." The tactic did not amuse Marcella. She really did not feel like bantering with Spense and his pushy actions.

"All right, darling, shoot me," Spense babbled as he floated through the door.

"If you insist," Marcella answered in a tone that left no doubt in Spense's mind that she was not amused.

"I will get to the point instantly." Suddenly, Spense became businesslike. "First, I am delighted that you have taken over *Haute*."

"Have you told your close friend, Sylvia, about your delight?" Marcella interjected.

"Of course not. I am too young and too beautiful to die. Getting to the point, you remember the XSPENSE Collection? My little bargain line?"

"Hardly a bargain, but certainly less money than your regular line of clothes."

"That collection is going to be launched early in July. I decided to offer it in time for the buyers to become educated to the fact that they, too, can have Spense instead of whatever drab little frocks they have been forced to sell their customers before this glorious day."

Marcella was purposely silent.

"Well, Sylvia had promised me a layout in either June or July, and I know that you, being the marvelously ethical person you are, will honor your lesser predecessor's words."

Marcella doubted that Sylvia had actually promised Spense the layout. He was attempting to pull something. But an idea was forming in the back of Marcella Todd's mind. An idea that might just save the June issue.

"Is the collection finished?" she demanded.

"Yes. XSPENSE is perfection."

"Are all the model samples made?"

"Yes."

"I want the entire collection delivered to my apartment this afternoon."

"Darling, there are more than three hundred pieces in

the group. Why don't you come over to my showroom and select what you want?" Spense suggested, surprised his lie had apparently been swallowed so easily.

"Fine. On your way out make an appointment for me to come by sometime in December." Marcella went back to work, ignoring the designer.

"They will be there this afternoon."

"Get going." Marcella waved Spense out of her office. As he turned toward the elevator, she raced toward the stairs that led to the editorial department.

"Where is Zack Jones?" she demanded as she whizzed through the door.

"In the darkroom," a startled receptionist answered. Marcella pushed through the blackened revolving door that kept all outside light from the darkroom and entered the dim yellow-lighted collection of individual cubicles.

"Zack, where are you?" she called.

"Hey, Marcella." Instantly, Zackery Jones was beside her. "What's going on? You have to be the first big boss-type ever to invade this territory."

"I need to talk to you privately."

"Okay. Come into my office." He guided her through the yellow darkness into his tiny developing room. Negatives hung from wires strung across the ceiling in long black tendrils. "So, shoot."

Marcella poured out the story. She explained the ruined issue and came quickly to the point. "The photos from Paris are the worst. The clothes are silly and impractical. The models are made to look like cartoon characters. I have an idea about using these photos as a backdrop for a layout of the new XSPENSE Collection accentuating the contrast between Spense's affordable clothing and the Paris excess."

"For the August issue . . . maybe." Zack was figuring the production time.

"It *has* to be for June," Marcella insisted.

"We could get models on short notice," Zack admitted. "Everyone wants to work for *Haute*." He was already planning the shooting in his mind.

"I don't want to use an agency. I absolutely do not want any hint of what we are doing to leak. If we save the June issue, I want it to seem as if there had never been a problem, that everything has been under control."

"Do you have the clothes?" Zack asked.

"They will be at my apartment this afternoon."

Zack thought for a moment. "I have an idea about the models. We have a super-looking girl from Texas working here. Her name is Buffy Sarasota. She isn't a model, but she should be. She could do it without anyone knowing. She isn't connected with any agency."

"What is her coloring?" Marcella asked.

"She's a redhead and tall, with the greatest green eyes."

"Fine . . . she will be right for the greens, the rusts, and the blacks. We need a second model — someone who will play off the redhead and wear the blues, the off-whites, and the beiges." Marcella thought furiously.

"How about you?" Zack suggested.

"I don't model anymore, but you've given me an idea. Have you ever seen my daughter, Diane?"

Zack nodded.

"She wants to model, and she has the right look," Marcella added.

"She looks just like you."

"Like I *did*," Marcella corrected.

"Let's see. We have the photographer. We have the models. We have the clothes. We need a crew. Making this layout work will require about forty excellent shots. That means we need people for makeup and hair and women to iron the clothes. We will need maybe ten people." Zack was not telling Marcella anything she did not already know only too well. "We can get Bonnie Vincezo to help with the makeup and hair."

"She could write a sidebar piece on the new American face," Marcella said, becoming more excited by the minute.

"And we can shoot everything on the streets of New York." Zack's creative energies were moving into high gear. "We can contrast the opulence and decadence of the Palace of Versailles to the reality of life in the big city."

"Perfect!" Marcella's spirit was soaring.

"We will have to shoot this weekend. If it rains we shoot in the rain. If it snows . . . well . . ."

"We can't have snow in the June issue."

"It will just have to rain if it is going to do anything." Zack's mind was planning furiously. "I'll go out today and do some Polaroid shots of several locations that might be right for the spread. Can you look at them this evening?"

"You bet."

"Is the layout full color?"

"All the Paris photos are color, so the pages will be color." Marcella felt a tightness in her stomach when she thought of thirty-two pages in full color being shot during a single weekend. Normally, months would be spent on such an important layout.

Zack was already pulling on his leather jacket. He felt like a kid working on his first assignment after arriving in New York. He touched Marcella on the arm as they walked out of the darkroom. "Don't worry," he said. "We can do it."

Chapter Twenty-One

"How would you like me to make you a star?" Zack asked Buffy Sarasota. "What do you think of that, little girl?"

"Just forget the star bit, honey," she cooed in her sexiest Texas twang. "Jus' make me." Buffy was glad for Zack's company. She had been sitting behind her barren desk all morning with nothing to do. The assistant managing editor in charge of handling untalented daughters of rich and influential people had long since decided the only purpose Buffy Sarasota could serve at *Haute* was to collect her weekly salary of $116.73 after taxes.

"Sugah." Buffy had laughed upon opening her first pay envelope. "Ah spent more than this fo' my lunch. Ah jus' don't know why y'all insist on paying me what Ah am worth. Ah can jus' thank mah stars that Ah got a rich daddy."

"Look, Buffy," Zack continued, "I want you to do some modeling with me."

"Ah bet you want me to take off mah clothes." Buffy smiled. "Not that ah am complainin'. Y'all are the best-lookin' hunk of man Ah have seen since Daddy sent me here. Ah declare, this place is worse than the convent —"

"I'm serious, Buffy," Zack interrupted. "I have a real top-secret assignment that I have to shoot over the weekend, and I want you to model. You'll get paid."

"Ah want to shoot it at a nice hotel. Ah absolutely refuse to shoot any more photos in a hotel that costs less than twelve dollahs a night, honey. Ah am used to the best."

"I am not joking." Zack sounded frustrated.

"You aren't." Buffy dropped the accent momentarily. "If you are talking about a real honest-to-god modeling job, then I can answer you right now. No!"

"What?" Zack was shocked.

"I've been watching these models. You gotta know what you're doing to be a model. I am just a dumb little ol' rich girl from Texas whose talents lie — or should Ah say lay? — in other directions."

"You are beautiful," Zack said, pleading.

"Sure, Ah know Ah look good. Whole football teams have told me that, darlin'. But Ah just ain't talented in this modelin' stuff."

"Look, you are. How about this? I have to take a look-see around the city today to select locations," Zack said quickly. "If you aren't too busy, come along."

"Do Ah git to see your apartment?" Buffy teased.

"No, you get to see New York."

"Well, just let me grab mah purse," Buffy said. "Ah might have ta buy a growin' boy like you some lunch." She looked closely at Zack with the kind of head-to-toe appraisal men usually used to rate women. A little over six feet tall. Thick black hair. Blue eyes hidden behind glasses. She could tell even through his clothing that he had a farm boy's body with big shoulders, and still had a thirty-inch waist even though he had been a well-fed New Yorker for a few years. He was probably hung like a Texas Longhorn bull, she decided.

"Ah think Ah will *have* you fo' mah lunch," Buffy teased.

"Oh, come on. I'll make arrangements with your boss. This project has top-level approval." Zack looked around for the assistant managing editor.

"Hell, honey, she wouldn't miss me if I were gone for a month," Buffy said. "Ah don't do nothin' around here anyhow but go to lunch, and where you are fixin' to take me isn't it."

"Sooner or later," Zack said.

Zack and Buffy made a striking couple as they waited for the elevator. When the car arrived, Buffy turned to Zack and said, "Just remember, honey, you can have mah body any way but on film."

Zack Jones smiled.

In her office, Marcella had been watching the clock. She knew Diane would probably go home for lunch since her grandmother's house was so close to the high school. At 12:10 P.M. she dialed the number.

Diane answered. Marcella was glad she did not have to explain everything to her mother first. "Diane," she said.

"Mother, what's wrong?" Diane was surprised by the phone call.

"Nothing. Look, if you are serious about wanting to be a model —"

"You know I am," Diane interrupted.

"Look, I am in a bind and I need someone with your kind of looks. Someone I can trust."

"Oh, Mom!" The voice on the other end of the phone was becoming very excited. "You mean it?"

"I want you to come to New York."

"When?"

"This afternoon. There is an American flight out of

Youngstown Municipal Airport at two-twenty-five. I have arranged for tickets to be waiting.''

"Mom! Are you serious? What about school?''

"I will call the school. Do you have any money?''

"Sure.'' Diane's head was reeling.

"Then take a cab to the airport. If you ask your grandmother to drive you, she will only make a fuss, and we don't have the time. I will talk to her later.''

"Okay . . . Mom, what should I bring? Do I need makeup or anything? How about clothes?''

"Just wear whatever you are wearing now and get to that plane. I will have the limo at LaGuardia to meet you. And, Diane, thanks.''

"Thank *you*, Mom.''

Marcella Todd was starting to sense good things about the shooting that was ahead of her. What had at first seemed defeat would not only be a success; it would be a Marcella Todd success. She intended to triumph.

A few blocks away at a hot-dog stand at the edge of Central Park across from the Plaza Hotel,, Zackery Jones was finally buying Buffy Sarasota lunch.

"Four chili dogs with onions, two diet Dr Peppers, and some chips,'' Zack told the pushcart vendor.

Zack had managed to convince Buffy to pose in some of the shots so that he could gain a better perspective of how the setting would look with the models. The results surprised Buffy.

"Let me look at those pictures again,'' Buffy said.

Zack handed her the pile of Polaroid test photos. "Ya know, honey, you sure are a good photographer to make me look this good.''

"You look great,'' Zack reassured her.

"You sure are talented,'' she said emphatically. "Just

think how great the pictures will be when you get yourself a real model."

"I have got myself a real model." Zack handed her a chili dog. "You are exactly what I wanted."

"Ah don't want to mess up your shooting. You said it was very important. Ah don't want to make you look bad." For once Buffy was not joking. She was still staring at the photos taken by a man who saw something in her that she had never seen in herself. "You know, these pictures don't look like me at all. Ah never look that good."

"You do to me," Zack said softly. "You have looked that way to me since the first time I ever saw you."

"Get serious, boy." Buffy was attempting to rekindle her sense of humor, but her eyes were studying the pictures and then they turned to the man who made them. "If you think Ah won't wreck your layout, well, Ah guess Ah could give it a try."

Zackery bent down to where Buffy was sitting on the Cental Park bench holding a chili dog in one hand and a stack of photos in the other and he kissed her on the cheek. It was the most innocent kiss she had ever received in her life from a man who was not kin.

And the most exciting.

Chapter Twenty-Two

Marcella and Bonnie had spent the entire previous day and evening going through the piles of clothing that were the models' samples of the XPENSE Collection. Some sixty outfits, dresses, suits, evening clothes, coats, hats, gloves, purses, shoes, and jewelry had been selected, notated on four-by-six cards, and numbered so that later when the identification lines were written for the pages of *Haute* there would be a complete description of every item.

Bonnie had spent the night at Marcella's since it was almost three in the morning when they had finished the selection process. During that time Marcella had learned that Bonnie was an efficient fashion expert with impeccable taste. The new editor of *Haute* had plans for the future of her frumpy, albeit enthusiastic, beauty editor.

The secret photo-shoot began at 6 A.M. on Saturday when two huge rented motor homes arrived in front of Marcella Todd's apartment. One was to be a rest-and-changing area for the models; the other held the clothing and additional camera equipment. At exactly six that morning, Zack rang Marcella's buzzer.

"It's about time," Bonnie teased. "What did you do, sleep in or something?"

"Hell, I haven't even been home yet," Zack quipped. "You know how we New York playboys are."

"Just be quiet, you two," Marcella said. "Diane is still sleeping." Both Bonnie and Marcella had insisted that Diane go to bed at 9 P.M. even though Diane swore that she had never been in bed that early in her life and there was not a chance that she would sleep.

Zack exited to one of the motor homes where his two assistants, a lighting man and another photographer, were triple checking the piles of equipment. Zack gave the chauffeur a map showing each location and the order in which they would be shot. He had picked his sights according to where the sun would or would not be at different times of the day. Zack was attempting to seem calm, but he was nervous.

Marcella was nervous. Diane was very nervous. Only the surprisingly unflappable Bonnie Vincenzo seemed totally calm and organized as she scanned checklists and barked orders.

Precisely at 6:30 A.M. a cab squeaked to a halt on questionable brakes only a few inches behind one of the motor homes and out stepped Buffy Sarasota.

"If'n y'all think Ah look like shit this morning, don't be worried about hurtin' mah feelin's if ya might just wanna dump me," Buffy commented.

"You look great," Marcella reassured the girl.

"Wonderful," Bonnie added.

"Absolutely beautiful," Zack said, gazing deep into Buffy's eyes.

At almost that same moment, two hairdressers, friends of Bonnie's who were eager for the opportunity to get their initial exposure in *Haute*, a makeup artist, and several gofers and assistants arrived.

"Are there always this many people?" Diane asked her mother.

"Sometimes there are many, many more," Marcella said. "I have done shoots where there have been more than one hundred people behind the scenes."

Diane was impressed.

"Your hair is fabulous. Absolutely fabulous," one of the hairdressers twittered as he experimented with Buffy's luxurious mane of auburn hair. "This is heaven."

"Ya know, honey," Buffy said, "Y'all are jus' the kind o' boy mah Daddy sent me to New York to meet." She smiled at the hairdresser menacingly.

"Forget it, sweetheart," the hair expert kidded. "I can love you only for your hair."

"Lately, that is the *only* portion of mah anatomy that has seen any action," Buffy laughed. "But a girl will take a what a girl can git."

Both Buffy and Diane had been pulled into the motor home where the makeup people and hair stylists draped them in smocks and started their work. Marcella and Bonnie were keeping a careful watch on the results.

"Here is the order of shoot." Bonnie passed out a list of the location sites that would be used throughout the day. "We start at Battery Park, at the tip of Manhattan. The models will be wearing the rain looks. Greens for Buffy and the white for Diane." She held up the numbered ensembles so the crew could see them.

"Wagons ho!" Zack yelled. The two huge motor homes lunged forward toward Park Avenue, where they would turn south to Battery Park. When they reached the park, while Zack and his lighting man raced about holding light meters in the air, the other assistants started putting sun reflectors and lights into place. A portable generator for extra power was started with a noisy rumble.

All the cameras and lights were in place in a matter of minutes. Normally, it might take hours to situate lights and models for this kind of layout, but Zackery was working faster than he ever had in his life.

Marcella looked at the setting and lighting with the practiced eye of a person who had worked in similar settings for more than a decade. "It's a little hot over there," she said, pointing to a place where a high-intensity light was too bright.

"Thanks," Zack said as he ran to correct the problem.

"Hey, arteests!" Bonnie bellowed in the models' motor home. "They ready yet?"

"Bonnie, dearest," one of the hair designers said, "you are extremely fortunate that I am a genius."

"Aren't we." Bonnie was keeping the conversation at a teasing tone to prevent the tension that could easily develop.

The entire crowd, including three winos who had been occupying the park bench next to where Zack intended to shoot, bcame silent in approval when Diane and Buffy appeared. Marcella realized that for the first time she was viewing her daughter not as a little girl, but as a woman. Buffy was nervous but was beginning to respond to the enthusiasm of the crowd.

"There is some ham in you," Zack teased Buffy when she appeared to be getting herself into character.

"No ham, honey," Buffy returned. "Ah feel like Texas prime rib . . . center cut."

The three winos began to slither away to less visible human refuge dumps. Zack wanted the vagrants' photos.

He stepped in front and said, "Hey, buddies, you don't have to move. Just stay where you are while I take the ladies' pictures."

"Go to hell, mister," one of the winos snarled.

"Why, honey," Buffy purred in her best Southern sex-kitten voice, "don't you want mah picture taken with y'all?" She slipped her arm through one wino's tattered sleeve. Then with her other hand, she clutched one of the other grubby characters. When she turned, the light caught her exactly right, and she started walking toward Zack with the two men on her arms, while the third derelict was weaving behind them.

"J.R., honey . . . are ya ready to take me to the Cattle Barons' Ball?" She exchanged flirtations with the bedraggled trio. The men on her arms took on a kind of fleeting dignity. How long had it been since either of them had had a beautiful woman at their side? They looked proud through their rags.

Zack was frantically snapping pictures with the four cameras that were hung around his neck. Each was set for a different exposure to get different effects. Something seemed to have come over Buffy. She was moving, changing her expressions and gestures in rhythm to the clicks of Zackery's cameras.

Then came the shot that would make her world-famous.

She pulled the green plastic Australian bush hat she was wearing over one eye and placed both arms around the necks of her seedy escorts, drawing their faces close to hers in a Texas bear hug. All three smiled. Her pose was dazzling. Theirs was snaggletoothed. When the photo appeared on the cover of the magazine, it became the symbol of the new *Haute*, of the new American fashion industry.

The day became a blur. From the rainwear shots at the Battery, they went to suits and business looks in the deserted area of Wall Street, sports clothes in Chinatown, dresses at Herald Square, and . . .

But it was at Herald Square that something happened that made Marcella very happy. Just as Diane and Buffy were running through a flock of pigeons and baby prams, a cab stopped and Jayne Caldwell got out.

"I have been chasing you all over town," she told Marcella. "Look, I know what you are trying to do and I want to help," she said, making it clear that she supported her new boss. Marcella knew Jayne had too much integrity merely to latch on to whoever was in power; she sincerely wanted Marcella to succeed.

For the rest of the day, Jayne would do whatever needed to be done, whether it be sewing a torn hem, holding some mustard-covered pretzels that were to be used as props in a shot, or convincing irate policemen that they should allow two huge motor homes to double-park on Fifth Avenue in front of Tiffany's.

"Officer, I know we have the photography permits someplace," she lied, because Marcella had neglected to purchase the necessary permits from the City of New York. "They must be in that pile of clothing. But, Officer, I was just thinking — this layout is about the real New York. By the way, let me introduce myself, I am Jayne Caldwell, the managing editor of *Haute* magazine. What was I saying? Oh, yes, this layout is about New York, and we would really appreciate it if you two policemen would be in a photo with our models."

"Why, sure," one of the cops, of obvious Italian extraction, said. "My wife reads your magazine all the time."

"Can I have your name for the identification?"

Jayne asked politely as she produced her always handy pen and paper.

"Antonio Spago — that's S-P-A-G-O." The officer was obviously pleased. "My partner is Jerry McCandless. M-C-C-A-N-D-L-E-S-S. Don't worry about anything, lady."

For the next hour, officers Spago and McCandless, of New York's finest, became the unofficial assistants and bodyguards to everyone on the set. When Zack wanted crowds in the background, Spago would signal for a group of onlookers to start walking — or else. He even halted traffic in both directions at Fifth Avenue and Fifty-ninth Street for almost five minutes while Buffy and Diane pretended to be directing the flow in one of the world's busiest intersections.

The afternoon became evening and the women were modeling formalwear at Tavern on the Green, in Central Park.

"Honey, if'n Ah don't eat some of this food, there is goin' to be one photographer who will never fathah any children, and that would be a mighty terrible waste," Buffy threatened.

"I second that motion," Diane added.

"We will eat right after we finish the photos with the horse-drawn carriage and the doormen," Zack promised.

"Hurray!" came a chorus from the crew.

When the photo session finally came to an end, everyone headed for the restaurant. Zack sat next to Buffy at one of the large round tables reserved for them at Tavern on the Green. Buffy was cold and moved closer to the fireplace, where a log fire was crackling. "Do you always photograph summer clothes in the middle of March?" she asked Zack.

No, this is kind of late. Usually we do it in January

and February," he explained. "Swimwear is almost always photographed in January."

"That sounds awful, honey," Buffy complained lightheartedly. "Why, a gal could freeze something mighty important doin' that."

"That's the reason we usually go someplace warm like Aruba or Jamaica to photograph," Zack explained. "You ever been to Jamaica?"

"Do they have a football team?" Buffy smiled.

"Why do you say things like that?" Zack asked seriously. "That isn't you. You pretend to be cheap and easy, but that is not what I see through my camera. That is not how you appear in my photos."

"How do I appear?" Buffy, too, was serious.

"You appear tender and caring and vulnerable. You are a woman. There is intelligence and dreams and ambition. You are beautiful in every way."

"Do you really mean that, Zack?" Buffy asked softly.

"I really mean that."

Chapter Twenty-Three

Everyone should have been exhausted following the Saturday marathon photo session. They should have been, but they were not. So at midnight, the two motor homes were parked in front of the *Haute* offices while the anxious crew waited to see the first transparencies.

Marcella Todd had called in staff to open the executive dining room and was throwing a small party for the photo technicians, the hair and makeup people, the models, the drivers, even Officer McCandless, who had joined the party at the end of his shift and was showing an intense interest in Jayne Caldwell, who did not mind his attentions at all.

Champagne was flowing in the executive offices.

In the photo lab, Zack was supervising as six technicians being paid triple-time wages carefully developed the one hundred twenty-three rolls of film he had shot since early that morning.

Buffy Sarasota was waiting with him. She was excited, but not so much for herself. She had not quite realized that this frantic day had made a difference in how she would perceive herself for the rest of her life.

"I know the stuff is going to be great," Zack said nervously. "I could tell it would be when I was shooting. A photographer can sense when a shoot is going right. Marcella could, too. She would never have invited everyone back here if she thought the pictures would not be good. She even called in the art director to start thinking about a layout tonight."

Buffy listened to the excited photographer and she watched him. There was a man with pride and talent, and he had seen something in her that he thought was special. He was a man she wanted as she had never wanted any other man.

A technician entered the room. She was wearing a stained white smock and holding a plastic file box filled with slides. "You want to see the first of them tonight or wait until Monday?"

"Hell, yes — tonight!" Zack roared.

He turned on the light under a huge white Plexiglas-topped table and spread the first slides across the illuminated surface. The images of the slides came to life.

The first photos were those of Buffy and the vagrants at Battery Park. Zack stopped breathing when he caught sight of one picture in particular. A professional photographer would snap thousands, maybe millions, of frames of film during a career, but only a few times did he produce a photo that was more than an image, a photo that attained the level of art.

The contrast between the perfection and richness of Buffy's face and the wrongness of the winos' visages told the story of the success or failure that was life in New York City. It was the finest photo Zackery Jones had ever taken. For the rest of his life, people would remember that photo.

He turned to Buffy. "You are wonderful." He walked to her and put both arms around her waist, lifting her off the ground. "You are great. Wonderful. Fantastic."

"Oh, Zack . . ." Buffy was laughing.

Then they both realized their mouths were close together. Zack kissed her, a hard, excited, almost violent kiss. Zack and Buffy breathed hard and in unison as the kiss continued.

Thoughts flashed through Buffy's mind. She seemed to be drifting in space far away from the viewing room and *Haute*. Even farther from Texas. She had found someone who actually made her feel the passion she had only pretended to feel with so many men. *Oh, please, God,* she prayed, *make him feel the same way about me. I have to hold on to this man.*

"Do you know how much I care about you?" Zack asked. His hands clutched her body in gentle rhythm with his breathing. "I have so much I need to tell you."

I have to hold on to this man, Buffy thought again as a kind of panic started to churn her stomach. *I must hold onto this man. I will do whatever I have to do to hold on to this man.*

As the urgent kiss continued, her hand moved to the zipper at the back of the strapless sundress she was wearing. As she had done so many times before, she released the zipper silently and the tight dress loosened. "I can do better than that," she whispered in Zack's ear. "Much better."

Zack's body tensed. Still breathing heavily, he pulled away from Buffy and glared at her. She recoiled upon seeing the anger in his eyes.

"You don't understand anything." Zack was almost crying. "I really care about you and you act as if I am just one of your football-player lays. You don't have to sell yourself to me. Jeesus Christ!"

"I just want to make you happy." Buffy, too, was

crying. "I know how to make men happy. I can show you." Frantically, she continued undressing. "You will like me, Ah promise, you will like me."

Zack felt sick. "What am I, just another . . . I mean . . . you know I like you. I more than like you . . . I don't know what I'm saying." Zack sat down on the couch and rested his head on his hands. "I don't understand you."

"Don't you want me?" Buffy was genuinely confused.

"Not like this, lady. Oh, I want you, all right, but I want the woman in the picture, not the rich little whore who is standing in front of me right now." Instantly, Zack regretted his words. "I'm sorry."

Buffy was sobbing heavily. She had been called a whore before. She had even called herself a whore, but the words had never hurt so much as they did coming from Zackery Jones. Suddenly, she felt naked and exposed and very, very cheap. She had done it again. She had messed up her life. *Why can't I do anything right?* she thought.

"I'm so sorry," she cried. "Ah am so *very* sorry."

She turned and ran through the empty editorial department toward the elevators. Zack suddenly realized she had left him. Jumping up, he ran after her but entered the reception hall just as the elevator doors were closing.

Inside the elevator Buffy was sobbing and pounding her carefully manicured hands against the wood paneling until she reached street level. "Ah am no good. Ah am a whore. Mah Daddy is right. An . . . ah . . ." Her sobs dissolved into hiccoughs.

A few dozen floors up, Zackery Jones cut his knuckles as he slammed his fist into the closed elevator doors that were blocking him from Buffy. Slowly but violently, he pounded the bleeding knuckles against the steel doors over and over until the shiny metal surface was streaked with his blood.

"What have I done?" he asked aloud. "What have I done?"

He pressed the button to call back the elevator, but before the car could arrive, he heard the voice of Marcella Todd.

"Here you are," she called out happily. "We all have been looking everywhere for you. I saw the slides out in the viewing room and they look great —" She stopped talking in mid-sentence when she saw Zack's bleeding hand and the bloodstained elevator door. "Your hand, Zack! What happened?" She grabbed some tissues from a dispenser on the receptionist's desk and carefully cleaned the blood from his knuckles. "Come with me."

She led Zack into the ladies' room, where she stuck the bleeding hand under the cold-water faucet and soaked some paper towels into compresses. "Are you going to tell me what happened?" Marcella questioned.

"Just a case of artistic temperament." Zack attempted to make a joke of the situation, but his voice was still shaking. "Look, I would rather not talk about this right now."

"Sure," Marcella said.

"So you saw the photos," Zack said, trying to change the subject.

"They are wonderful. You did a terrific job. So did Buffy." Marcella paused. "Where is Buffy? Does all this have something to do with her?"

"I don't want to talk about it."

"She is all right, isn't she?" Marcella's voice took on a harsh quality that Zack did not understand. "You didn't hit her or anything like that, did you?" Marcella's mind was flashing through long-buried memories of the last time she had seen blood on a man's fist. It had been her blood. She glared at Zack.

"Hit her!" Zack was shocked. "I couldn't hit her! I love her!" He felt anger building inside him, anger directed at Marcella. "How could you even *think* that I would —"

"I'm sorry," Marcella interrupted, realizing instantly someone like Zack would not be the kind of man who would attack a woman. "It was just something . . . oh, Zack . . . I *am* sorry."

"Look, I have to finish going through the photos," Zack said in a flat, beaten voice. "It's late and we're all tired. Things just snapped. Let's forget it."

"Done," Marcella agreed.

But Marcella stood alone in the hall looking at the bloodstains on the elevator doors for long minutes after Zack left. Those stains and what had happened had shaken and surprised her. Maybe she did not trust men. Maybe Burt Rance was right and she was burying herself in her work because she was afraid of being caught up in any emotional entanglements. She did know one thing; she was never going to be hurt by a man again — in any way.

She wanted to talk to Burt.

Chapter Twenty-Four

It was four in the morning and Zackery Jones was glad he lived in New York City, the city that never closed, as the tourist commercials stated. Only a few minutes earlier the crowd that had gathered to look at the photos had finally dissipated. There were hours of work ahead to transform the pictures into a slick magazine fashion layout.

But everyone was enthusiastic.

Zack knew where Buffy lived. It was in one of the posh high rises where corporations kept overdesigned yet sterile apartments for the use of top executives when they were in New York City. It was Buffy's father's apartment.

On the way to the apartment, Zack had commandeered one of the huge motor homes for transportation. He had stopped at an all-night liquor store and bought three bottles of champagne and some candles. Then he found a Chinese restaurant where he ordered ten cartons of food that included almost everything on the late-night menu.

Zack pushed the gas pedal to the floor and the giant vehicle bounced down Second Avenue, from pothole to pothole, at speeds approaching fifty miles per hour, racing, toward Buffy's high rise.

When he arrived at the building, he realized there was no place to park a sixty-foot super-sized mobile home in midtown Manhattan. There was probably no parking space large enough to accommodate the monster vehicle east of Albany. So Zack flicked a series of switches that ignited an extravaganza of warning lights on the top, sides, back, and front of the mobile home. He was amazed at the computerization available on the motor home, which included a keyboard for typing out messages that would appear in lights at the top of the front of the bus and along the sides.

He typed a message that immediately started flashing in white light from the front and sides of the mobile home, causing bursts of illumination to flood the front of the building.

"What the hell is going on out here!" yelled the doorman-security guard. "Get that thing out of the road. You're blocking the whole street."

"Look, buddy," Zack said evenly, "this is important to me."

"I don't give a fuck!" the doorman snarled. "Move it!"

Zack handed the doorman a one-hundred-dollar bill. The doorman looked at the bill and his snarl turned to a smile. "Now that you explain it that way, I will watch that thing."

"What is Buffy Sarasota's apartment number?" Zack demanded.

"I have to announce you. Them's the rules. No exceptions." The doorman was serious again. "I could lose my job."

"I want to surprise her," Zack said as he pulled out another hundred. "Look, it's all cool."

The doorman took the bill and said, "Well, I don't think you could be too dangerous showing up in a thing like that. You sure aren't trying to hide nothing. She's in 6408 in the east tower." The doorman smiled. "You ain't too crazy, buddy; she is sure a swell-looking babe."

But Zack was already running to the elevator with a bottle of champagne in one hand and two glasses in the other. The first bank of elevators ended at the fortieth floor, so he had to take another elevator to the sixty-fourth floor. He started unwrapping the foil around the cork, but he was nervous and his hands were clumsy.

Inside the huge chrome-and-glass-decorated apartment, Buffy was sitting in the dark still wearing the partially zipped dress she had worn hours earlier when she was at *Haute*. When she was with Zack. She finally had stopped crying but the remains of her eye makeup still streaked down her exquisite cheekbones.

Zack pounded on the door. "Buffy, open up!" he demanded. "I am a jerk. You are a jerk. We are both jerks. Dammit! Open this door!"

She jumped to open the heavy steel doors but fumbled with the multiple security locks and electric sensors that protected the apartment.

"Open the door!" Zack bellowed.

"Ah am trying, honey!" exclaimed Buffy. Without pressing the digital combination that turned off the security, Buffy finally undid the master locks. In the security office deep in the basement of the building, a warning flashed that all was not well in apartment 6408.

"Oh, Zack," Buffy began, "I feel —"

"I love you," Zack interrupted.

"Say that again," Buffy demanded.

"Didn't you hear me, you crazy woman? I *love* you. I love everything about you," Zack sang.

Buffy clutched Zack and kissed him. She was like a lioness who wanted to devour the man emotionally, this man who really loved her. In the background the elevator doors opened and two armed guards stepped out. Buffy saw them over Zack's shoulder but waved them away with a hand signal indicating that far from there being something wrong in apartment 6408, everything was in fact, very, very right.

"You better come on in," she said between kisses.

"No," Zack said, suddenly remembering. "You come with me."

"But Ah am a mess!"

"You are *my* mess. Now, come on." He pulled her into the elevator. They kissed until they reached the fortieth floor. They kissed until the elevator arrived to take them to the lobby. They were kissing when the door opened onto the lobby, where the doorman and the two security cops stood. They kissed right up to the moment when Buffy noticed the flashing neon extravaganza of the motor home. "Oh, my." She was amazed.

The lighted sign in the front of the bus proclaimed "BUFFY . . . I LOVE YOU . . . BUFFY . . . I LOVE YOU . . . BUFFY . . . I LOVE YOU" in a sequence that repeated itself again and again as the message ran across the signboard. The huge flashing sign on the side of the mobile home, the sign that was illuminating the entire outside of the skyscraper, read WILL YOU MARRY ME? in foot-high letters.

"Well . . . ?" Zack prodded her.

"Oh, Zack."

The inside of the motor home was lit with candles and more champagne was already opened. The Chinese food was scattered over the teakwood table.

"Hungry?" Zack asked.

"For a Chinese breakfast!" Buffy was laughing. "A Chinese breakfast at five in the morning."

"Did I goof?" Zack looked alarmed.

"No, honey, you didn't goof." Buffy hugged him again. "You just didn't realize what Ah was really hungry for." She kissed him again.

"I am so sorry if I hurt you," he whispered as they both fell to the floor of the motor home. "It is just that you are so special to me." He realized that they were about to make love. "So very, very special."

"Zack . . . were you serious about wantin' to marry me?" Buffy asked.

"I couldn't be more serious," he answered.

"Then Ah have made a decision. Let's wait till we are married to make love."

Zack paused. "Wait." He thought. "Well." He thought some more. "I guess."

"Then we won't do it till we are married," Buffy continued.

"Whatever you say." Zack touched her cheek.

"Then get this thing fired up, honey. Ah think the closest place to get married tonight, or today, is Virginia or someplace like that," she said. "While Ah have my *mind* set on waiting, the *rest* of me is not too anxious for an extended wait, if'n you get my drift."

"You mean . . . go get married now?" Zack asked.

"If you are too tired to drive, Ah guess Ah can handle this thing myself," Buffy said, laughing. "Ah will tell you one thing, Mr. Zackery Jones, we are goin' to be in the weddin' bed before this day is over."

As the huge motor vehicle rumbled across the George Washington Bridge, which linked the world of Manhattan with the outside universe including Winchester, Virginia, the home of the instant wedding, Buffy Sarasota, about to become Buffy Jones, poured champagne and fooled with the small computer that controlled the sign on the side of the bus. For the next eight hours, that sign would flash ALMOST MARRIED . . . SO LONG TO ALL YOU COWBOYS!

A few hours later, in a parking lot outside the office of a justice of the peace in that small Virginia city, the motor home rocked gently as Buffy and Zack made love.

"Darlin', they are never gonna believe this in Dallas," Buffy said with a strong Texas twang. "Damn . . . if'n you ain't the real thing!"

Buffy looked at Zack. "Honey," she said, "Are ya pants too tight or are ya just glad to see me?"

"I can take care of the pants," Zack smiled. They both laughed. Zack and Buffy had made love without removing their clothing.

Facing each other, they slowly started undressing. As their clothes piled between them, they studied each other's body.

Buffy took a long elegant fingernail and gently traced the vein that ran down Zack's neck into his arm. She could feel his heart beating.

Zack lifted her toward him and started kissing her neck. His powerful hands seemed to be stroking every part of her body at the same time. Those wonderful hands caressed her legs as he gently kissed her stomach.

"I love you," he whispered.

In that moment their two bodies became one. Buffy

felt tears welling in her eyes and then cascading down her cheeks.

"Is it all right?" Zack whispered.

"Oh . . . yes." It was so very all right. Buffy Sarasota had made love to hundreds of men and this was the first time, she realized, that everything was right. Her breaths were short and gasping as he enveloped her body.

Again they loved. Her fingernails dug slightly into his neck. Then she felt something she had never felt before. Her trembling body was suddenly hot . . . so hot! She wrapped a long leg around Zack's torso as her back arched naturally. The white heat continued as both bodies churned.

They both climaxed at the same time and they could feel their warm body fluids mixing. Buffy Sarasota had never reacted like that before. It was her first.

Both Zack and Buffy stayed entwined during the stillness that follows lovemaking. He gently rubbed her back. She moved her lips close to his ear and whispered.

"Honey . . . Ah . . . Ah . . ."

"Me, too!"

Then Zack Jones started kissing his bride on her neck again . . . and again . . . and again.

Chapter Twenty-Five

Zack and Buffy Jones waited in the phone both in Winchester, Virginia, while the motor home idled impressively a few feet away.

In New York, Marcella Todd picked up the phone in her apartment and recognized Zack's "Hello!"

"Zack, where are you? I was at the office all day today and I certainly could have used some imput from our head photographer," Marcella said rather angrily. "This isn't like you at all."

"Marcella —" Zack tried to interrupt.

"We are attempting to select the cover and everyone likes the shot of Buffy with the winos at the Battery, but do you think it should be a close-up of her face with just a hint of the winos on either side of her face, or a longer view?" Marcella was anxious for her photographer's opinion.

"The close . . . I mean, Marcella, listen to me a second." Zack was almost laughing.

"We couldn't find an exposure list for that series of photos. Can you bring it right over to me? We need to decide which of the hundred or so photos you took of that grouping will appear best in the magazine."

"Sorry, I can't come over right away." Zack finally managed to spit out an entire uninterrupted sentence.

"You *what?!*" Marcella was shocked. Usually Zack was far more cooperative.

"I'm in Virginia and —"

"Virginia! What are you doing in Virginia?"

"I . . . we . . . Buffy and I got married."

Marcella was stunned. Both ends of the phone line were silent for a moment. Then she said, "Why didn't you tell me that in the first place?"

"I guess it just slipped my mind." Zack was actually laughing now. "We just decided to get married last night — well, actually, early this morning — and we drove to Virginia and got married this evening."

"I'm sorry. What am I saying? Congratulations, you two. I didn't realize that you were . . . I mean . . . this is a bit of a surprise." Marcella was embarrassed that she had centered the entire conversation on the magazine, when Zack and Buffy had something so very important to say. "Congratulations and best wishes and all that."

"Look, we should be back late Monday." Zack looked at Buffy, who was shaking her head furiously. "Maybe Tuesday."

"You kids have to have a honeymoon. You both have done plenty. We have the art here. Have a good time and we will see you when we see you." Marcella reached for a pencil. "Where are you staying?"

"You would never believe me." Zack started to laugh again.

"I want to send you something. What is the name of the hotel?"

"You know the motor homes we rented? Well . . . one of them has not been returned yet," Zack explained.

Marcella coud hear some commotion in the background. "Look, Buffy wants to say something."

"Marcella" — Buffy's Texas twang filled the phone — "tell that motor-home man that Ah want to buy this thing for sentimental reasons."

"Certainly." Marcella was laughing, too.

Then Zack came back on the line. "Look, we'd better go before she wants to buy this phone booth for sentimental reasons," he said. "Wait a second. Maybe you can help me. Where should I buy a wedding ring?"

"You don't have a wedding ring yet?"

"Not exactly," Zack said sheepishly.

"When you get back in New York I will have the best selection of rings in the city waiting for you at *Haute*. I would say we should have a little pull in the jewelry business. Now you two be happy."

Both Buffy and Zack yelled their excited good-byes and then hung up.

Marcella stared into space for a moment, then dialed a number she had memorized but seldom used, Burt Rance's number.

"Hello . . . can a lady buy you a drink?" she asked.

"Only if you get me drunk and take advantage of me. I know how you jaded career women are. You will just use me and toss me aside, forgotten and broken," Burt said.

"Oh, shut up and get over here."

"I'm on my way."

A few minutes later the buzzer rang, announcing that Burt Rance had arrived. Marcella had barely enough time to change into a long silk evening robe. She was wearing nothing underneath. *This is not like me,* she thought to herself. *It must be that I am getting caught*

*up in the romance of Buffy and Zack. Anyhow, Burt
will never know there is nothing between the luxurious
white silk and my skin.*

Burt noticed the clinging robe and exacty where it
clung to Marcella's body. "Omigod, this is going to be
hard on a healthy American male," he teased. "Oh,
boy!"

"I promised you a drink."

"I think I need a cold shower."

"Ice water, then."

"No, vodka!"

Both Marcella and Burt laughed. Then Burt pulled
her toward him and kissed her. His face was rough from
not shaving all day. She liked the feel of the slight
beard; a man's roughness had not been a part of her daily life for too long. He kept kissing her. On the lips. On
the back of the neck. On the breasts.

Marcella felt the silk robe fall open. Burt continued
gently kissing her breasts until her nipples became hard
and erect. Burt's powerful hands gently caressed
Marcella's back as he kissed her breasts and neck.

Marcella tried to remember. For so long, she had existed without a man in her life and had become independent. Yet, at this moment, all she wanted was this man
to love her and make love to her.

Burt too was excited. He wanted this woman. He
wanted to possess her. He wanted Marcella to be only
his, not to share with her career or *Haute*.

Slowly he lowered Marcella onto her couch. He could
feel himself becoming erect.

Marcella was enjoying her emotions. This passion
was so different from her past experiences. Love making with Burt Rance was totally enveloping. She ran her

long finger nails through his thick damp hair and kissed his hair while he continued kissing her breasts.

Burt was aware that Marcella, who was usually cool and controlled was rapidly losing control of her emotions. He did not want to rush her. So he clutched her in his arms and continued kissing her entire body without moving toward intercourse.

It was Marcella who made that move.

Aware of his erection, she turned her body to his and guided his penis into her body. They both climaxed at the same instant. As if they had both only discovered sex for the first time, and as if everything that had ever happened to their bodies before had only been in anticipation of these moments, they made love again.

Then both their bodies relaxed. Seemingly taking the same breaths Burt Rance and Marcella Todd held tightly to each other.

But thoughts of the outside world began to reenter Marcella's mind.

"Burt," she said as his lips pressed against her breasts. "There is something that I have to ask you."

"Ask me anything," he whispered between kisses.

"It's about *Haute*," Marcella felt him pull away the instant she mentioned the magazine.

"You can forget that cold shower. I don't need it anymore," Burt said as he moved toward the bar, where he poured himself a triple shot of icy vodka. He turned and stared at her. "I don't understand you, lady. I think I love you, but sometimes I don't even know you. What in the hell are you trying to do?" He was angry.

"I don't understand myself." Marcella suddenly felt nervous and exposed and, more than anything else, wrong. "I do care about you. I probably love you."

"We aren't children," Burt said softly and coldly. "You act one way. Look at the way you are dressed. I am not stupid; I know you want me and I want you."

"It might not be fair to you," she answered.

"And this is fair? Look, maybe some other man hurt you. Maybe he made you act the way you do, but I am not that man and I am damned sick of paying for what he did or did not do to you."

"You're right. You're absolutely right, but I am afraid not to be independent. I can't let myself need a man again." Marcella wanted to cry but could not find the tears. "I don't want to be hurt again. You could hurt me. You are the first man in years who could hurt me."

"So you care about me, even love me, so much that to protect yourself you have to keep me away. You will forgive me if I don't completely understand that line of reasoning. Would it be easier for us to build a relationship if we hated each other?"

"Things will be better once I have the magazine under control," Marcella promised. "It is all I can think about right now. I didn't realize that it was going to be so important to me, but it is."

"I wish I were that magazine," Burt said as he poured himself another three ounces of vodka. "But I am something less than the mighty *Haute* magazine, just a poor mortal man. How could I hope to compete for your love with all that passionate paper and ink?"

Marcella realized that she had hurt Burt Rance deeply, but she did not know what to say. She had already used her daughter as an excuse for not letting herself become more involved with this man. Then, when her passions almost overcame her emotional judgment, she had placed the magazine as a barrier between them. She did not want to lose this man, but neither did she want to belong to him.

Burt walked over to the door and pulled it open. He started down the stairs, then turned. "You know, you are starting to remind me of Sylvia Harrington. She had a fucking affair with that magazine, too. When you can be a woman again, call."

Chapter Twenty-Six

The heavy burgundy blackout drapes of Sylvia Harrington's bedroom had not been opened for days. The marble shell-shaped ashtray beside the bed was filled with cigarette butts. Some of the ashes had spilled onto the plush rose carpeting. On the bed, amid the soiled linen and ash-burned satin, lay Sylvia Harrington, alone and angry. Yes, more angry than desolute. Most of her fury was pointed toward Richard Barkley, Dickie, that little prick who had sold *Haute*, her *Haute*, out from under her.

There was a weak knock at the bedroom door.

"Miss Harrington," came the maid's voice. Sylvia glared at the rose-satin-padded walls and lit another cigarette.

"Miss Harrington, are you all right? Is there anything you want me to do?" There was a pause. "Miss Harrington, I hate to bother you, but you forgot to leave my check."

Ah, another person who truly cares about Sylvia Harrington, Sylvia thought. She got out of bed. Her legs hurt. She walked to her purse and groped inside for her check-book.

"Miss Harrington?"

Sylvia pulled open the double doors, startling the heavy woman. "Here's your check. Now get out." She walked toward the windows that faced the Fifty-ninth Street Bridge. The maid quickly slipped out the rear door of the apartment.

Sylvia realized that there was too much silence in her world. There were no telephones ringing. No special-delivery couriers bringing packets of payola to the apartment. No calls from the doormen to announce that there were flowers in the lobby and to ask if she wanted them brought up to the apartment. There had not been even a bothersome knock from that little bitch from the rental company who wanted to sell her her own apartment. The apartment was still and lifeless. She was lifeless. *Haute* was her life. Without her magazine, she was dead.

She had thought of suicide.

She was still thinking of suicide. Perhaps if there had been enough pills in the apartment she might have taken them. She did not own a gun. Jumping out the window was a bit too melodramatic. So it was not that Sylvia Harrington had rejected the idea of suicide; it simply was not convenient enough.

She decided to water — no, mist — her orchids instead. She had never been a plant lover, but a fashionable public relations man had given her some orchid plants. He had a mania for them and the ones he gave her refused to die.

"I always thought these things were supposed to be so fragile," she said to herself as she squirted the mister over them. "Maybe that is what is to become of me. Just a little old lady tending her orchids in her New

York apartment." The idea repulsed her. She noticed some dead leaves and reached for the sharp scissors that her maid used to tend the orchids. She looked at the blades — the blades.

Almost in a trance she turned and walked toward her bedroom with the scissors gaping open in her hand. "Cut away the dead. That is the answer. Cut away the dead."

She entered the rose room with the padded walls and became very still. The only sound in the room was her breathing. "Cut away the dead. It is so right. Everything will be right if I cut away the dead."

She raised the open scissors and plunged them into the padded silk fabric on the walls, making a tearing sound. "Cut away the dead." She sliced into the walls again and again. Then she hacked at the burgundy drapes until they were ribbons and the sunlight filled the room. "Cut away the dead. Cut away the dead." Finally, she sliced into the luxurious bedding, ripping the silks and satins and scattering the eiderdown feathers into a cloud in the suddenly sun-filled room. "Cut away the dead." She said the words in the rhythm of a children's playground chant. "Cut away the dead. Cut away the dead." She smashed the scissors into the expensive glass and crystal figurines and fixtures. "Cut away the dead. Cut away the dead." The room — her sanctum — was destroyed. She stopped and looked at the shambles and smiled. "I did it. I cut away the dead."

She turned toward the telephone and dialed a number that she found after a few minutes of searching through her phone book. "Barry Dobene, please. This is Sylvia Harrington."

"Oh, yes, Miss Harrington," the impressed voice on

the other end of the phone gushed. "I know he will want to talk to you right away." Sylvia smiled. So her name still was important, her name still was power.

"Sylvia." The voice on the other end of the receiver was unmistakably that of Barry Dobene, the interior designer protégé of Beverly Boxard, dragon lady grande dame of *Architecture Now*.

"Barry, remember a few months ago when you told me I probably needed to do something about my bedroom?" Sylvia began.

"I hope you aren't —" Dobene was worried Sylvia was calling to vent her anger.

"Not at all," she interrupted. "You were absolutely right. I have been meaning to do something about that room for years, and, frankly, today I just took matters into my own hands and made a mess of everything."

"I am sure I can help."

"I really need someone over here as soon as possible to cart out the mess and redo the room. Be a dear and take care of it."

"It will be my pleasure," Dobene reassured her. "I will have a crew there this afternoon."

"That would be wonderful. See you then."

After Sylvia hung up, Dobene walked over to the desk of one of his assistants and said, "You would not believe that call. Sylvia Harrington wants me to redo her bedroom, the room nobody has ever seen. Seems it was torn apart or something. I'm going over this afternoon." His thoughts were rambling. "I wouldn't miss seeing that for anything." He paused. "I wonder if it really is black leather . . ."

But Sylvia Harrington had already put the ruined room out of her mind. She was making more calls. Again she dialed. Again the phone rang. The receiver was answered on the other end of the line and a voice said, "Please hold." A minute later a professional-sounding voice came on, saying, "Melissa Fenton's residence." It was the answering service. Normally, Sylvia would have slammed down the receiver, but this time she wanted to know where she could find Melissa Fenton.

"Would you like to leave a message?" the voice asked carelessly.

"No, I would not. I want to know where Melissa Fenton is," Sylvia demanded.

"If you will leave a message, I can ask her to call you." The voice remained uninterested.

"This is Sylvia Harrington. I can tell you that Miss Fenton would want to speak with me right now, and if you do not stop wasting my time and tell me where she is, I am sure Miss Fenton will can your ass!" Sylvia thundered. "Do I make myself clear?"

"Oh, Miss Harrington." The voice on the other end was suddenly alert because her company did a lot of business with *Haute* and *Haute* clients. "I am sure she would want me to tell you. Oh, I apologize. I didn't realize."

"Shut up, you ninny, and tell me where she is!"

"She has been working on a project with Mrs. Parker . . . yes, that is the name. She has been staying with a Mrs. Parker at her New York apartment. I don't have the number. She calls in several times a day. I will give her your message."

Sylvia slammed down the phone. She knew who Mrs. Parker was. That was obviously Vice-President Parker's wife, Miranda Dante.

Sylvia dialed Miranda Dante's apartment on Fifth Avenue.

It was Miranda, the fading star herself, who answered the phone. She must have sent the servants away for privacy. *Miranda Dante probably had not answered a phone since she got her first free one installed after giving Alexander Graham Bell a case of the clap,* Sylvia thought.

"Miranda, my dear, how wonderful to hear your voice."

"Who is this?" Miranda sounded as disinterested as did the twit at the answering service.

"Sylvia Harrington."

"What can I do for you, Sylvia?" Miranda's voice went from bored to chilled.

"I understand that Melissa has been visiting you —"

"She *lives* here," Miranda interrupted.

"For a few days." Sylvia continued, as if Miranda had not spoken. "I need to talk to her."

"About what?"

"*Really*, Miranda, it is something I should only discuss with Melissa. When did you say she was coming back?"

"For you? Never." Miranda said flatly.

"Oh, I am sure she will find the time to talk to me sooner or later. I know I am most eager to talk to her. I really feel that I have misunderstood the girl."

"Sylvia, I hear you are out of a job."

"Not exactly out. There has been some reorganization at *Haute*, but I am still on the masthead. This just means that I have some more free time to do some of the things I really want to do, like that project your husband mentioned — that government liaison thing to the fashion industry."

"So you want the job?" Miranda suddenly felt more secure.

"You might say that," Sylvia replied.

"It's a cruel world out there," Miranda was making a deal. "Quite often in order to get what you desire, you have to give up something else you want. You *do* understand what I mean?"

"I understand perfectly." And Sylvia did.

"Then I will call my husband immediately and tell him I have managed to get you to accept the position."

"At slightly more salary than he suggested."

"He never told you how much the job pays."

"I know, but I still want slightly more. There must also be no complaints if I continue collecting a salary from *Haute*."

"Whatever." Miranda felt the conversation was almost finished. "I take it there will be no need to tell Melissa that you called?"

"None whatsoever," Sylvia agreed.

"And you don't intend to try to see her?" Miranda still seemed worried.

"I am sure I will be too busy with my new position to have any time for other interests."

"Fine." The line went dead. Miranda was not one for civil good-byes. Sylvia smiled. She had gotten what she wanted from that call, *everything* she wanted. And she had given away nothing, nothing that had ever really meant anything to her.

Now for the final call.

"Hello." The voice on the other end of the phone seemed hostile. There was irritation in the tone. Sylvia was delighted to hear that irritation.

"Dickie," she cooed with false animation.

"Sylvia. How in the hell did you find me?" Richard Barkley was not delighted to have Sylvia Harrington reappear in his life, but he preferred hearing her voice to the one he had expected when he rushed to answer the phone.

"Don't you know I know everything about you? I know you better than anyone, Dickie. My, we sound irritated. Have we struck out — that *is* the right baseball term, is it not?"

"What do you want, Sylvia?"

"It seems, Dickie, dearest, that we might be stuck with each other. We might detest each —"

"Try hate each other's guts," Barkley interjected.

"Isn't it amazing how well we work together? Well, I figured that by this time there might be trouble in paradise."

"Everything is fine here," Richard Barkley lied. In truth, things were terrible in the sprawling mansion at Key Biscayne. After a few days, during which Richard had thought he could never have been happier, Tom Andrews went into one of what Richard called his "But-you-see-I-am-really-straight-even-though-I-like-to-suck-an-occasional-cock" moods and started making telephone calls, first to the stewardess he met on the flight from Rio, and then to some little trollop he met in a bar on Collins Avenue. She had called earlier and Richard had managed to intercept the call before Tom heard the phone ring. It was she whom he had expected to be on the line. Instead, it was Sylvia Harrington.

'I am very happy," he continued.

"Oh, I *am* delighted. Look, I just wanted to say that while I think you are a bastard, I do understand you, so —"

"So what?" Barkley was becoming annoyed with the all-too-familiar tone of this conversation.

"I just wanted to let you know that when you decide you need me, and you will, you know, we will be together again. Old habits are . . . you know what I mean.''

"You are out of your mind!" Barkley roared.

"We will see. Tata . . . Dickie.'' Sylvia calculated how much money would be Barkley's share of the four-hundred-million-dollar sale of *Haute*. Probably twenty million, or as much as thirty. That would not be enough to start another magazine, but she might have a use for that money someday. And poor little Dickie, when his baseball player dumped him, and it was only a matter of time until that happened, he would have no one but Sylvia Harrington. He hated her, she realized, but she was the only person who could give him success. Richard Barkley did not realize it, but he needed success. He would not be content being another rich aging Miami gay. He would be back in New York and he would come back to her.

In Miami, Richard Barkley looked out over the calm waters of Biscayne Bay. He was thinking about Sylvia Harrington. He was afraid that she was right again — always right. He should not have sold *Haute*. Without *Haute*, Sylvia Harrington was still Sylvia Harrington, but Richard Barkley was nothing.

He had thought that by selling the magazine, he would finally have his revenge on the woman who had belittled him all his adult life. He had hoped to destroy her. Instead, he had destroyed himself.

Chapter Twenty-Seven

The big white Corniche convertible sped down Canon Drive. Marti Golden preferred driving in Beverly Hills. She was late in having her hair finished at Umberto's and was meeting her interior designer, Phyllis Morris, at the Bistro Garden. She could have walked the few blocks, but she wanted the car left in the parking lot at the restaurant.

"Good afternoon, Mrs. Golden," the red-jacketed parking lot attendant greeted her. He backed the ultra-expensive and luxurious car into the most visible space in the lot, the first position among a collection of Rolls-Royces, a Lotus, and Phyllis Morris's beige Corniche.

"Thanks, Ramon. I'm late."

She walked through the long hallway into the paneled inner room of the Bistro Garden. The maître d' greeted her. "The usual table?" he queried.

"Yes," Marti said as she headed toward her somewhat off-the-chic-area table in a remote corner of the outdoor garden. She always liked this more private area when Sol was going to join her for lunch. Phyllis was already waiting.

"I have to say that your husband has set a new standard for gift-giving — even for Beverly Hills," Phyllis teased as Marti sat down at the umbrella table. "There isn't a woman in town who doesn't want her own four-hundred-million-dollar magazine."

"*Haute* is really part of Golden Limited," Marti corrected her. "Sol just bought it for the company because I wanted it."

"I want to hear all about it." Phyllis was curious. The real story behind the takeover that had made page one of the *Los Angeles Times* would be the choicest of Beverly Hills gossip.

"I'd rather see the renderings of what you have planned for the executive offices," Marti said.

"Ah, business. If there is anything I like better than gossip, it is business." Phyllis reached beside the table for a thick portfolio of designs her staff had completed. "I especially like profitable business. Now, before you look, I want to remind you that you said you wanted nothing but the best — and the best, my best, is expensive."

"I expected nothing less." Marti laughed.

Marti thumbed approvingly through the renderings. "I like this idea of disguising the security doors to the offices," Marti said with a smile, "but where are you going to find bulletproof Lalique?"

"In Beverly Hills anything is possible." Phyllis shrugged. "Actually, I have been putting that in a lot of shower doors since, you remember, that actor's boyfriend took a shot at his lover while he was taking a shower with his wife."

"Whose wife?" Marti had not heard this story. "Oh, you're putting me on."

"I'm not so sure. It probably has happened at least

once." Phyllis Morris had been around Beverly Hills for a long time.

"Mrs. Golden." A busboy interrupted the conversation. "Mr. Golden called and said he would be unable to make lunch. He said if you needed him, he would be at home."

"Sol Golden at home in the middle of a weekday afternoon!" Marti was really alarmed. "Something must be wrong."

"When my husband comes home in the middle of the afternoon, it is usually a sign that everything is great." Phyllis was attempting to be reassuring. "He loves matinees."

Marti could not hide her worry. "No, Phyllis, this magazine takeover took a lot out of Sol. He has been very tired the last few weeks. I have to tell you I have been worried. I wish I had not insisted that he buy the damned thing."

"Then you're serious." Phyllis stopped joking.

"When Sol Golden stops working in the middle of a weekday afternoon," Marti said, "you can bet that I am worried."

"Then what are you here for?" Phyllis put her hand over her friend's hand. "Why don't you go home?"

"If you don't mind, I'll do just that." Marti walked away from the umbrella table, past the maître d', who looked alarmed that one of the best customers was leaving without having eaten lunch, and proceeded out to the parking lot, where the alert Ramon was already maneuvering the Rolls-Royce out of its prime parking place.

She gunned the powerful car along the narrow road that led to her house atop Beverly Crest Drive. As she turned the bend and the iron gates appeared, she pressed the electronic button to open the gates in time for the big automobile to pass through. She ran into the house, leaving the door of the car open and the motor running. Marti found Sol in their bedroom. He was sitting on the bed fully clothed and looking very gray.

"I'm calling a doctor," Marti said.

"No, honey." Sol reached out his hand. "I'm fine. Just a little tired. Come here and sit by me." They nestled against each other in the massive bed. Sol looked over at his wife and smiled. "You know, you are more beautiful today that you were the day I married you."

"And you are more handsome." She smiled and clutched his hand.

"No, I am just a fat old man, not the skinny boy with lots of hair. That was the boy you married." Sol seemed to be breathing easier.

"I prefer the man I have now to that boy I married," Marti whispered. "Oh, Sol, I do love you so much. It scares me so when something like this happens."

"My darling Marti" — Sol leaned over to kiss his wife — "how I do love you." Then suddenly he started to gasp for air.

"What's wrong? Sol!" Marti screamed.

It was as if the old man were strangling. In a few seconds his face had gone from ashen to red, and now a purplish tint was creeping into his complexion.

Marti jumped from the bed and grabbed the bedside phone, pressing the button for the servants to come at once. Sol had lost consciousness and had stopped breathing. Calmly, Marti cleared Sol's throat and started mouth-to-mouth resuscitation. She had taken a first-aid course years earlier when Sol had suffered a slight stroke, but this was the first time she had needed to use it. Breathe-two-three-four . . . she counted silently and the old man lay still in the bed. Then his body began to shake in convulsions.

A maid appeared at the door. The Mexican girl looked frightened.

"Call the paramedics!" Marti yelled. "Move!"

Marti started heart massage, alternating with the mouth-to-mouth. She was attempting to remember that course. "Oh, God, please let me do this right. Don't let him die yet." The determined woman tore open the silk shirt she had ordered especially for Sol. She could hear the sirens coming far down the hill. Marti did not notice that the gardeners, the butler, several of the maids, the cook, and the garage man had entered the bedroom and were looking helplessly at one another. All she could see was her husband. It was only when the paramedics entered the room and gently led her away that she understood there were more than a dozen other people around her.

She clutched both hands together tightly and her carefully sculpted nails dug into her palms. As the paramedics worked over Sol attaching equipment, radioing for instructions, and administering drugs, Marti watched and prayed. Finally, the activity stopped and one of the paramedics looked at the distressed woman.

"I'm sorry, ma'am," he said.

"What do you mean, sorry?" Marti asked in a voice that started almost calmly but became more shrill at each word.

"He's gone, ma'am." The paramedic walked toward Marti and was prepared to help her if she fainted. But Marti Golden did not faint.

"Who are you to tell me my husband is dead?" she

demanded. "You are not a doctor. Get him into that ambulance and get him to the U.C.L.A. Medical Center."

"But, ma'am —"

"Now!"

The paramedics knew not to argue with her. Carefully, they loaded the dead man onto a stretcher and, with Marti holding his hand, drove to the Medical Center. For two hours, Marti Golden held her husband's hand until their family doctor finally managed to administer a sedative and led her to a room. Marti, throughout the ordeal, was very calm on the surface. There was no crying. It would be days before she would be able to accept the loss enough to cry. She felt only one emotion — guilt; she blamed her obsession with owning *Haute* magazine for the death of her beloved Sol.

Chapter Twenty-Eight

Sol Golden had been dead for only three hours when Arthur Lavery, the chief counsel for Golden Limited, entered Mrs. Golden's hospital room and awakened her.

"Mrs. Golden," he said softly, "I know this is a difficult time, but there are necessary things we must do."

Marti understood. Sol and his lawyers had a carefully orchestrated plan of how the estate would be handled. There would be papers to be signed and details to be arranged in the few hours before probate and Internal Revenue people descended on the Golden fortune. It had been only a few weeks earlier that Sol had insisted Marti review the procedures she should follow. He must have known there was something wrong. He had even joked at the time, saying, "When I die, I want to die at about two in the morning. That would probably save you a couple of hundred million dollars."

She had not understood what he meant by that remark. Soon she would.

"Your husband was one of the richest men in the world," Lavery began in his legal voice. "There will be a tremendous amount of publicity surrounding his death. Since Golden Limited is owned solely by Sol Golden, his wife, and his heirs, the actual accountings of the money are not public knowledge. I can tell you, Mrs. Golden, that the amount of the estate that will have to be made public is in the area of two billion dollars.''

"I know that." Marti was not surprised.

"Since your husband died at approximately three in the afternoon, the word of the death leaked to the wire services in time for the eleven o'clock news on the East Coast. I also expect it to be on the front page of every morning paper in the country. Our original plan was to transfer a large portion of the fortune to a blind corporation your husband created ten years ago in the Bahamas, but because of the immediate publicity, that avenue is out of the question.''

"Does it really matter?" Marti asked. "How rich do I have to be?" She knew that even if she were taxed on the two billion, there had already been hundreds of millions in currencies, bonds, and investments hidden in Switzerland and Monaco. "Why don't we pay the taxes and forget about it? Frankly, I don't care.''

"It is not quite that simple," Lavery continued. "Your recent cash purchase of *Haute* magazine left the American parent company without its usual reserves of liquid cash at this time. The taxes could reach the five hundred million mark, which means that you might have to produce some of your foreign holdings to cover the debt.''

Sol would never approve of her revealing the carefully secreted foreign investments, Marti realized. She knew what she would do.

"Sell *Haute*," she said.

"Mrs. Golden, please do not misunderstand me. No

one is going to force you to liquidate a valuable asset such as *Haute* magazine for immediate satisfaction of taxes. I am sure I can work out a plan with the government that will be equitable to all parties and at the same time permit you to maintain all of the business ventures. Golden Limited is a very sound company that is of great benefit to the United States, especially under its current management and ownership."

"You don't understand," Marti said. "I want to sell *Haute*. I would sell that magazine anyhow. It was my fault that Sol bought *Haute*, and I think the pressure of making that deal is what killed him."

"Oh, Mrs. Golden, I strongly doubt —" Lavery did not approve of undoing the deal he had just spent months creating with Sol Golden.

"Sell it!" ordered Marti Golden, now the chairwoman of the board of Golden Limited.

Marcella Todd was removing her makeup while the television played softly in her bedroom. She thought she caught the name Sol Golden in the promo for the eleven o'clock news. *I wonder what he has bought now*, she thought as she turned up the volume of the set. *That man never stops*. She smiled as she thought of Marti and Sol back in Beverly Hills celebrating another business victory.

She watched the screen as a commercial for a mass-market plastic surgery clinic flashed new faces for old ones at bargain rates. She made a note to have someone look into such clinics for a possible story.

The sleek and pancake-bronzed news reader looked sternly into the camera. "In our top story of the night, international communications and publishing magnate Sol Golden died suddenly this afternoon at his palatial

Beverly Hills mansion." The screen flashed to a photo of the huge house in the distance behind the heavy security gates. Marcella recognized Marti's white Rolls-Royce with the door still open parked crossways in the driveway. "Golden, whose fortune is estimated to be somewhere between two and five billion dollars [another photo of the Golden Building in Century City came on the screen], was the world's leading communications power. Because his fortunes were not publicly owned, details of the vast estate are unavailable, but the Internal Revenue Service and California state officials have already frozen records of Golden Limited, the parent company."

Marcella's fingernails dug into her palms as the commentator continued. "Mrs. Golden, his wife of more than four decades, was with her husband at the time of death and is resting at the University of California at Los Angeles Medical Center, where her husband was pronounced dead. In a brief statement, Golden Limited chief counsel and executive vice-president Arthur Lavery said that Mrs. Golden had instructed him to dispose immediately of certain Golden Limited properties to pay the expected whopping estate taxes, which are estimated to be the highest ever paid in the United States. For more details stay tuned to a special edition of "Night Views," following this newscast, which will examine the Golden empire and the effects this death will have on world communications. Now, on a hap ——"

Marcella shut off the seat and dialed the Golden house in California. The lines were all busy into the house. Poor Marti, Marcella thought, how she loved that man. All this must be cutting her to pieces. Marcella was thoughtful. *I wonder if there is enough pleasure and satisfaction in loving and being loved to make up for all the pain.* She dialed the phone again. Still busy. she put down the receiver.

Her phone rang.

Marcella instantly recognized Marti Golden's shaken voice on the line. There was a long silence as both women tried to find the proper words.

"I am so sorry for you. I just do not know what to say. I can come out there," Marcella offered.

"No," Marti said. "I want some time to myself. I have decided to make the funeral very small and private or it will become a media event. Then I am going to stay at the Palm Springs house until I can stand coming back to this bedroom." Marti finally began to cry.

"I'll come and spend some time with you there if you want me," Marcella offered. "He was such a wonderful man, and you two had so much happiness."

"I know." Marti continued crying. "I blame myself for this."

"How?" Marcella was shocked.

"I didn't know his health was as bad as it was. He somehow kept the problem hidden from me. When I made him buy *Haute*, I am afraid that the pressure of making the deal . . ."

"No, Marti." Marcella wanted to reassure the stricken woman. "He was enthusiastic about buying the magazine."

"No." Marti had stopped sobbing. "He bought that magazine because I wanted it. He did it for me and it killed him. I hate that magazine and I hate myself. I wanted you to know — before the press gets hold of it — that I am selling *Haute*."

"Are you sure you want to do that?" Marcella was numb and the announcement of the impending sale of the magazine somehow did not seem very important.

"Yes. The money will pay the taxes — or almost pay

the taxes — and I won't have to own the weapon that killed the man I love." Marti's voice was stronger.

"I understand," Marcella said.

"I wanted you to know first. I have always felt so close to you. I know that you have a lot of yourself involved with the magazine now —"

"Don't ever worry about that," Marcella interrupted. "Marti, if Sol bought that magazine it might have been to give you something he wanted for you. He enjoyed giving you things. It might have been that making the deal helped to keep him alive longer because he wanted to make you happy."

"That's a nice thought," Marti said, "but I will never know the truth of it. I will have to live the rest of my life with all the possibilities and without Sol."

Both women silently held the phone for several minutes. Marcella regretted that she could not be with her friend to comfort her. Finally, Marti whispered, "Thanks, and good-bye," and the phone went dead.

Some forty-odd blocks north of Marcella's apartment, Sylvia Harrington was watching the "Night Views" special on the Golden empire. As the newscaster listed the hundreds of magazines, newspapers, television stations, motion picture companies, and service industries owend by the late Sol Golden, Sylvia was thinking of only one of those properties . . . *Haute* . . . her *Haute*. The broadcaster had commented that one of the strongest rumors around the employee network of the Golden empire was that its latest and one of its most expensive acquisitions, *Haute* magazine, would be soon on the auction block.

It would take four hundred million dollars or more to buy *Haute*. If Marti Golden were willing to sell, it would not be a forced sale at a bargain cost. Sylvia Harrington started calculating. Richard Barkley's money was a start, albeit a small beginning. Perhaps she could work a deal with one of the other big publishing empires to become involved in her repurchase. She certainly knew a lot of the richest people in the world. Somehow, she would raise the money and she would have *Haute*. What business organizations could afford the magazine? The Hearsts. The Newhouses. The Chandlers. She had never before realized how many of the publishing greats had close affiliations with California, and she had her feelings about Californians. In New York there were Malcolm Forbes and Burt Rance. Both men seemed unlikely possibilities.

Sylvia took a notebook and started writing names, monied names of people who owed her something. Tomorrow morning she would leak to the press that she was forming a syndicate to make an offer to purchase *Haute*. With her name and Richard Barkley's name affiliated with the proposed purchase, a lot of investors would feel secure that their money would be safe. Richard Barkley and Sylvia Harrington had always seemed to be the real inspiration that had made *Haute* great. *Seemed?* Hell, she *did* make it great! Still, a lot of potential investors would feel better about putting money into *Haute* if Richard were involved. Sylvia knew she would be up all night, calling Richard Barkley and explaining her plan, then thinking of ways to make it happen.

Marcella Todd was thinking, too. Why did she care so much that *Haute* would be sold? She had been connected with the magazine for only a few weeks. It was silly. But she did care. *Haute* represented ambition and success to her. She had traded love and her family for that amibition and success, but now it was going to be taken away, too. No, it would not happen. She would find a way to keep *Haute*. There *had* to be a way.

Chapter Twenty-Nine

When the first of the staff arrived at *Haute* the following morning, Marcella was already in her office planning her takeover of the magazine. She sat behind Sylvia Harrington's ornate desk, which had not yet been removed in spite of Marti's orders to purge the office of the Harrington image. For hours she sat in the silent offices and slowly formulated her plan.

Her scheme would require Marti's cooperation. She wanted *Haute* to be purchased by the employees. There were three thousand people working in varying capacities for the magazine and its subsidiaries. She had heard about other companies being purchased by their employees. It would work for *Haute*. It would *have* to work.

As the employees drifted into the complex, there was an abnormal silence. They had all heard of Sol Golden's death. With all the upheaval of the takeover and buyout now coupled with the new owner's death, there would be morale problems among the staff members. Marcella feared that key people were probably considering looking for more secure employment. That would have to be attended to immediately. Maybe a staff meeting would be the answer, Marcella thought. No, she did not want to have to answer the obvious questions that would be asked until she had decided exactly what was going to happen. However, there should be some kind of memorial service in honor of Sol. But what did he mean to those people, most of whom had never even seen him? There was a man with so much power, yet only hours after his death that power still existed to be controlled by another. Power. It was far stronger than any individual who attempted to possess it. Marcella contemplated that thought.

Jayne Caldwell appeared at the door. "It's just awful. I feel so terrible for Mrs. Golden. And you." She looked closely at Marcella. "They were very close to you, weren't they?"

"They were my family," Marcella realized.

Jayne was silent. Then she looked as if she had just remembered something. Something important. "Marcella, have you forgotten that Diane is flying in for her spring break this morning?" Jayne asked. Marcella had forgotten. "Look. If you want, I could meet the plane or send Sandy."

"Send Sandy. I need you here." Marcella realized instantly the underlying meaning in those words. She had promised Diane, and herself, that the spring break was going to be their special time, but that was before Sol's death and the *Haute* sale. Diane would have to understand. "I'm going to need you here all day today," she said to Jayne.

Both women realized there would be enormous staff attitude problems to be overcome in the following days. Jayne, accurately, feared that somehow the death could affect the future of *Haute*. "Do you think *Haute* might be sold to pay the taxes?" She asked.

"I know it will," Marcella said emotionlessly.

Both women were silent. Then Jayne asked, "Do you have any thoughts about what is going to happen? How soon . . . ?"

"Nothing I want to talk about yet. I would appreciate it if you would say nothing to the staff about the sale. Now, if you could let me alone for a few minutes . . ."

"Of course," Jayne said, and excused herself.

Marcella stared into space. She needed advice about this employee buy-out idea. The only man who might have the answers was Burt Rance. She called him.

Burt listened to the problem and Marcella's solution. "I figured that it would probably be *Haute* that would be sold," he said. "It was just a hunch, but it makes sense to raise the money by selling the latest acquisition that does not already require a lot of corporate management from the home office. Golden ran a tight operation and called the shots from Beverly Hills. All the top management is there. His heirs could not sell any of the other companies without cutting loose some of their own top personnel to run them. *Haute* was still autonomous. There had not been time to transform it into a Golden operation."

"So what do you think of my plan?" Marcella asked.

"It doesn't have a chance," Burt replied.

"Are you just saying that because it was my plan?" Marcella asked in an angry, hurt tone. "Are you being so pessimistic because you are still upset with me?"

"I am merely telling you a few cold, hard business facts of life. The employees of *Haute* could never afford the takeover." She could hear Burt operating his calculator. "If I can figure roughly, each employee would be assuming about a $140,000 share of the debt, and that follows the hardly probable premise that every employee would want to participate in the buy-out. Even if the employees would go for it, which I doubt, none of the big lending companies would be interested in such a gigantic outlay under the current circumstances."

"What circumstances?" Marcella asked.

"Almost all the top management that were responsible for the immense success of the magazine are gone. Harrington. Barkley. You do not even have the resources and track record of Golden Limited behind you. As for you, sure you are a respected talent, but a few weeks as top management of a company is not bankable for a four-hundred-million-dollar loan."

Marcella could understand the truth in what Burt was explaining.

"But some employee takeovers do work," she said, praying for some hint of hope.

"They usually work in firms that are already in serious financial trouble and everyone is willing to sacrifice to save their jobs. The principals of the company usually sell at fire-sale prices and the employees and unions agree to massive pay cuts. I can tell you that will not happen at *Haute*. It makes a lot of money and many of your employees are badly underpaid anyhow. Sylvia Harrington believed in slave labor."

"I didn't think about any of that," Marcella said very softly.

"Well, you should have. Marcella, you are a hell of a writer and a good editor, but what you don't know about the business side of a magazine could fill a few hundred thousand pages." Burt was being very, very blunt.

"I might have learned." Marcella felt defensive.

"You no longer have the luxury of time," Burt added.

"Now, if you have any other solutions I shall be delighted to listen to them and offer my actually very expert opinions."

"I was hoping that you might offer a few suggestions." Marcella had an almost pleading tone in her voice.

"I might. I might have a lot of suggestions about what you should be doing." Burt was not only referring to advice about Marcella's professional life.

"I should like to hear them!"

"I have an offer for you. I had planned to go out to a farm I own in Bucks County and think a lot of things through. And most of the thinking concerns you. If you should happen to come with me, we could discuss everything at once."

"Oh, Burt . . ."

"Look, I promise to devote most of the time thinking of ways you can keep your precious magazine and very little of the time discussing the fact that I do happen to love you. It's up to you. You want my advice? Come to the country, where I am going to be. Strictly business."

"I'll come."

Burt's voice was husky, as if he were attempting to hide his emotions. "I wish I could understand what goes on in that brain inside your beautiful head. One thing I would like to know. Are you coming to Bucks County to find out what we mean to each other, or to pick my brains about ways of keeping *Haute*? No, don't answer that. I don't want to know, after all. I'm afraid to know."

Marcella was glad, at that moment, she did not have to answer the question.

The *Haute* limo glided to a stop in front of Marcella's

apartment and she got out and started for the door. Then she saw Diane. "Oh . . . have you been waiting long?"

"Awhile. I stayed in the car until Sandy got the call to go back to the office. I didn't know it was for you or I would have come along." The excited girl threw her arms around her mother's neck. "It's no problem. I'm just glad you are here. So you decided to leave the office early to be with me." She kissed her mother.

"Didn't you hear?" Marcella's voice was strangely cold.

"Hear what?" Diane was confused.

"Sol Golden died last night. Everything is a mess. Don't you ever read a newspaper or look at a news show?" Marcella's words stung her daughter.

"Mother, I went to bed early last night and left first thing this morning to catch the plane," Diane said defensively. "How could I know? I'm sorry. Are you going to the funeral?"

"No . . . I'm not."

"Then you did come home to meet me." Diane looked hopeful.

Marcella was embarrassed . . . worse than embarrassed. Right then she did not like herself very much. Still, there were things she needed to do. "*Haute* is going to be sold and I have to do something about it," she said.

"Sold . . . oh, no." Diane felt the loss, and for a moment the two women shared their ambitions for power with each other. Neither wanted to lose the magazine as part of her life. "What can you do?"

"I am going to try to buy it."

Diane looked shocked and impressed.

"I have asked Burt to meet with me to discuss ways I might be able to purchase the magazine."

"Your boyfriend?"

"He's not really a boyfriend. He . . . he . . . I don't know what he is to me. I do know he is an expert on magazines and I want his advice."

"Sure. I can understand that. I'll talk to you tonight. Maybe I'll have a brilliant idea." Diane wanted to do something that would help save the magazine that had become a part of her life and future, too.

"I won't be home tonight," Marcella said flatly. "I am going to Burt's farm in Bucks County. We thought it would be a good idea to get away from all outside influences until we found a solution."

"Outside influences?" Diane exploded. "You mean like your daughter! Oh, yes, your daughter, who puts so many demands on you, like forcing you to spend a spring break with her once every sixteen years. No, Mother, I would not think of interfering with your talking business for a few days with your boyfriend in some businesslike farmhouse in Pennsylvania. I wouldn't want to take you away from your work."

Marcella slapped her daughter.

Diane flinched slightly but just stared at her mother. "I just thought of something interesting. It was too bad for Sylvia Harrington that she was so ugly. Because of the way she looked, people always expected her to be cruel and selfish. She looks cruel. But you are so beautiful. No one would ever believe how much you two are alike."

Her daughter's words sliced through Marcella. For a few seconds the two women just stared at each other, both searching for the right words.

"I'm sorry," Marcella said. "You mean everything to me. So much is happening." She walked toward her daughter and embraced her. "I love you so. I want you with me. I want to be the kind of mother you deserve, but . . ."

"I think I understand," Diane said. "You just can't handle everything right now."

Marcella was silent.

"I'll go back to Ohio . . . for now. But I know you want me. I know we are going to be a real family, you and me. It's going to happen because we want it to happen, Mother."

And Marcella Todd knew she *did* want that to happen. As the limousine drove away toward LaGuardia Airport, Marcella knew that someday she and her daughter would be together again.

Chapter Thirty

The silver Ferrari roared through the cold gray early spring weather toward Burt Rance's house in New Hope, Pennsylvania.

Marcella nestled in the soft gray leather seats. The car smelled of leather. The late-afternoon air in the countryside was clean and seemingly held a cold treat feeling. How different it all was from the frantic, ambitious, and soiled pace of New York, she thought. "I didn't know you had a car like this," Marcella said, breaking a silence that had started all the way back in Manhattan.

"She speaks." Burt smiled. "I was beginning to think you had decided you were a kidnapping victim being dragged away to the boonies."

"No," Marcella said. "It wasn't that. I was just thinking how different things are out here than back in New York. When you're in the city, it seems that it is the only place in the world, and yet, out here, you realize there is a whole country filled with people living lives of their own."

"That's one of the reasons I own this car," Burt said.

Marcella looked confused. "I don't understand."

"This isn't a New York car. It could not survive

there. One week of driving it around the city and it would be a dented mess — or stolen. This is my escape car. The country is my escape place. When I get into this car and drive out here, I am leaving behind everything about my city life." Burt pressed a bit harder on the accelerator.

"This is supposed to be a business trip," Marcella reminded him.

"I know," Burt said softly. "I just thought I would share something of a side of myself you have not seen. Maybe there is a side of you I have not seen."

"I don't know anymore." Marcella thought of the country girl she had been once. She thought about the insecure wife she had been once. She thought of when she started taking control of her life. She questioned whether there were still bits and pieces of all those women in her now. "Maybe. Maybe."

The car turned into a long driveway that seemed to be nothing more than a graveled woods path. No house could be seen from the road.

About a quarter of a mile later, the house appeared. Marcella was surprised. She had been to many country houses. Usually, they were large sprawling places that would fall into the category of country chic. What she saw was a small clapboard house with dark green shutters and a new addition that was just a little too architecturally obviously added. It was not unlike the house in which she lived as a girl and where Diane still lived.

"I know it's not much," Burt said. "I didn't want something elaborate. This is my private place. Only a few of my friends have ever been here. Most people do not even know it exists."

"This kind of house brings back memories," Marcella said.

The house was basically a center core of two stories with a pair of tiny bedrooms upstairs and a small kitchen and bath below, built around 1800. The other part was a large living room with a floor-to-ceiling stone fireplace at one end wall. Burt had built part of the room himself when he bought the property ten years before.

There was a fire going in the fireplace.

"The house is pretty self-sufficient. I have a caretaker who checks on the place; he started the fire and stocked the refrigerator," Burt said. "But I wanted the place to have some of those pioneer qualities. It can be heated by that stove built into the fireplace, and there is a place to cook if the kitchen appliances are not working. I even have the old ice house set up so that it still works. The original owners could return today and find the house inhabitable." It was in this house, and not in computerized, heated, electronically arranged Manhattan that Burt felt the most independent.

Marcella moved toward the blazing fire. Burt walked across the room and kissed her immediately.

"I thought this was business," she said.

"Pleasure before business." He continued to kiss her as the firelight flickered on their faces.

Marcella was ready to be kissed. In that setting so far from New York, she was reminded of the times in her life when she had been touched by a man, when she had wanted to be held by a man. And at that moment, she wanted to be held by Burt Rance more than she had ever wanted a man.

They lowered themselves gently to the Oriental rug that was warmed in front of the fire. They were not talking. Only the marked increase in their breathing indicated what was affecting them. Marcella looked at

Burt's face as his big hands undressed her gently. She stared into his eyes. He was a man of passion, but not lust. He wanted to make love to her, yes, but she was starting to believe he really did love her. And maybe, too, she loved him. Marcella studied the man's face for the answers to her questions. Was that the face of a man she could love? Did she know how to love a man anymore?

As Burt removed her clothes carefully, he marveled at her. He had fantasized about her so many times, he feared that reality might be something less than his dreams. But it was not. Her body was as perfect as her face. Even the way she lay on the Oriental rug, slightly taut, was erotic.

One of his hands touched her face delicately and then explored her body from the neck to the breasts. Both hands outlined her contours from the waist to the hips to the insides of the thighs. Marcella felt a heat that was more than the fire, a heat that she had never realized. Her long nails went to the muscles of his back as she pulled him toward her. He could feel the nails digging into his flesh with a mixture of pain and passion. Marcella closed her eyes as his body covered hers. She forgot about ambition. She forgot about being insecure. She forgot about the magazine. She luxuriated in the kind of passion that could not be bought by the richest, most successful of women, the passion that could be given only in love. And they made love. They loved as if they were making up for all the times they had denied themselves. Hours passed in passionate silence before they finally nestled under a quilt in front of the fire.

Marcella and Burt seemed to instinctively understand each other's bodies. As the fire flickered on the muscles and curves of their two bodies, the lovers twisted into a single entity of passion.

"I love you," Burt whispered.

"Me, too," Marcella said in a hushed tone.

"Then say it." Burt was suddenly serious. He turned and looked at the woman who was curled into the crook of his body. "Say it."

"I love you," Marcella said.

"God, how I have wanted to hear you say those words." Burt kissed her again and again. "Why has it taken us so long? I knew I loved you from the start."

"You did?" Marcella was truthfully surprised.

"Didn't you know that . . . ? No, I don't think you did. You had done something to yourself that tuned love out. You wouldn't let yourself feel anything."

Marcella knew he was right. She was afraid of love. Perhaps she was still afraid of love, but she realized that she was no longer afraid of being loved. She had never been loved as Burt had just loved her.

"Let's have some brandy." Burt stood and walked to a table where liquor bottles were arranged with a collection of heavy crystal barware.

"Put on your pants," Marcella joked.

"Why?"

"There is something too decadent about a naked man pouring brandy," she said.

"How about a naked woman drinking brandy?" Burt laughed as he pulled on his jogging pants.

"That's different." Marcella sipped the warmed liquor.

"Just like a woman," Burt added.

"Just a fact. Women were meant to drink brandy naked, and men should always wear their pants while pouring brandy. It's in Emily Post, the revised edition, I believe," Marcella teased.

"I stand corrected."

"I would rather you sit down corrected," Marcella said as she pulled Burt toward her again. "I have never known a man who can make me feel the way you can."

"One had better be enough," Burt said in mock seriousness. "I want to be enough man for you. I want to be the *only* man for you."

"You are."

"Then when do we get married? Since you have used me, I want you to make an honest man of me." Burt started to kiss her again.

Marcella was suddenly tense. "Isn't all this a little fast? We don't have to be married. If we know how we feel about each other, marriage is not so important." Marcella felt a new tension spreading through her body.

"I have some strong feelings about marriage. People like us need to make a permanent commitment to each other. Our lives are too fast. We need that piece of paper to hold us together."

"I don't need that piece of paper," Marcella said.

"I do. You do, too." He hugged her. "I know you had a bad marriage, but ours won't be that way. I adore you. I want to give you everything. You can do whatever you like. If you still want to do some writing . . . fine."

Marcella was startled. "What are you saying? That if I marry you I am going to quit my career? Quit everything I have built?"

"You will be starting a new career as my wife and partner. I need you to be with me. I can tell you that being my wife will be a full-time job." Burt seemed so clear in what he was saying and thinking.

Marcella was quiet. After a few minutes of silence, she said, "It sounds like a well-upholstered version of my first marriage, where I was the dedicated wife. I love you, Burt, but I cannot give up my independence. I've worked too hard for it."

"I'm not your first husband." Burt sounded hurt.

"I know that. I'm sorry. I phrased that badly. It is just that part of what I am, an important part of what attracts you to me, is my independence. I would be a different woman if I were just your wife. You might not even like me."

"That is ridiculous." Burt's voice was growing angry. "If you don't want to marry me, just say so, but for God's sake, stop this convoluted philosophizing. Do what you feel, not what you reason to be right."

"I feel what I am doing is right," she said. "Maybe in the future things will be different, but now with Diane feeling neglected and the problems at *Haute* . . ."

"That damned magazine!" Burt's voice was cold. "That is the real problem. You aren't worried enough about your daughter to make any real efforts there." Marcella's eyes flashed angrily. "You are interested only in the power you have at that magazine. To hell with the rest of us poor mortals who can only love you. You want the magazine, which can give you power."

Marcella feared there was truth in what he was saying, but she did not want to consider that truth. "I don't want to fight with you right now. I do care about you. We had better talk about something else. Let's give ourselves time to think all this through."

"Very rational," Burt said dryly. "After all, you did come out here to discuss ways of saving your magazine, and here you had to suffer through a seduction."

"I didn't suf ——"

"Here are the possibilities," Burt interrupted. "Plan A: you ask Marti to hold on to the magazine long enough for you to float a public stock offering to raise the money for a buy-out."

Marcella was interested in the conversation in spite of her inner urge to take Burt in her arms and say she loved him and would leave everything for him. She listened carefully.

"The problem is this might take several years to clear the Securities and Exchange Commission, and I don't think Marti wants to hold *Haute* any longer than she has to."

Marcella knew that was true.

"Plan B: you can interest some other magazine chain in purchasing *Haute* and retaining you to manage the operation, but then I am sure you are already working on that possibility."

Marcella nodded, rather ashamed she was so engrossed in the conversation that must be causing emotional pain to Burt.

"Plan C: you could form a company with the established names associated with the magazine, such as Richard Barkley and Sylvia Harrington, and attempt to secure loans to purchase the magazine. Perhaps Marti would retain a partial interest that could be slowly accumulated over, say, a ten-year period.".

Marcella contemplated that potential solution.

"Why don't you think through those plans by yourself for a while? When you have made a decision, I will put you in contact with the right lawyers and money men. Now, if you will excuse me, I am going upstairs to bed. I know you have a lot of really important things to consider and I don't want to intrude."

"Burt . . ." Marcella held out her hand to the hurt and angry man.

"I will talk to you in the morning. Shall we go back to New York first thing? I know you must be anxious."

"Burt . . ."

"Good night Marcella." Burt walked from the room, leaving her huddled under the blanket in front of the blazing fire.

Marcella looked into the flames and started to think through her life seriously.

Chapter Thirty-One

Sylvia Harrington stood outside the entrance of her apartment building and looked at the snow that had changed the grayness of East Fifty-ninth Street to pristine white. No limousine waited for her.

For the first time in years — decades, actually — Sylvia was walking. But she was still walking with the erect and sure Harrington posture and determination. She took a deep breath of exceptionally clean air.

"I'm not beaten," she said to herself as she walked toward First Avenue. "I don't think I can be beaten." Sylvia Harrington was not at an end; she was at a new beginning.

"Marcella Todd." She said the name softly as she crossed under the Fifty-ninth Street Bridge, her feet crunching determinedly in the fresh snow. "She is only getting what I have already had. Now let's see her keep it. See if she knows what she has got, and what I am going to have again."

Marcella Todd did not leave Burt Rance's farmhouse early the following morning. Nature, in the form of a late spring storm, had left a foot of snow in the long drive.

"It's going to be fine," Burt reassured her. "Just give me a few hours to dig the drive out with the tractor and you will be headed back to the city." He disappeared into the machine shed and emerged atop a smoke-belching, aged John Deere tractor that had been a part of the farm for longer than Burt had.

Marcella watched as Burt methodically began plowing the snowdrifts from the drive with the snow blade of the tractor. He seemed to be lost in the work. She could tell by the look of satisfaction and calmness on his face. That was a part of Burt she had not considered. Here was a man who ran an empire valued at hundreds of millions of dollars, a man who ruled in the boardroom, and he looked more peaceful behind the wheel of this decrepit piece of machinery than she had ever seen him. Burt had found peace out here, Marcella thought. *He has power and success, but he . . . he has learned to enjoy things that are so basic, so simple.*

The nearly nonexistent muffler did little to diminish the noise of the tractor, which echoed through the trees and snow. Even when he was out of sight, down the winding drive, Marcella knew Burt was working to clear the path to take her back to her outside world. Something inside Marcella wondered whether she really wanted to return to that world.

She loved that man, and she knew he loved her. Yet, when he had asked her to be his wife, she feared losing her freedom and independence more than she wanted to have his love. Why must there be a tradeoff?

Marcella decided to walk through the clean snow. How different the country snow was from the city snow, which lay feebly on the sidewalk only to be soiled and trampled to death by the feet of the ambitious. This snow was free, she thought. It blew into drifts that would last for weeks, even if the weather turned warmer. The snow was permitted to behave as snow should, so it would never be slush. Marcella pondered that thought.

Burt was still working somewhere. She could hear the tractor nudging its way toward civilization, her civilization. Marcella decided to check with the office. She returned to the house and dialed Jayne Caldwell's private line.

Jayne was most anxious to talk to her. "I received a call from Sylvia this morning," Jayne began. "She asked for my help. She and Richard Barkley have put together an investors' group and intend to make an offer to repurchase *Haute*.

So Burt was right about that, Marcella thought. "What did they want from you?" she asked.

"They wanted me to be a spy to report back what is happening here. They wanted to know what you are going to do." Jayne sounded very matter-of-fact.

"And you refused," Marcella said.

"No," Jayne returned. "I told them I would consider what they asked. It might be a good idea for me to continue a relationship with them."

"Yes, it might." Marcella felt sick. Here was Jayne, one of the most honorable people she had ever known, trading in her ethics and integrity to help Marcella retain control of *Haute*. Or maybe to remain on the right side of the people who very soon might be returning to take control of the magazine. Marcella closed her eyes. Why did she have to live in a world where people must continually search out the hidden motives of others? Whatever happened to innocence?

Marcella continued in that train of thought for more than an hour after Jayne's call. She was so deep in contemplation she had failed to hear that the noise of Burt's tractor had stopped. It was only when she heard the stomping of feet on the porch and the banging of the heavy door that she realize he had finished plowing the drive.

"Look, I've been thinking," Burt said.

"I have, too." Marcella looked at the man she knew she loved.

"I can't force you to decide what to do with your life. I realize that. I sat on that tractor and tried to imagine if the positions were reversed, and you asked me to leave my work — but it just does not seem the same," Burt said. "My companies are me. I built them and I own them. I just could not make the comparison."

He looked at Marcella with a sadness in his eyes. "There is one thing that is certain. You have to make some decisions in your life. I want you, but you really have to want me completely. I have decided to stay out of your life until you know whether or not you want me. That might sound silly, but right now I hurt and I want somebody to soothe that hurt. If I can't have you, then I want to keep looking until I find someone who can fill your place. If that is . . ." His voice drifted away.

Marcella was unable to speak. It was not so much that she was choked with emotion as she did not know what to say. Here was the first man she was sure she wanted, and she was accepting the fact he would be seeing other women, women who might replace her in his life.

She began to gather her coat and scarf in preparation for the drive back to New York.

Both of the passengers in the sleek gray Ferrari were lost in their thoughts during the silent ride to Manhattan. Soon the country lanes became the crowded bumpy city streets. Noise replaced quiet. The soulful brayings of a lone dog several hills away were traded for the rumbling of the subway underground.

Burt drove straight to the offices of *Haute* magazine. He did not have to ask Marcella where she wanted to go. He knew. As he watched her walk through the revolving door, he felt so alone. He was overcome with the kind of loneliness a man could know only when he had learned how fulfilling and satisfying his life could be.

It all seemed so wrong. Finally, he had met a woman whom he wanted for the rest of his life, and he knew she wanted him; yet she wanted something more. No . . . he would not permit this emptiness, this loneliness, to hurt him anymore. Tonight, he would not be lonely. Tonight he would be loved.

When Marcella arrived in her office, she looked down to the street and saw the Ferrari pulling away from the curb. She thought of Burt. She thought of her life. Then came other memories. She recalled some of her high-school girlfriends back in Canfield. At a reunion they had all seemed so envious of her. She secretely enjoyed that envy. They wanted her glamour, her success, and her money. She could certainly understand that. Only now did she realize what they had . . . or most of them had. Most had an uncomplicated love. A man who wanted them and whom they wanted. A family. A little security. Shared worries. Someone who depended on them. Someone on whom to depend.

It would surprise many of those former friends to know what the successful Marcella Todd was thinking as she stood at the windows of her plush office overlooking her world, her empire of chic.

"Enough of this," she said aloud, even though she was alone in the office. She pressed the intercom and said, "Tell the art department to send in whatever they have completed on the June issue. I want to start okaying pages."

Minutes later dozens of pages pasted on huge sheets

of cardboard were scattered throughout the office. Page by page, Marcella filled her mind with the images of June, warm images of beaches and tans and clothes that let the breezes caress the skin . . . all the while attempting to suppress an image of a cold night and a fireplace, and a man holding a snifter of brandy.

Hours passed as she marked the pages. A change of a word here. An enlarging of a photo there. A remake of a page that did not seem to say what she wanted it to say.

The digital clock on her desk read 3 A.M.

Marcella reached for the phone and dialed the art department. "Look, I'm sorry. I didn't realize it was so late. You people go home and get some rest. I really apologize."

She put down the receiver.

She could hear the ring of the elevator arriving on the floor below through her open office door. The art department was leaving quickly. Marcella walked to the bar in a corner of the office and poured herself . . .

. . . a brandy.

She looked into the rich mahogany-colored liquid. Then her face took on a determined look. "No!" she said aloud in the room that was empty except for herself.

Without even taking her coat, she walked out of her office, which had been Sylvia Harrington's office. As she strided out of the building, she whistled with two fingers to her lips and a cab skidded to the curb. She gave him the address.

At Burt Rance's town house, she pressed the doorbell and waited for a light to appear in the room above her head, the light from Burt's bedroom. She heard the shuffle of his bare feet on the cold marble of the entrance hall.

The door opened and Burt looked out at her, confused. "What does this mean?" he asked.

"It means I want you," Marcella said, looking into the man's eyes.

"Come in," he said.

The two stood in the marble entrance hall and tried to find words. Then Marcella saw a third image at the top of the stairs. "Burt . . . what is it?" came the voice of the third person.

Marcella looked at the woman who was wearing only a red silk gown. The woman was tall and beautiful, with long blonde hair.

"She looks like me," Marcella said to Burt.

"I know," Burt answered softly.

The woman walked down the stairs carefully. "So you are the one," she commented as she eyed every inch of Marcella. "I knew there was someone. He had to be taken home. I found him drunk in a bar last night. I knew he was too good to be . . . don't worry."

"I'm not worried," Marcella said.

"I'll get you a cab," Burt said to the woman. He flicked a switch that started a small yellow cab light flashing in front of the house. While the woman changed, Marcella and Burt stood silently in the hall.

She reappeared just as the honk of the waiting cab's horn sounded outside. As she started for the door, she turned and took a hard look at Marcella. "If I thought there was a chance, I would stay and fight you for him, but I know there isn't. I could tell that this guy was hung up on someone." She opened the door and paused, turning back again to face Marcella. "You are the luckiest woman I know — whoever you are, lady." With a slam of the brass door catch, the woman was gone.

"I *am* sorry." Burt looked miserable.

"I understand. I really do understand." Marcella and Burt continued to face each other.

"I want to be your wife," Marcella said. "There are many things I want in life, but I want to be your wife the most. I will try it on your terms." She looked deeply into Burt's eyes.

"It won't work that way," he said.

"What do you mean?" Suddenly, Marcella felt fearful. A hot, burning fear . . . a fear she had lost what she had only so recently learned she wanted.

"I was wrong. *You* are the woman I love. All of you. Not just your brains or your kindness or your beauty or even the fact that I know you love me. It is all of you that attracts me. I realized that tonight when I tried to find a substitute. She was your image, but she was not you. She didn't have your drive, your ambition. I guess . . . I . . ."

"I want to be the woman you want," Marcella said.

"You are," Burt whispered. "You are. But tonight, when I realized that I could not — did not want to — change you, I made another decision."

Marcella looked curious.

"I guess we are going to have to be a threesome — you, me, and that magazine. I have to consult with my partner, but I am ready to buy that blasted magazine and share it with you if it will share you with me."

"Your partner?" Marcella asked. "I never knew you had a partner."

"I don't, unless you agree to accept the position. Well, do you want to be my partner in life?" He gently placed a hand on each of Marcella's shoulders.

"Partner," Marcella said as she looked straight into Burt's face.

We hope you have enjoyed this
KNIGHTSBRIDGE book.

We love good books just as you do,
so you can be assured that the
KNIGHT ON THE HORSE
stands for good reading, every time.